About the Author

Rachael Lucas has written sixteen novels for adults and teenagers, including the Carnegie nominated *The State of Grace*, which was selected as an Outstanding Book for Young People with Disabilities by IBBY. She lives on a beautiful stretch of coastline in the north west of England with her family and two very enthusiastic spaniels. When she's not writing at the kitchen table with a cup of coffee by her side, she's out walking the dogs on the beach or in the nearby pinewoods.

Keep up with Rachael - follow her on Facebook @rachaellucaswriter where you can hear the latest book news and behind the scenes updates.

## ALSO BY RACHAEL LUCAS

# THE LIGHTHOUSE LIBRARY

RACHAEL LUCAS

*This one's for you, old boy.*

# CHAPTER ONE

Meg trundled slowly up the inside lane of the motorway, hoping she looked braver than she felt. The journey from South Yorkshire all the way to the west coast of the Scottish Highlands was a long one for someone who hadn't driven further than to the local supermarket in years.

Her husband Michael had always insisted on driving, telling her she didn't have the confidence and that he'd be happier behind the wheel. She'd had a few cautious, experimental trips since selling her little car and buying the campervan, but nothing to prepare her for a drive of over four hundred miles. Her little corgi, Eliza, sat beside her on the passenger seat, strapped into her little doggy harness and looking out of the window with her habitual cheerful curiosity.

It was funny, Meg thought, that there was something about a campervan that just seemed to intrigue people. Before signing on the dotted line at the showroom and handing over a hefty sum in exchange for a set of keys for the six-month-old van, she'd never so much as looked inside one. Selling up

1

everything she owned and buying a house on wheels had seemed the biggest gesture she could make towards changing her life completely. So she'd parted with the cash, swallowed any vague sense of unease she might have felt, and decided to go for it.

After a couple of hours, they stopped at a service station to stretch their legs. There were long parking bays, which were specifically laid out for drivers like her. She pulled in alongside a beaten-up van with stickers all over the back doors, mismatched streaks of paint where the rust had been covered over, and a side door with several dents in it. She was just taking it in when the side door slid open and a tall boy in his early twenties appeared, a tin mug of coffee in one hand and a half-eaten sandwich in the other.

'Alright?' He tipped his head in greeting as she put the window down to lean out and double check she'd parked within the lines.

'You've got loads of room there,' he said, smiling cheerfully. 'Nice van.'

She looked across into his little house on wheels. Colourful Nepalese flags hung on the wall, and a still-steaming kettle stood on top of a blue gas stove. Striped rugs lay on the floor and the whole interior looked cool and hippy-ish.

'I think mine is a bit more traditional than yours – luckily my friend's promised to make me some nice crochet blankets to brighten it up a bit. I'm going to house sit for her,' Meg added.

'Cool,' said the boy, sipping his coffee. 'Doesn't matter what it looks like, though, it's the ethos that's important. Freedom is everything.' He patted the battered side of his van affectionately.

'Freedom is everything,' echoed Meg. 'I like that.'

He looked like the sort of person who was designed for van life. She felt like a bit of a fraud in comparison.

Eliza gave a gruff bark of excitement and pulled against the travel harness, making it almost impossible to unfasten the two safety clips that held her secure on the front passenger seat where she'd been sitting on a blue and white fleece blanket folded neatly to protect the brand-new upholstery. The blanket already had a light dusting of the ever-present golden hairs, which her little corgi left as a calling card wherever she went.

'Come on then,' she said, as Eliza hopped down from the seat and navigated the climb down to ground level. Her little legs bustled along as they made their way to the grass where she found the young man leaning against a wooden picnic table.

'We meet again. Oh look at her, she's a sweetie.' He bent to give Eliza some pats then straightened again, laughing as she wagged her little tail with excitement as his two graceful lurchers sniffed her in greeting.

'I hope they're passing on some travel tips in doggy language.'

He chuckled. 'They know their stuff these two – they've been all over the place. Spain, Greece, all the way down to Turkey...'

'In your van?' Meg tried to keep the surprise out of her voice.

He nodded. 'Tough old bird, is Esmerelda.'

'Your van has a name?' Meg laughed.

'Course she does. What's yours called?'

'I... well, it's just a van.' She felt a pang of guilt for her poor nameless vehicle.

'It's not just a van. That's your home, it is. Treat her well and she'll do the same for you.'

3

'I'll give it some thought.'

'Happy trails,' he said, reaching out a hand and shaking hers, taking her by surprise with his old-fashioned manners. He smelled of patchouli oil.

'And to you.' He gave a wave and loped off, his dogs trotting along behind him.

She popped Eliza back into the campervan and headed into the café to pick up a coffee and something to eat, musing as she waited for her coffee. One suggestion her therapist had left her with was the idea that she start thinking about the things that made *her* happy, rather than things she felt she ought to do. She'd been married to Michael for twenty-five years and in that time she'd always bent to his will. *He'd* have had no time for nonsense like naming an inanimate object. She frowned at the thought, and paid for her food, still so lost in thought that the girl behind the counter had to remind her to take the brown paper bag containing her bagel.

Try as she might, she couldn't quite get her head around giving the van a name, but she did listen intently to a podcast Helen had recommended as they made their way up through the borders of Scotland, and along the very plain and unappealing motorway that led towards Glasgow.

*'Rising from the ashes of a toxic relationship is hard, but it's not impossible...'* said the voice through the van speaker.

# CHAPTER TWO

Gabe Anderson sat in the beaten-up Land Rover Defender and frowned as he double checked the list of names. He'd picked up the printout and a clipboard from the forestry office first thing, ready for the new recruits who'd passed through the vital health and safety training. The wind blowing over the Highland moor was so strong that it rocked the vehicle slightly, parked as it was on the ridge of the hill. When he looked left, there were blue skies and sunshine. To his right was a bank of heavy cloud, which he hoped was on the way north where it could break somewhere convenient like John O'Groats and not over the head of his new planting crew. He rubbed his chin absently and gazed ahead, gathering his thoughts.

Down in the distance, far below, he could just make out the tiny dots of the white houses and buildings which made up the village of Applemore. They nestled in around the bay, guarded by the distant islands which were half-shrouded in grey clouds.

Early that morning, when Gabe had opened his curtains,

he'd looked out at the islands from the window of his cottage. They'd been a strange purplish grey then, lit up by the sun which was rising in the east. He'd been startled out of a deep sleep by the sound of his phone buzzing unexpectedly with a message from the other side of the world. By the time he'd showered, he returned to his bedroom to find the alarm on his phone bleeping insistently.

But that was a couple of hours ago, and now it was nine in the morning.

'Come on, you.' He opened the door, dodging out of the way to allow Stanley, his black cocker spaniel a chance to jump out from the back of the truck for a quick leg stretch.

Stanley shot off, nose down and tail wagging, in search of the scent of rabbits. Gabe only had a couple of minutes before he had to get to work, and he wouldn't be able to focus with a spaniel in hunting mode. After a few moments, he whistled and Stan darted back, sitting neatly at his heels.

'You can wait in here out of mischief,' he said and opened the door to let him hop back inside. Stanley immediately curled up on an old blanket, ready for a morning of intensive snoozing. His ability to switch off was enviable. He leaned over and ruffled Stan's ears, checked the bowl of water he'd left in the footwell, and headed across to the group of people who were waiting to be inducted.

'I've got a brand-new group of victims here for you,' Ed called in his lilting Orkney accent. As one of the forestry managers, he'd been detailed with giving the new group their introductory health and safety briefing before delivering them to the moorland site. This week they were planting tiny baby fir trees, which were part of a bigger environmental project, funded by a big investment bank in London.

'We meet again,' said Gabe, grasping his hand in a brief greeting. 'How's it going?'

'No' bad,' said Ed. He was short and stocky with fair hair and blue eyes, which suggested his Viking blood. 'I've given them the health and safety pep-talk – don't eat the trees, don't drown in a peat bog, you know the drill.' His eyes twinkled with amusement.

'Excellent,' said Gabe, drily. 'That should cover it.'

'Hang on, now I think about it, I've left the papers back on the passenger seat,' Ed said, dashing his palm to his forehead. 'I'll go and grab them.'

'No problem,' said Gabe. 'I'll get them. You get off.'

He fell into step beside Ed as he headed back to his vehicle.

Ed stooped, bending to pick up a long piece of blue baling twine which was caught on a gorse bush, 'Looks like they're a decent bunch this time, no' like that group of tree-hugging hippies we had the other week.'

Gabe grinned. 'They were alright once you got to know them.'

Ed shook his head. 'It's forestry, not fairy tales.'

'They mean well.' Gabe had a more sympathetic view, having only worked in the industry for six months.

'Och, yes,' Ed agreed. 'I just don't think there's any room for sentiment in this business.'

'I don't think anyone's ever called me sentimental before,' said Gabe, taking the papers as Ed handed them over. 'That's a new one on me.'

Ed grinned. 'As long as you don't start wearing beads and chanting to the forest fairies we'll be fine.'

'Never going to happen.'

'Excellent.' Ed waggled his eyebrows. 'If you get any inclinations in that direction, let me know and I'll take you down to the river and dunk your head in.'

'I'll bear it in mind.'

'Talking of which I'm off for a meeting with the ecologists.'

Ed said the word with a roll of his eyes.

'You love them really.' Gabe chuckled, watching Ed's reaction. He was old school, and his favourite pastime was cutting trees down – the bigger the better.

'They're a necessary evil, if you ask me. The trouble with ecologists is they have a habit of spotting rare species on sites I want to clear. I swear they'd find a great crested newt in the kitchen section of Ikea, given half the chance.'

Gabe grinned. He was still laughing at Ed's intransigence as he drove away, raising a hand in farewell as he headed off down the narrow single-track road which twisted through the heather-clad moorland.

*Right,* thought Gabe, turning back to see the gaggle of new workers.

He'd got used to giving the introductory talk over the last few months. It didn't seem that long since he'd been standing there himself, slightly apart from the others, pondering his life choices and wondering what on earth had possessed him.

He looked at the group, musing as he always did what had brought each of them to work as a tree planter in the far north of Scotland. As he spoke, the thought stayed with him.

'Hi everyone,' he began, looking around to include everyone. 'I'm Gabe, and the first thing I'll tell you is that this job is as easy or as hard as you want to make it. Six months ago, I'd never planted a tree in my life, and now I couldn't count how many of the trees on this hill I'm responsible for.'

He lifted one of the tiny young seedling trees, smelling the fresh pine scent of its needles as he balanced it on his palm.

'The main thing,' he went on, 'is to make sure the roots go in the ground and the tree stays above it.'

He heard the chuntering of a pheasant somewhere in the undergrowth and caught a flash of the bright feathers of a male bird scuttling in search of his mate.

It was an impossible contrast. For most of his working life, he'd shuttled back and forth across the Atlantic, sitting in billion-dollar boardrooms as a systems architect. Now he was standing on the side of a heather-covered moorland, hoping someone would smile at his terrible attempt at an ice breaker.

A couple of smiles, a groan or two and a headshake with a wry smile gave him the answer he was looking for. At least they were receptive. That was always a good start.

As he ran through some of the details of the job, he took in the latest group of workers.

He could already make a guess at who was who, simply from their clothing. The four young lads in their early twenties who stood laughing and chatting were clad in work boots and trousers. The collars of their high-visibility coats were turned up. It was almost a certainty that they knew the job better than he did, so he didn't want to patronise them with a long spiel which would bore them to death when time was money.

Then there was a tall blonde girl of about thirty-five and what he assumed was her partner – although they could be twins, they looked so alike. He'd put money on them being German – their long legs were clad in sturdy walking trousers and the colourful scarves wrapped around their necks were a giveaway.

They would have been recruited – as he had been – online. In six months, one of them could easily give the same pep-talk he was currently detailed with. Things moved quite quickly in the forestry world, he'd discovered.

The advert on Facebook had enticed people with views of huge, breath-taking Scottish moorland and the promise of a fun, hard-working way to make a difference to the environment. They skipped the part about sideways wind whipping torrential rain into your face, boots layered so thick with peaty mud that you ended the day a foot taller than you started, or wrists which ended up covered in a red rash from the pine oils which leached out from the tiny baby trees they were detailed with planting.

He didn't mention those elements in his introductory talk, either. It would become self-evident pretty quickly, and the attrition rate in the first couple of weeks made it clear that you were either up to the task, or very definitely not.

He outlined the task in hand briefly. Each of them would take two bags laden with trees – the size of which varied depending on the job. This week would see each of them planting thousands of tiny seedling fir trees into a moorland which stretched as far as the ridge of the hill on the other side of the river.

'So to summarise,' he finished up, 'one fact I was told when I started working here was that every time you plant a tree you're helping to save a salmon. So if you're a fan of smoked salmon sandwiches, consider this an investment in your future.'

The four lads were eager to get to work. They got the joke, one of them giving him a brief wink of acknowledgement.

'If you're ready to get on, be my guest.' Gabe gestured to the stack of tree-filled sacks which were ready to go. In seconds, the four young men had bags strapped over their shoulders and had shot onto the moorland, knowing time was money with the job being paid by the number of trees planted.

'Any questions, anyone?' He leaned back against the mud-covered Land Rover, watching with amusement as the lads got to work at the speed of light. They were, as he suspected, seasoned workers who'd stop only for fleeting breaks, making as much money as they could before getting to work on the next project.

'We are ready to go,' said the blonde girl in a gruff German accent. He'd guessed right.

'Yeah, I think we're sorted.' The four shaggy-haired gap-year students, none of whom were dressed particularly warmly, looked at each other and nodded. One turned up the collar of his fleece jacket, zipping it up fully. He was wearing tracksuit trousers and a pair of walking boots. Gabe put money on him coming to ask if there were any spare warm clothes going begging before the end of the morning. Una, who ran the forestry office, was kind-hearted and always made sure there were spare coats and waterproofs available for the workers who turned up on a sunny day not realising that the weather in the Highlands could change three times in an hour.

'Actually, I have a question,' said a short girl with tufts of pink and yellow hair peeking out from under her woollen hat. She glanced at her friend, a cheerful-looking person who had a buzz cut and piercings through their nose (one in each nostril and one through the middle) and both eyebrows.

'Go on,' said Gabe, checking the list of names on the clipboard.

'Well, I'm a vegan,' she began.

'Of course you are,' said a sardonic voice in a northern accent, which came from the rough shaven man with an earring in one ear and a tumble of untidy dark grey-black hair which reached the collar of his jacket. Despite the dry edge to his tone, his eyes were twinkling with amusement. He looked around at the new crew.

'Love a bit of salmon, I do. Can't beat it,' he continued.

The corner of Gabe's mouth twitched in amusement, but he was relieved to see that the pink-haired girl took the teasing in good part.

'There's a seafood stall down in Applemore that you'll

want to check out, in that case. Fresh off the boat – it's amazing.' Gabe's stomach growled as a reminder that he hadn't had a moment to grab breakfast.

The vegan girl raised her eyebrows and looked at her friend.

'And The Applemore Hotel has a very good vegan menu, apparently, as does the new café by the harbour,' Gabe added to appease her and was relieved to see she perked up immediately. The last thing he wanted was to have ructions in the ranks of his first ever crew.

'You see,' he added, trying his best to prevent rumblings of dissent in the workforce before he'd even got the rest of them sorted out with their tree-planting kit and sent on their way, 'there's something for everyone.'

'I just want to make a decent bit of cash,' said the man, looking around for someone to agree with him. 'My van's on its last legs and a new exhaust isn't cheap.'

There was a general mutter of agreement. Most people were up here to make a quick buck – happy to camp out in cheaply converted campervans or share digs in the village where locals let out rooms.

'Well, you've come to the right place. Planting one of these –' Gabe picked up a tiny young tree with a tiny root ball, only a few inches high '– will earn you 11p. The fastest planters are making two hundred pounds a day.'

He watched as the girl frowned, seemingly confused by the calculation. Gabe pointed to the lads who were already a good distance away, bending to plant a tree, marching forward, reaching into the sack, taking out another and starting all over again. They moved at lightning speed.

'Those lot will do about four tiny trees a minute,' he said, and several mouths dropped open in shock. 'They don't mess about.'

The girl took off her bobble hat and shook her head before placing the hat carefully back onto her rainbow-coloured hair. 'I was still trying to figure out how planting a tree was going to save a salmon.'

Gabe grinned. 'I wondered if anyone was going to pick me up on that.'

He held out one of the tiny trees on the flat palm of his hand, extending it out so everyone was focused on it.

'It's like this. Years ago, dense woodland would have covered all this land around us. The streams and rivers that cut through it were shaded and protected by the trees, which kept the water cool so the salmon could breed and spawn there. Then insects and bugs would fall from the leaves and needles of the trees into the water to feed the young fish. Meanwhile, the roots stabilised the sides of the rivers, which slowed erosion and allowed the clean water that salmon need to survive.'

He paused for breath, surprised to discover that rather than being bored, everyone was waiting for the next part of the explanation.

'Fallen trees and branches create breaks in the currents so pools can form for the fish to rest and shelter, and the decomposing tree matter then provides food for aquatic insect life, which gives the salmon something to eat. So basically, the next time you eat a salmon sandwich, give a nod of thanks to a tree – or at least you can do once we get this lot planted. You're doing your bit for future generations.'

He inclined his head towards the UTV on a trailer behind the pick-up. It was piled high with white sacks, each one packed full of baby trees.

'Right then, that's enough of me rattling on about salmon. Let's get to work.'

Once he'd demonstrated the planting technique to the

newbies, Gabe got down to work himself, hefting the sack over his shoulders and marching along planting the tiny firs into the heaps of soil that had been pre-prepared by another of the forestry workers. It was oddly therapeutic on a day like today when the weather was on their side – almost meditative. Over the last six months he'd discovered a strange satisfaction in doing the same thing over and over and over again, turning when the bag was empty and heading back to pick up another one from the stacked pile a hundred yards down the forestry track.

He'd replied to the Facebook job ad on the spur of the moment. It was one of those seconds where you balance on the edge of a precipice and something – bravery or terror or maybe a little of both – prompts you to take the leap. He'd been convinced he'd stick out like a sore thumb, turning up gym-fit but never having done hard outdoor work, throwing himself into it from the first moment just like the gang of new starters he'd inducted that morning.

The job attracted all sorts – from hardened forestry workers to tree-hugging hippy types, disenchanted office workers like him, and more than a fair proportion of people from the edges of society, who'd stepped outside of the neatly marked lines of conventional life. If someone had told him twenty years ago that he'd fit into that category, he'd have burst out laughing. Hard working, with an expensive car and a stylishly decorated apartment in a fashionable part of the city, he'd fit the part of a successful high-flyer perfectly. If someone had told him he'd throw it all away – hand it over and walk away with nothing – he'd have thought them completely and utterly insane.

# CHAPTER THREE

After a night sleeping in a cute little campsite surrounded by oak trees by the side of a river, Meg was rested and ready to set off early in the morning for the final leg of the journey. She'd made the bed (which was incredibly comfortable, although it should be, given the cost of the thing) and wiped up the little kitchen, tipping the leftover water from the kettle outside to save filling up the waste-water tank unnecessarily as she'd been instructed, and putting her cup and plate and cutlery away in their little holders. Now she was driving along, listening to 90s music and singing tunelessly. Eliza was by her side, curled up and snoozing on the passenger seat after a walk through the cool woods, which had clearly worn out her stumpy little corgi legs. Meg smiled at her as she glanced across before looking back at the sat nav map. Two hours to go, most of it winding down country roads to get to the little village where her best friend Helen had settled with her husband ten years after they'd left art school. He'd been a local there, and she'd been welcomed into the community and supported with kindness when he'd walked out a few years after their daughter was born. Now she'd lived there so long it was hard to imagine her being anywhere else. Meg felt a pang of regret that she hadn't been to visit in so long, but things had been... well, the podcast about toxic relationships that her friend had recommended had made a lot of sense of why she'd lived the small little life she'd been stuck in since she met Michael.

Little by little, he'd chipped away at what small self-confidence she had, suggesting that she stop working for the company in York where she'd found her niche creating websites. As his furniture design company grew, he said he needed someone there to take care of the back-office side of things and keep their website up and running. As social media had become a thing, she'd set up pages for the company, acting as the cheerful voice who shared photos and fun facts with potential clients.

Eventually the company had grown to have a huge following online – something that anyone other than Michael might have put down to Meg's skill in understanding how it all worked, not to mention her design qualifications. He would veer between briskly dismissive and then unexpectedly complimentary, managing to fly her skilfully as if she was a human kite. Somehow, the bad days were always just outweighed by the good – or just good enough. After an unhappy childhood, where her late mother had picked on every fault and failing, it seemed to Meg that the status quo of being ever so slightly miserable all the time was... no more than she expected.

So she'd found her joy in working hard on the house and garden, making it pretty and homely and welcoming – not that they had any guests.

The company grew, but with her social life tied to

Michael's disinterest in doing anything (he was always too tired from working on an installation or would say he was worn out from working at exhibitions…) there was nothing to spend the increasingly large sums of money that the company made. So she splashed out on gardening bits and pieces, or the occasional trip into York where she'd splurge in bookshops. She'd take time buying thoughtful presents and packaging them up for friends and sending them in the post. Eventually, though, a lot of the friends seemed to get lost in the flotsam and jetsam of life, not helped by the fact that Michael always had an excuse for skipping a get together or dissuading her from attending an old art school reunion.

When they'd first moved into the house, she'd spent long hours outside digging and planting, weeding and tidying. The old man who'd lived next door told her it took eight years to see a garden to maturity, and twenty years after she'd begun, she'd left the place looking quite beautiful. Thick ropes of wisteria tangled over the pergola, hanging in long deep violet bunches in early summer. In spring, the place was beautiful in a stark, skeletal manner. The magnolia blossom was pink and pretty in the corner overlooking the patio of golden stone she'd laid one weekend when Michael was working in Paris. She narrowed her eyes in thought, realising in that moment that… well, she'd never know. Had he, in fact, been working? Had he been doing what he said? There were so many unanswered questions.

Helen had remained steadfast, despite it all. She didn't seem to mind that Meg hadn't been to visit in years. She'd travel down from the Highlands to visit and ignore Michael's ungracious lack of welcome. Meg lived for the weeks when she turned up, full of joy and trailing colourful, arty scarves and an air of nonchalance. Her daughter Phoebe was a delight, filling the house with chaos and noise. Then her neighbour

Janey had moved in next door, and she seemed to somehow *get it* too. It was no surprise that Michael had thoroughly disapproved of *her* as well, but living next door he'd had to swallow his disapproval and politely accept the invitations to dinner parties and Sunday summer barbecues. Meg suspected privately that Janey got a kick out of making him uncomfortable. She'd been amazing when he'd died, turning up with two bottles of red wine and a shoulder to cry on until Helen had arrived, rushing straight down from Scotland to stay for those early, confusing days, helping her to clear out papers and unearth all sorts of things - not the sort of things that most new widows had to deal with. Meg grimaced, remembering.

Meg reached over and ran a hand down Eliza's back. In return, she was given a lick on the wrist as a thank you, which made her smile. Her little corgi had been a delight, making her laugh and keeping her going over the last eighteen months as she'd come to terms with everything.

It was funny how driving all these miles seemed to give her time to mull things over. She smiled to herself as she checked the side mirror and indicated to overtake a horse trailer, which was trundling along even slower than she was. All those long-distance truck drivers must be like zen masters with all the time they had to think.

The time sped away, the road clear and the sky bright, and before she knew it, she was driving down the narrow curving lane that led down towards the tiny seaside village of Applemore. The hedges were still skeletal and dark, but the starry pinpricks of white blackthorn blossom danced among them, and the fields were shaded with the first tinges of acid green suggesting that spring was just around the next bend in the road. As was the village, she realised with a happy sigh, at last.

## WELCOME TO APPLEMORE
### Twinned with La Mardelle, France

The sign was freshly painted and decorated with hanging baskets of pretty violet and yellow pansies and greenery which swung gently in the breeze. She slowed down a little more to take in the view as she navigated the twisty road which led down to the village.

It had been so long since she'd visited Helen in Applemore that the place felt quite different from her memory of it. Parked in the car park at the start of the main street was a sleek silver Airstream caravan which - judging from the queue of people waiting to be served – was selling something in great demand. Despite the chill of the early spring day, people were sitting on the sea wall eating takeaway food from white cardboard cartons, wrapped up in waterproof coats, their hair blowing in the wind. All the way along the street on the seaside, jaunty multi-coloured bunting flapped between the lampposts and the metal railings which edged the sea wall were freshly painted a cheerful sky blue. The last time she'd visited the village had seemed much more faded and work-manlike. At the far end of the street opposite the tiny harbour, the Applemore Hotel looked positively stylish with a modern-looking black sign above the door and flowers filling the windows. She couldn't take it all in – conscious that the road was narrow, Meg felt a vague sense of panic that something might appear and she was going to have to manoeuvre herself in the still unfamiliar – and very large and unwieldy – campervan. With a row of cute little cottages on her right, she indicated left and trundled at a sedate pace towards Helen's place, surprised that it all suddenly felt quite familiar.

The road was lined with leafless hedges and inclined upwards slightly, curving round for a moment before the lighthouse came into view. It stood tall and brightly painted on the sea's edge, surrounded by the rocky outcrops which led down to one of the tiny beaches which edged the Applemore shore. As she reached the white-painted gate, Helen appeared at the door of her cottage, both arms waving madly as she dashed through her garden and up the gravel path towards her.

'I'll get it, hang on,' she yelled, motioning for Meg to stay put. She unlatched the gate and swung it open, motioning for her to pull forward, and then closed it securely behind her.

'Lambs,' she explained, pointing in the distance to where a collection of white specks could be seen. 'We have to be careful with the gate at this time of year or they make a run for it, and then Finlay the farmer's son gets cross when he has to herd them back when he'd rather be in the pub.'

'Well, that makes sense.' Meg glanced over at Eliza, who had both front paws on the dash and was peering out with interest. Luckily, she wasn't in the least bit interested in sheep – or any other fluffy creature, for that matter.

'Oh it's so lovely to see you,' Helen exclaimed, pulling the door open and reaching up to squeeze Meg so hard she gasped and laughed in surprise. 'Stick the van over there on the gravel. I've made us some soup and bread for lunch, and we've got so much to catch up on before I leave for Chile.'

Meg climbed down from the driver's seat and Helen held her for a long moment in a hug that made her eyes prickle unexpectedly. She smelled of the same lily of the valley perfume she'd always worn.

'Excuse the garden,' Helen said, gesturing to the tangle of daffodils growing through the faded brown leftovers of last summer's planting. 'I had every intention of getting it all done in the autumn, but I got caught up in a series of paintings, then – well, you know how it is.'

Meg shook her head, laughing. 'Never apologise. It's so lovely to be here.'

Helen's cottage had been built for the lighthouse keeper over a century ago, and stood in the shadow of the tall tower which had guided boats safely into the harbour of Applemore ever since. There was a disused outbuilding which joined the two, with a separate door and windows looking out over the bay.

Helen opened the gate to the garden, which was surrounded by a stone wall about four feet in height.

'Come on, you two,' she said, beckoning Meg and Eliza inside. Meg brushed against the dried stems of last summer's lavender, catching a momentary scent which reminded her of the garden she'd left behind.

The cottage was tiny and cosy, and a million times more chaotic than it had been the last time Meg had visited. Back then, her daughter Phoebe was still living at home and that had clearly meant Helen's hoarding tendencies were kept under wraps. The place was stacked with piles of everything under the sun – books, yarn, craft equipment, boxes of unopened paints, and potted plants covering every surface.

Helen glanced over at Meg, who kept her face as neutral as possible.

'It's a bit of a bomb site, isn't it?' Helen said, mistress of understatement.

'I'm here to see you, not the house,' said Meg, which would have made sense – except they both knew that she was there to house sit.

'Well me *and* the house.' Helen made a face. 'I tried to clear up a bit, but I was so busy getting packed up for the trip – there's so much stuff that Phoebe can't get over there in Santiago.' She motioned to a heap of suitcases. 'And I hate under-packing.'

'I remember.' Meg grinned at her friend. 'What have you got in there, out of interest? The entire contents of the M&S food hall?'

'Never mind the food hall, it's the knickers. She sent me a huge shopping list and nice underwear was at the top. You know what it's like when you've had a baby and your –'

Meg raised an amused eyebrow. 'I don't, I'm relieved to say.'

'You know what I mean.' Helen shook her head and cleared a space on the sofa, patting the cushions to indicate to Eliza that the space was meant for her. Eliza, tired after a busy morning of snoozing in the passenger seat, hopped up politely, circled three times and collapsed in a neat little pretzel shape, her chin resting on a brightly coloured crewel-work cushion.

'She approves of your handiwork.' Meg ran a hand over her soft fur and followed Helen into the kitchen, which was – even worse. Despite the muddle, the room smelled of freshly baked bread, and there was a pretty jug of creamy narcissi on the big wooden table which dominated the room.

'Just shove those things over to one side,' said Helen, 'and we can have lunch. I'm assuming you must be hungry after all that driving. You didn't eat on the way up?'

Meg shook her head. 'I was saving myself for your famous sourdough.'

Helen beamed. 'I made one especially for you. Talking of which, that's on the list of things for you to do while I'm gone.'

'Make sourdough?'

'It's not hard. There are loads of tutorials on Instagram if you get stuck, but I'll leave you an instruction manual. You don't have to make bread if you don't fancy it, but you need to feed her twice a week at least, to keep her sweet. I'll put her in the fridge before I go.'

'Her?'

'Mildred. My sourdough starter.' Helen waggled a crusty-looking jar which had been sitting on the windowsill beside a vigorously flowering and very pink geranium.

'It has a name?'

'She is very temperamental. Well, she's not if she's well looked after, but we had a serious talking to the other month when I went to Edinburgh for a week, and she didn't like the water.'

Helen sold her art at galleries all over Scotland, so it wasn't unusual for her to travel south to deliver paintings.

'Funnily enough, I had someone tell me yesterday that the van ought to have a name as well. There must be something in the air.' Meg surreptitiously stacked up a pile of travel magazines and a pile of yarn strands and shifted them sideways to make space before sitting down on the bench at the clearest end of the table.

'Abeona,' Helen pronounced, as she placed a heavy Le Creuset pot down onto the scuffed wooden tabletop.

'I'm sorry?'

'Goddess of departures. That's what you should call her.'

'It's an inanimate object, not a *her*.' Meg accepted a bowl and a spoon.

'All travel things are female, I think. I can't remember why. It's a nice name for a van, anyway. I shall think of her as Abeona in my head when I think of you travelling the world in her.'

'Travelling the world might be pushing it a bit. I've made it to the Highlands from Yorkshire, and even now I'm staying at your place, not even camping out.'

Although, thought Meg, as Helen ladled some of her delicious smelling vegetable soup into bowls, if the spare bedroom is as chaotic as the rest of the house, I might just be sleeping in the van for the next two months out of self-defence.

'Butter?' Helen slid the dish across and passed her a knife. There were a few minutes of silence as they both busied themselves spreading cool pats of thick butter onto the still-warm bread, the only sound the ticking of the old wooden clock on the wall. It chimed one o'clock as Helen started to speak.

'So how was the journey? You managed okay in the van?'

Meg nodded. 'Good. Admittedly, I was a bit spooked to start with, but once you get going, it doesn't really feel like you're driving something huge. I think I might need some work on my reverse parking, mind you. I can't imagine getting that thing parked in the supermarket in town.'

'You don't need to worry about that. I've sorted the car for you – even had it cleaned and serviced. It's so pristine you might want to sleep in there while I'm gone.' Helen gave a chuckle.

'Oh that's amazing, thanks.'

'Least I could do. I couldn't really leave this place empty for two months, and it's hardly in the sort of state for listing on Airbnb, is it? Talking of which, if you felt the urge to do some of your magic while you're here, I'd be more than eternally grateful.'

Meg looked across at her friend. Her long red hair was threaded with silver highlights now, which glinted in the sunlight that shone in through the side window. She looked exactly the same as she had the day they'd met in the first week of art school, and yet... completely different at the same time. It was the strangest thing to watch your friend age alongside you. It didn't seem any time at all since they were turning twenty, and now here they were thirty years later.

Helen hadn't changed in lots of other ways, too – she'd always been chaos to Meg's order. When they shared a flat together as second and third-year students, Meg had always been the one following along behind her, clearing up and making the place look nice.

'Some of my magic?' Meg said, after a moment, knowing exactly what her friend meant.

Helen waved an arm. 'Your decluttering magic. I mean you don't have to. If you want to leave things exactly as they are I would be equally delighted. Having you here to stay is saving my life and Phoebe's delighted, as well, as you can imagine. It's nice to have your mum around when you're having a baby, especially when you're living on the other side of the world. But if you felt the urge to – I don't know, organise it all a bit? That would be fine, too.'

'I'd love to.' It was the least she could do. Helen had been there, always. Decluttering and tidying were her thing. Having a purpose would get her stay off to a good start, and then – after that – perhaps she'd have a think about what she was going to do with the rest of her life.

'Nothing's off limits,' Helen said, breaking into her thoughts. 'I mean there's nothing you're going to find that's going to freak you out. I don't have any dead bodies hiding in the cupboard under the stairs, or anything like that.'

They exchanged a look.

'Sorry, that's probably not the best analogy, under the circumstances, is it? If you could make some sort of order out of the chaos, maybe I could sort it properly when I get back.'

'I'd love to.' Meg glanced around the room. A plan was already formulating in her mind.

'I don't want you thinking I'm taking advantage.' Helen fiddled with the petals of one of the flowers from the jug between them.

'I'm staying in your house, for one thing,' began Meg.

'But you've bought a campervan so you can travel the globe.'

Meg wrinkled her nose. 'I'm not sure I'm quite globe travelling material. Not when I can't even park the thing.'

Helen waved her hands airily. 'Whatever. I mean – what I'm trying to say in my usual roundabout manner is I'd be really grateful if you did manage to do some sort of decluttering magic, but you don't have to do anything at all.'

'I promise you; I'll love doing it. It's therapeutic for me. I can listen to one of your podcasts while I'm working.' Meg waggled her phone to illustrate the point.

'Talking of which, did you like the one I sent? I thought it was pretty apposite under the circumstances.'

'Painfully so.' Meg grimaced. 'It's not very edifying to realise you've spent the best part of your adult life unhappily married to a man who's been living a double life.'

Helen's brow furrowed as she thought for a moment. 'Perhaps you were so busy trying to make everything look okay from the outside, there was no time to think about what was going on the inside?'

'I think you might be onto something there.' Meg tore a piece of sourdough crust off and spread a little more butter onto it. 'It's hard to look back and realise I wasted so much time trying to make someone happy when I wasn't the problem.'

'It's not easy, though, is it?' Helen stacked up a little pile of colourful post-it notes as she spoke. 'Grief is complicated.'

'You're telling me. All those people at the funeral telling me how heartbroken I must be to have lost Michael, and I'm standing there thinking about the fact he died in a hotel room with a woman he met at a conference.'

Even now, saying it out loud sounded crazy. The whole situation had been so shocking and unexpected. And embarrassing. That had been the worst thing, dealing with the awkwardness.

Helen shrugged slightly. 'There isn't a rulebook for how to act as the grieving widow of a man you weren't particularly happily married to, is there?'

'Funnily enough,' Meg said, pushing a stray strand of hair back behind her ear as she leaned forward as if to confide in Helen, despite the emptiness of the room, 'it turns out that there's a whole world of women out there in the same boat. You search on Google, and there they are. Thousands of us. Millions, probably. There are forums where people share their stories.'

'I can't believe you stayed. I can't believe you didn't tell me how bad it was until after he'd gone.' Helen grimaced. 'I mean it was pretty evident it was – he was – awful. But all the cheating and lying on top of it was the worst kind of icing.'

'The worst kind of icing on a cake nobody in their right mind would want to eat.' Meg straightened her knife, laying it neatly on the plate and absentmindedly arranging crumbs into a line beside it as she spoke. 'All those trips away and exhibitions.'

Helen shook her head in sympathy.

'I feel guilty. I knew you were trapped, but you seemed – well, I always thought if you wanted to get out, you'd find a way.'

'We talked about this after the funeral. It's that old saying about boiling a frog. Maybe if we'd had kids, it would have been different. Maybe I'd have escaped then, because I'd like to think I wouldn't have made someone else live with it.'

Helen reached across the table, closing her hand over Meg's for a brief second.

'The thing is, it's a mind game. It's how they control you. You mustn't blame yourself.'

Meg shook her head. 'Weirdly, I don't. The therapist said the same thing. It feels more like I was under some sort of spell, and as soon as he died, it broke. Then I could see things for what they really were.'

'Weren't you tempted to let people know the truth? You could have stood up at the funeral and told them what you'd found out in the days after he died. All the emails, the second phones, the trips he took abroad with other women when you thought he was on top secret business…'

'You know I thought about it.' They'd discussed it over wine in the days before the funeral, when Helen had shot down to be with her on a moment's notice. Janey next door had been in on the secret, too, but apart from that, nobody else had the faintest inkling that Michael was anything other than a loving and hardworking husband who'd tragically died on a business trip at the shockingly early age of fifty.

'But there would be so much to it. All that drama.' Helen nodded.

'People feeling sorry for me. People wondering what I'd done to drive him away. You know what gossip is like. That's why I couldn't face staying there. It would have come out one way or another in the end, and I didn't want to be the person people were talking about the moment my back was turned.'

'I get it.' Helen cut another thick slice of bread, then split it in half, passing one over to Meg. 'Believe me, when Tommy left me here, I had years where people couldn't help but bring it up whenever they saw me. It's exhausting being the subject of pity, even if it's well meant.'

'Exactly. The only blessing is that for whatever reason, between selling off the business and the life insurance policies, I never have to think about money ever again.'

It had been eighteen months since Michael died. It had taken time, and a fair amount of expensive therapy to get to a place where Meg could say calmly and objectively the facts as they lay before her: her marriage had been miserable, and she'd felt trapped and lonely - but now she was free to live the rest of her life on her terms. All she had to do was work out what exactly it was that she wanted.

Helen raised her soup spoon in a toast. 'To Michael, who got one thing right at least.'

Meg gave a wry smile. 'To Michael, indeed.'

# CHAPTER FOUR

The spare room was slightly less chaotic than the rest of the house, which was a relief. The first of the two drawers in the scrubbed pine chest were empty, and Helen had emptied *almost* all of the wardrobe, which smelled of her perfume. All that remained on the hangers were a couple of very dated and tiny dresses which looked like they hadn't seen the light of day since the 1990s. Shoeboxes filled the floor of the wardrobe, along with a noticeable layer of dust. Meg closed the door on the problem and decided she'd deal with it once Helen had set off on the long journey to Santiago.

She left her things in the van and brought in a change of clothes and her toilet bag, leaving them on the end of the bed before heading back down to find Helen cuddling Eliza on the sofa, the two of them snuggled up on a rainbow-striped crochet blanket.

'I wish we'd timed this a bit better. I should have arranged the flight for a few days later so we had some time to hang out.'

Meg sat down on the sofa beside them. The room itself

was incredibly pretty – pale walls the colour of thick cream were set off by solid dark stained wooden beams. A thick wooden mantel stood atop a fireplace which held a sturdy black log burning stove. Two comfortable sofas sat against the walls, one facing the fire and the other looking out of a wide window which faced out to sea. A chunky wooden coffee table sat in the middle of the room, piled with heaping mountains of books and magazines as well as countless colourful crochet projects and skeins of yarn.

'We'll have it when you get back. You've got a new baby to wait for. When is Phoebe due?'

'The eighteenth. I'm working on the assumption that she'll be late going into labour, because I was a week over with her, but I want to get there and get settled and get some time with my baby before we welcome *her* baby. I still can't believe I'm going to be a granny.'

'You can't?' Meg laughed. 'I'm still coming to terms with you being a parent. I remember the time you nearly killed us cooking a saucepan of boiled eggs for three hours when you passed out fast asleep drunk on the sofa after that quiz night when we were students.'

'Fifty is quite young to be a grandma, to be fair. I never expected Phoebe to take after me in that regard.'

'She's like you in lots of ways. She's sweet and kind and she'd do anything for her friends.' Meg gave Helen's knee a squeeze.

'Fortunately she's not like me on the organisational front.' Helen raised an eyebrow and inclined her gaze towards the chaos on the table.

'It was going to go one way or the other. She turned out to be a neat freak.' Meg laughed.

'I'm trying to think of all the things I need to tell you before I go. I was going to write a list but life sort of got in the way, and I was so busy focusing on making sure I had every-thing packed and triple checking I had everything I needed for the travel documentation that it kind of slipped my mind.'

'I'm sure it's quite straightforward. I'll be here, hanging out with Eliza, watching the baby lambs skipping about in the field outside and enjoying my own company. I probably won't see a single soul the whole time you're gone, apart from when I drive to the supermarket. That'll suit me perfectly. I take it the big store is still that one in the town on the way towards Inverness? I've forgotten what it's called.'

Helen's eyes had widened in surprise. 'Yes, there's that one, but there's also a little mini supermarket in town now – that caused a bit of a drama, but that's another story – and we've got a farm shop in the grounds of the big house, and...'

'Are you okay?' Meg watched as Helen stood up and went over to the window, peering outside and then turning back again.

'Me? Yes, fine. I remembered there's one minor detail I forgot to mention.'

Eliza hopped down from the sofa and pottered over to the stove, sniffing it thoughtfully.

'Go on?'

'The library. Well, it's not so much a library as a – well, it's a little free library. More of an exchange, really. Hang on, I'll show you.'

Meg followed her friend through the back door of the cottage and out into the garden. The grass was shaggy and sprinkled with daisies and dandelion flowers. An early bumble bee, warmed by the first of the spring sunshine, was sleepily buzzing between the flowers, trying to find the choicest nectar.

'What do you mean when you say library?' The sky might be azure and the sun bright and high in the sky, but the wind off the sea was biting as she followed Helen through the little garden gate and onto a path that led down to the beach. There on a wooden post stood a glass-fronted box with a sign above it on which someone – if she had to hazard a guess, she'd say Helen, from the familiar curled lettering and pretty flowers that decorated the sign – had written THE LIGHTHOUSE LIBRARY.

'It completely slipped my mind. I'm so used to doing it that it didn't even occur to me it would be a problem, but when you mentioned not seeing a soul, I realised you'd get the fright of your life if I didn't explain.'

Meg opened the door to look inside at the shelves. 'Go on,' she said, leaning in to see that there were – inexplicably – two cartons of eggs on the bottom shelf, along with a jumble of slightly tatty looking paperbacks.

'You might not remember, but we had a little bookshop in the village – it limped along for years, but it never really did very well and when the lease came up, the girl who ran it decided to give up and move back to be near her family in Glasgow. Anyway, what with the mobile library service stopping because of cuts in funding, we decided it would be an idea to set up a little free library here in the village.'

Meg's eyebrows, which were already well on their way skywards, raised a little bit further. She looked around at the lighthouse, and the cottage, and down towards the white sand of the beach.

'This isn't exactly in the village.'

'It's not as far as you think – it's only a five-minute walk along the beach path. It only takes longer by car because of the way the road goes. So there's always someone passing by, walking their dog or taking their children for a run about on the beach down here, because we get the best rock pools after high tide. Anyway, it doesn't take long. All you have to do is keep an eye on the books and make sure nothing untoward is being left in there.'

'Nothing untoward?' Meg looked at the shelves once again. 'Like eggs?'

'Oh no, the eggs are fairly standard. Kathleen along the road has a very bad chicken habit – she can't stop buying them, so she has far too many eggs, so she puts them in the library for anyone who might need them.'

'Do they leave the payment in the library?'

'Oh no, they're free to whoever needs them. Food's expensive these days, especially if you've got lots of little mouths to feed. And it's not always easy finding work up here in the middle of nowhere in winter when the tourists aren't around.'

Meg's heart squeezed in empathy at the thought. 'Oh that's such a kind thing to do.'

'Yes, Kathleen is a sweetheart. I'm sure you'll bump into her when she's doing one of her egg deliveries.'

'Maybe I won't be quite as isolated as I was thinking.'

Helen pursed her lips and widened her eyes in an expression that Meg knew of old meant there was more to the situation than met the eye. 'Possibly... not.'

Meg followed her back towards the cottage, her love of Helen battling with the vague sense of unease that she'd been sold a pup and this idyllic eight week break in the middle of nowhere was going to be something very different indeed...

# CHAPTER FIVE

'You sure you don't want to come down for a drink after work? It's a long way to Friday, after all.'

Ed, who had returned with the van to collect the planting gang, looked at Gabe and waggled his sandy eyebrows.

'Honestly, I'm whacked. I don't have the stamina you lads have. I'm an old man, remember.'

Ed gave a laugh and shook his head, continuing to wheedle in his sing-song accent. 'Old man my eye! You're fitter than half the other forestry lads out there.'

'Wait until you see me tomorrow morning and tell me that. A day up there planting and I feel like I need a hot bath and an early night.'

'Friday, then. Is that a deal?' Ed cocked his head in query.

'It's a deal.' Gabe shook Ed's outstretched hand and headed back to the Land Rover, stopping to pick up a piece of plastic wrapper which was caught on the branch of a gnarled hawthorn bush. Litter really did get everywhere, even up here on the moor three miles from town.

He stood apart from the others and watched as the hills

emptied of people, the heaps of empty bags collected up and packed in the back of the trucks. Tired, aching workers were laughing and groaning as they rubbed their backs before heading down to the village where they'd decamp – after a few drinks in the village pub – to their assorted lodgings for the night before it all started again the next day.

The rows of tiny trees sheltered with their little casings dotted the landscape which stretched down the valley towards the peaty water of the river. It was strange to think that twenty years from now the place would be thickly wooded, creatures sheltering beneath the branches and the ecosystem restored. Thank goodness for the owners of the land who'd invested their money in making a difference. He shook his head, smiling to himself, as he cast a final glance around and climbed into the cab of the truck to head back down to the village below.

Twenty years into the future this place would be thick with trees. Twenty years before, the landscape had probably looked much the same. His landscape, though, had looked completely different. On a Monday evening at 4.30pm the Gabe of twenty years before might have been two hours into a board meeting about financial projections for the next quarter, or flying to New York for a conference. He'd have been dressed in an expensive suit and ordering something in for dinner, not brushing mud and pine needles off a pair of work trousers before stopping at the farm shop to grab something from the freezer to sling in the oven.

The wheels of the truck rattled over the cattle grid as he left the moorland track and joined the road that curved down to Applemore, and he took a left and headed up towards the farm shop, crossing his fingers he'd catch it before it closed.

A woman with dark hair tied back in a ponytail was doing something with the sign as he approached the gateway that led to the Applemore Farm Shop and he slowed for a moment, opening his window to try and get a better view. Was she changing the sign to 'closed'?

'Am I too late?' he called out, crossing his fingers in hope.

'No, the shop's still open. Go on up,' she said, turning and giving him a welcoming smile. 'I'm just putting the new sign up. Or trying to, anyway. Darling, have you got those nails Mummy asked you to hold?'

A cute little girl of about six with a matching ponytail appeared from behind a hedge, proudly brandishing a handful of long metal nails in one hand and a slightly sticky-looking rainbow lollipop festooned with pieces of grass and distinctly muddy in the other. 'I fell over, but I didn't drop them,' she said, proudly.

'Well done, Kitty,' said her mother, rolling her eyes in amusement as they exchanged glances. 'We might need to give that lolly a bit of a clean before you –'

At that moment little Kitty's tongue darted out and she took an experimental lick of her lollipop. 'It's okay,' she said, looking pleased with herself.

'Too late.' He burst out laughing. 'I'm sure the grass and mud coating give it a whole new flavour.'

'What's that old saying about children eating dirt to keep themselves healthy? I suspect this one's going to be as strong as an ox if that's the case.'

'Good luck with the sign,' Gabe said, giving a wave as he headed up the road towards the farm shop. The verges were neatly trimmed, and he noticed as he drove further into Applemore Estate that the work someone had mentioned when he was in the pub at the weekend was well underway. The massed rhododendron bushes which had lined the drive had been cut and cleared, leaving bare earth and only the stumps which would be ground out and removed. Funny how something that looked so pretty could be such a problem. Now he'd learned about the plant's invasive nature, he seemed to spot it everywhere – another example of how his outlook had changed since he'd arrived in Applemore. In the old days, he wouldn't have known an ash tree from an oak.

'Hi,' said the tall blonde behind the counter as he walked in. 'You didn't happen to see someone down at the gate, did you?'

Gabe took one of the wicker baskets that stood by the door and grabbed a couple of the crusty bread rolls that were left on the display, putting them into a paper bag as he replied. 'Yes, she's down there with a little girl – says she's trying to put the new sign up?'

The blonde woman grinned and gave an affirmative nod. 'Aha. Yeah, that's my sister-in-law, Rilla. I told her to wait until I was finished and I'd come and give her a hand, but she insisted. Stubborn as a blooming mule, she is.'

'I won't be long. Just need to grab something to eat.'

'Take as long as you need.'

Passing the shelves full of handicrafts which were strung with tiny fairy lights, he headed up to the back of the shop, his stomach growling again at the prospect of something decent to eat besides the substandard lunch he'd thrown together that morning.

'You've timed that well,' she called out cheerfully. 'I've just restocked the freezer.'

The shop was a treasure trove of local produce, but right now all Gabe wanted was to grab hold of something he could shove in the oven for half an hour to reheat. He knew exactly what would happen – it would cook while he unknotted his muscles under a scalding hot shower and then collapsed in front of something mindless on Netflix, and he'd fall asleep with Stan curled up on the sofa beside him, half an hour into the programme.

The freezer was stacked to the brim with handmade freezer meals, which were ridiculously expensive but delicious. He snagged a multi-pack of Coke and headed for the till.

'Good luck with the sign,' he said as he left.

'Oh, she'll have it sorted by the time I get there,' the woman said, shaking her head in amusement. 'I'd put money on it.'

Sure enough, when he got back down to the junction there was no sign of the dark-haired woman or the little girl, and the white paint of a brand-new sign was glowing brightly in the gathering dusk.

Half an hour later, a lasagne heating in the oven, he stood under a furnace-hot shower, letting the jets of water pummel all the aches out of his shoulders and back. Village life had taken some getting used to. Six months ago, when he'd arrived, he'd been discomfited to find that the person behind the checkout in the little village store asked where he'd come from or what he was doing, or that a passer-by on a walk might strike up a conversation out of the blue. Now, though, he'd become adjusted to it – so the impromptu chats he'd had up at the farm shop seemed perfectly normal.

He rinsed the citrus scented suds from his eyes, and reached out for the towel that was hanging on the heated rail by the door. It might have been bright and sunshiny earlier, but spring could be deceptive and there was a distinct nip in the air when he'd got back. He towelled himself dry, glad he'd lit the wood-burner which would be warming the sitting room.

The cottage kitchen was a tiny galley, big enough for two people – or one and a dog. Gabe smiled to himself a few moments later as he nudged a hopeful Stan out of the way and pulled open the oven to check on dinner. Only half an hour later did he remember the text from Jacob that had woken him this morning, picking up his phone and scrolling through WhatsApp. Something about the wording of the message had rattled him. He and Jacob had a warm enough relationship – he'd been fourteen when Gabe met his mother, long past the age where he might have been looking for a replacement father figure. The situation at home had made things more difficult. Gabe didn't blame Jacob one bit for choosing to travel to New Zealand as soon as he finished high school, attending university over there where his father had lived and worked for many years. It seemed a perfectly logical explanation to the outside world, and so no questions were asked or eyebrows raised. When his dad had died suddenly a couple of years later, Jacob had insisted that he was happy and settled where he was. Since then, they'd kept in touch, with Gabe acting as a go-between until the marriage had broken down irretrievably. Now he felt a sense of responsibility for a young man who lived almost as far away as possible, in a time zone which made picking up the phone for a chat a lot more complicated than it might seem.

# CHAPTER SIX

'Are you absolutely sure you don't want me to drive you to the airport?'

Meg watched as Helen opened her travel rucksack for the fifth time, took out her passport and travel documents, checked them over, slid them back into the plastic envelope, then zipped them back in the compartment on the side of her bag.

Helen shook her head vigorously. 'For one thing you've driven all the way up from Yorkshire, for another I doubt my little car would make it all the way to Inverness and back without something vital falling off.'

'That's slightly alarming,' said Meg, drily. 'I'll take the campervan if I'm going outside of Applemore, yes?'

'Oh no, it'll be fine, I'm almost certain.' Helen beamed with a confidence that Meg definitely didn't feel. 'But third of all and most important, I've booked an Uber.'

'An Uber? In Applemore?' Meg's eyebrows shot upwards in astonishment. It looked as if the place had changed a bit since she'd last visited, but somehow the idea of booking an Uber in the tiny village was impossible to imagine.

'Well, it's not strictly an Uber, it's the all-new taxi service. I like to call it that because it sounds fancy. He only operates on Tuesdays and Fridays unless he's in the mood, so I timed my flight well. Otherwise, I'd have been on the bus to Inverness and staying overnight at the Travelodge near the airport.'

'What happens if you want a taxi any other day?' Meg was baffled.

Helen shrugged airily. 'I don't know. I've never tried. It's a luxury to be able to call one at all when you're living out here.'

Meg turned and looked out of the window. The sea was rough and iced with white waves; the wind battering raindrops against the window. The weather outside completely wiped out yesterday's hint of spring, and it could have been the middle of November. Eliza, no fan of wet weather walks, was flat out and snoring on the rug in front of the roaring wood-burner.

Half an hour later than planned ('don't worry, I'd factored that in,' said Helen, cheerfully) Malcolm appeared, and with a last-minute panic about the size of her cases which filled every space possible, Helen was crammed into the front passenger seat and left, waving madly and promising to call as soon as she arrived at Inverness Airport for the first part of her long journey. It would take almost a day and a half to get from Applemore to Santiago, flying from Inverness to London and then onto the long, long flight which would take Helen to the other side of the world where her daughter was waiting.

Meg closed the door firmly and perched on the edge of the sofa, looking with a smile at Eliza, who'd made herself at home. She was completely unruffled by the chaos that surrounded them. Meg, on the other hand, felt as if her brain was spinning off its axis and she was going slightly mad. If she carried on living in Helen's muddle, she was more than a little bit worried that she might end up just as scatty and disorganised.

First things first – a cup of coffee, a bowl of hot soapy water in the sink, and a list. Everything was better with a list.

The clutter in the kitchen seemed to be formed of layers like geological strata, or some kind of chaos lasagne. There was a vast amount of paperwork and bills, and below that craft equipment, then an assortment of shopping bags and boxes from online orders – some open, some with now overdue return labels taped on the sides with haphazard strips of sticky-tape. Meg stood at the head of the table and surveyed the room, taking it all in. What was that saying? There's only one way to eat an elephant – one bite at a time. She rolled up her sleeves. This was quite a big elephant.

She wandered through the cottage, collecting coffee mugs and water glasses which seemed to be scattered all over the place. Helen's studio where she worked was surprisingly tidy, with just one hand-thrown clay mug balanced on top of a pile of books on the windowsill. The rain had gone off quite suddenly as if someone had switched off a tap somewhere, and a shaft of sunlight broke through huge, dramatic clouds and lit up the room. In the distance, the shapes of the islands seemed to glow a strange purplish black against a slate grey sea. It was the perfect room for an artist to work in. Meg turned, one hand lingering on the windowsill for a moment, and then headed back downstairs.

The mugs would need a long soak as they were tide-marked with long-dried coffee, so she plopped them all into the soapy water and turned once again, frowning. The best thing, she decided, would be to get some cardboard boxes and set about sorting the table. At least if she did that she'd be able to sit down and have dinner in the kitchen, and then perhaps tomorrow she'd work on the sitting room, and then the rest of the house could fall into place a room at a time.

There had to be some big cardboard boxes somewhere – there was no way Helen hadn't stashed some away in an outhouse, or more likely stuffed them in the back hallway that led out to the garden. There was a key rack on the kitchen wall, which had an assortment of huge old keys hanging – unlabelled, of course. One of them ought to work.

Meg headed outside, pulling the front door open to discover that the sun had broken through. A determined patch of blue sky was trying hard to gain ascendancy over the clouds, and a rainbow shone over the hill that led up to the village of Applemore. The lighthouse stood tall overhead, and Meg gazed up at it in wonder. She'd been so busy rushing to get here, rushing to get settled, and rushing to see Helen off safely that she hadn't taken a moment to really notice how magical it was.

She tried several keys before she found one that opened the door to the building, which was sandwiched between the cottage and the lighthouse. Inside – along with several enormous spiders, a lot of dust and some random old pieces of furniture which looked like they'd been left over when the previous owner moved out twenty-five years ago – she found a towering stack of plastic storage crates. They'd be absolutely perfect.

On the opposite side of the room, held open with a plastic doorstop, was a solid, half-glazed door. Years before, she'd climbed up with Helen, who'd told her with a mischievous expression that she was absolutely not allowed to do this.

'But who's going to know?' she'd asked, and Meg – wide-eyed with worry – had followed.

But now she was older and braver, so curiosity – and the knowledge that it was very unlikely she'd be caught out – got the better of her. She took a final look around outside before tiptoeing through the doorway and heading up the cool stone steps.

Up and up she climbed, the backs of her calves aching as she stopped halfway for a moment to catch her breath. Bending over, she could feel the blood rushing in her ears. It reminded her of a time when she'd decided to walk up the central staircase at the underground station in Marylebone in London. Only a sense of pride and determination had kept her going as amused passengers had sailed past her on the escalator. She straightened up and trudged upwards, her pace slowing until she reached the window, which looked out across the bay. Galvanised by the sight of the houses of Applemore, she kept going, up the stone steps, round and round, the air cold and damp, until she got to the top.

She pushed open the door, puffed out and heart thumping, and was rewarded with a shaft of sunlight which had broken through the clouds and lit up the light room.

The sky and the sea reached out for miles, making her feel quite dizzy with the enormity of it all. The distant islands seemed smaller from up here, and far below she could see waves crashing on the beach. A few hardy people were out for an afternoon walk between rain showers. Turning, she could see the rolling moors and a patchwork blanket of fields and the dark green forest, divided by the grey of stone walls and thin, dark line of hedges bare of leaves. It was magical and made her feel strangely small and insignificant at the same time.

It seemed hard to believe that this breath-taking landscape was a few hours' drive from the bustling streets of Glasgow or Edinburgh. Stranger still to think that right now Helen was miles away, heading towards Chile, where she was hoping to visit a lighthouse there as part of a series of paintings she was working on. She wondered what the world would look like from the top of a lighthouse near Santiago. There was so much out there, and she'd missed so much of it. All those years married to Michael where she'd done his bidding and kept herself small and invisible, locked away her hopes and dreams in favour of keeping things easy and peaceful at home. And now here she was, on top of the world, with – she took a breath in, trying to steady herself – absolutely no idea what she was doing, where she was going or what the rest of her life held.

A wave of vertigo caught her unawares and her legs threatened to give way. She turned and headed back, round and round the spiral staircase and down to the safety of terra firma. Then, trying to gather herself, she grabbed four of the plastic boxes, stacking them one on top of the other, and headed back to the cottage. The wind whipped her hair across her face as she pushed open the handle with her elbow, the boxes toppling out of her arms and clattering onto the wooden floor in front of her.

'Sorry, darling,' she said to a curious Eliza, who'd been roused from her slumber by the commotion.

Content that they weren't being burgled, Eliza trotted off back to the warmth of the rug in front of the wood stove. Meg dumped the crates on the floor of the kitchen and had a sudden flash of realisation. Once she got to work, she had a habit of ploughing on until her stomach made it very clear that it meant business. This was Applemore, not Heatherby, and she couldn't call for a pizza delivery or drive to the 24-hour garage to pick up some snacks. If she was going to be practical, she should probably get herself to the shop and pick up some provisions.

She checked the fridge – to Meg's credit, there was a brand-new bottle of milk, some orange juice and a block of reasonable looking cheese. The cupboards yielded some pasta, a half-used bottle of olive oil, and an assortment of herbs and spices.

Her phone beeped on the kitchen table.

*So sorry,* said a message from Helen. *Just remembered in my panic to get packed I completely forgot to go to the supermarket and get some bits and pieces.*

*You read my mind,* replied Meg. *Don't worry, am on my way out now to explore and grab some dinner.*

There was a message from her old neighbour, Janey, too. The new people had been spotted, she announced, and didn't look half as nice as Meg.

She popped her head into the sitting room and was rewarded with some lazy wags from a corgi who clearly had no desire to get in the car and visit the Applemore shops.

'Shall I leave you here?'

Eliza didn't reply, but rolled onto her back and gave a heavy sigh.

'I'll take that as a yes. Don't get up to any mischief while I'm out.'

The sky was still a peculiar mix, with heavy purple clouds threatening to overpower the thin blue sky and pale spring sunlight. Maybe she'd walk into the village another time, but for now she was grabbing the keys to Helen's little Ford Fiesta and driving to the supermarket.

# CHAPTER SEVEN

Up on the moor at eight in the morning, Gabe had been unsurprised to discover that his merry band of tree-pickers had dwindled in number slightly. When he'd started the job six months before, he'd worked out quickly that the hard physical nature of the job, not to mention the repetitiveness of planting tree after tree after tree could be a bit much to deal with.

The advert he'd answered online had said that a good sense of humour was a pre-requisite, as well as the ability to work with others. It was strange, because most of the day was spent with only your own thoughts for company, and the sound of birds wheeling overhead. If you were lucky, you might catch sight of a stag on the moor or startle a hare and watch as it leapt off in horror, instinctively fearful of humans. But at the same time you had to be able to take orders, work in a gang, keep an eye on what your fellow workers were doing... oh, and be ready for any kind of weather.

'Was it something I said?' he said, laughing, as he counted

heads and prepared to get everyone set up for the day. 'Or do you think the weather forecast has put them off?'

They were three people down. The young lads who'd arrived in a converted van and had been excited to discover that the local pub was only a five-minute walk from the yard where they'd be situated for the season. The old boat repair yard had running water, a basic but functional shower, and an all-important electricity supply for charging their phones and electrical equipment.

'They seemed quite happy in the pub last night,' said Ed, who had appeared and was standing, his thick blonde brows furrowed, looking over the plans for the morning's planting.

'Maybe that's the problem,' said Tor, one of the villagers who worked as a tree planter in the winter and as a wildlife tour guide in summer. 'Perhaps they're still fast asleep.'

'I had a feeling they wouldn't last,' said the pink-haired girl, who was wearing a set of faded red overalls. She folded her arms, looking around at her co-workers with a faintly superior air.

'You might have spoken too soon,' said Ed, tapping Gabe on the shoulder so he turned around. In the distance, slowly crawling up the winding road on the hill in what looked like a painfully low gear, was the battered green van that belonged to the lads.

'Fair play to them,' laughed Gabe. 'Although if I had to take a guess, it looks like they might be spending their first week's wages on a new clutch for that van.'

Ten minutes later the lads had arrived, loaded up their tree bags and were hard at work planting today's tiny young seedling trees. A year from now, hopefully, they'd be a good foot taller, and not choked out by bramble or gorse, both of which grew like mad in the acidic peaty soil of the Highlands.

The rain came and went in five-minute bursts, stopping as

suddenly as it started as the bright sunlight broke through the huge, towering purple clouds. He'd quickly grown accustomed to the weather in Applemore, where you could expect four seasons in one day – often in more than one rotation. Now that spring was slowly creeping in, the hillwalkers were returning, following in the footsteps of the most determined who would climb in all weathers.

Stan barked as he spotted a couple in the distance. He'd been full of beans that morning, and Gabe had suspected that he'd be happier out and about sniffing the scents left by wildlife and keeping him company than snoozing in the back of the pick-up truck. Gabe whistled him back to heel and watched as the couple trudged up the track below them, pausing on the ridge to unfold a map which ruffled in the wind and almost flew out of their hands, making them both laugh. He raised a finger to his forehead in greeting then turned and bent back to the soil, tucking one of the millions of trees he'd planted into its new home. Stan returned to the important task of sniffing for rabbit trails, his plumed black tail wagging furiously and his long ears trailing on the ground as he followed a scent.

Gabe gazed down the valley, looking at the other workers all diligently planting. Everyone seemed to be getting on with the job happily, which was a relief. He felt a strange sense of responsibility for his groups, having been charged with inducting them after giving the health and safety talk that was necessary before heading out onto a planting site.

It was a strange thought to think that he was making a difference with this planting – that they all were. In that moment – all over the Highlands and Islands – forestry workers were hard at work, reforesting land that had lain bare for hundreds of years.

He was lost in thought when he heard a shout a while later,

vaguely aware that there was a voice somewhere in the distance, carried away by the wind.

'Gabe!'

He turned to see Pete, second-in-command at the forestry business, shading his eyes against the low slanted sunlight and beckoning him with a gloved hand.

'Sorry,' said Gabe a few moments later, puffing from his climb over rough ground. 'Didn't hear you.'

'No worries,' said Pete. 'I've got a call with a client in five minutes, but Donald's been on the phone asking if someone will pick up the mapping for the Lochbrannich Estate job. Would you mind nipping down for me?'

'Sure.' Gabe swung the half-empty planting bags off his shoulders. 'Is he coming here to collect them?'

Pete nodded. 'Think he's got to swing by and have a meeting with the duke himself, so he said he's printed off new copies of all the plans. The other ones are covered in notes – and if I know Donald, which I do, probably coffee cup rings and mucky fingerprints as well.'

Gabe grinned. 'Mission understood. Are they in the office?'

'Yeah, Una should be in there with them ready. Do us a favour and nip into the shop and get something for lunch break while you're down there?'

'For you or for everyone?' Gabe reached down to pat Stanley, who'd jumped up at his legs and was keen for attention.

'A morale booster for the troops – grab a load of cookies or something. And if you can grab me a pasty or a pie and a can of Coke as well that would be great. I was planning on heading down for a meeting, but it's been called off and I'm starving.'

'On it,' said Gabe, fishing in his trouser pocket to find the keys to the pick-up truck.

With Stan sitting happily on the passenger seat beside him,

he started the steep descent down the twisty moorland road back down to Applemore.

When he'd arrived six months ago, he'd been resolute that he wanted this job to be nothing more than the most straight-forward of manual labour, the absolute opposite of his previous career. He'd get up, spend all day doing an honest day's work, and go home exhausted but with nothing in his head but thoughts of what he'd have for dinner that evening. It was as simple as that.

Or so he'd thought. Somehow – by accident or design, he wasn't sure – he'd found himself being given responsibility here and there that he hadn't sought out. Running a crew, taking his first aid in forestry training certification and then a weeklong chainsaw training course so he had his ticket – the forestry term for a certificate - for felling trees and a ticket for brush-cutting which meant he could clear areas for planting. Donald, the easy-going owner of the business, was even making noises about sending him out on a fencing job so he could learn more about that. It was starting to feel like he was embarking on an entirely new career at the age of forty-nine, which was a pretty strange thing to happen when you didn't expect it.

But there was no arguing with the fact that life here in the Highlands was a dream. Where else could you have a commute to work like this – where the sky lit up golden at night as the sun set over the distant islands, and the air that filled your lungs was so clear it almost hurt to breathe it in deeply?

Applemore itself was a thriving little seaside village. He'd arrived at the end of the summer and caught the tail end of the madness that was the peak of tourist season – the little High Street was packed with visitors taking advantage of an unusually warm October. As he made his way down to the bottom of the glen and drove through the edge of the village he passed the little building which hosted the volunteer operated fire service and the tiny petrol station and garage where a tractor was currently parked. The door was hanging open and a black and white collie looked out at him.

It was starting afresh now. The weather was changing for the better and already there were cars lining the road by the side of the bay and a few little groups of visitors wandering about. A delivery lorry was parked across the entrance to the forestry office, so he turned at the end of the road and parked the truck down a side street.

'You stay there – and don't bark at any passing tourists,' he warned Stan, who wagged at him with an innocent expression.

Una was sitting behind her desk, a blue and white spotted scarf tied around her neck and a green gilet over her sweater to guard against the draught from a door that didn't quite shut properly. The huge printer was chuntering away in the corner, copies of the maps she was printing slowly piling up as the job was completed. She stood up and marched across the room, tucking the pen she'd been using behind her ear.

'Let me double check they're all there. I did the first batch and the blooming printer jammed.'

Gabe looked around as she counted under her breath. The walls of the office were covered in huge Ordnance Survey maps of the Highlands and Islands, some of them marked with coloured pins to designate sites that were being worked on. By the door there was a jumble of spare boots and shelf with a stack of neatly folded sweatshirts with the forestry logo on, alongside polo shirts in a dark forest green.

'Take one of those while you're at it,' said Una, turning to see Gabe looking at them.

'I'm okay,' he said, brushing down the dark blue sweater he

was wearing. It was a traditional fisherman's jersey knitted from wool, warm and breathable and waterproof. He'd bought it when he first arrived from the outdoor clothing shop at Applemore House, and it had proved itself a hundred times over.

'You're a bit pine-y,' said Una, heading towards him and plucking fir needles from the front of his chest, 'and more to the point if you're off to the big house I think Donald will want you in your best finery, so I think we can splash out on a sweatshirt for the occasion.'

'Oh I'm not off to the big house,' Gabe began, but Una had bustled off and was carefully doubling over the printouts, muttering to herself again as she searched in the stationery cupboard.

'I swear those plastic folders vanish when I'm not looking.' She passed him the huge sheaf of printed maps. 'I'll need to get an order done for some more. Meanwhile, I can rely on you getting these up to Donald in one piece, can't I?'

Gabe shook his head. Una was a whirlwind and a law unto herself. She'd obviously got the wrong end of the stick about him going with Donald up to the Lochbrannich Estate to meet with the duke, but there was no point arguing the point.

'You can rely on me, yes,' he said, feeling the edges of his mouth twitching in laughter.

'Right.' Una unwrapped the sweatshirt from the shelf, shaking it out and passing it to him. 'That's you all sorted. Donald told me he wanted two copies of everything, so I've done three. I know what he's like and he'll get coffee or goodness knows what all over them before you've got up to the big house, and the Duke of Lochbrannich is very posh indeed and I'm fairly sure he'll not want filthy scraps of paper all over his big expensive walnut desk.' She paused for breath.

'Have you been to Lochbrannich House?' Gabe tucked the new sweatshirt under his arm along with the folded maps.

Una shook her head, reaching under the desk and re-emerging with a tin of colourful boiled sweets. 'I have not. But I imagine that if you're a duke, you've probably got a very fancy desk. Want one?'

'I'm okay, thanks.'

'Don't get them dirty,' said Una darkly as he left.

'On my honour,' said Gabe, laughing.

# CHAPTER EIGHT

Meg was almost in the car when inspiration struck. If she was going to the shop, she really ought to check and see what Helen had in the way of cleaning products. It was going to be one extreme or the other – mountains of the stuff, or nothing. She headed back inside, where Eliza padded through from the sitting room to see what she was up to, wagging her little tail and nosing her in the hope of treats.

In the cupboard under the big white Belfast sink there was a tidy-tray with a bottle of furniture polish, a half-used roll of disposable J-Cloths, and a tin of Brasso silver cleaner which was rusted shut. Well, that answered that question. The half-empty bottle of washing up liquid on the kitchen window ledge wasn't going to get her very far, either.

'Back in half an hour,' she promised Eliza, pulling the door closed behind her and heading back to the car.

She drove into Applemore, surprised to discover that she couldn't find a spot to park the car on the main street. A huge delivery truck was parked at the far end, nose jammed up against a tiny orange Mini which looked like it must be about fifty years old.

*I must find another point of reference*, she reprimanded herself. For as long as she could remember that had been her mental line of demarcation for "quite old, really" but in less than a year she, too, was going to be about fifty years old, and she very definitely didn't feel it. Not that she knew what it was supposed to feel like, but somehow when she thought about people being fifty in her head they were in sensible shoes and possibly a headscarf and a cardigan, and not jeans and a hoody and a pair of snazzy pink converse trainers, humming along to Nirvana on the car stereo.

Anyway, that was enough thinking about that. She had a parking space to find, which wasn't something she'd thought was going to be an issue in the far northwest of the Scottish Highlands. She got to the end of the street and slowed up, trying to work out what to do. In the end, she took a left and turned into the petrol station up the hill, squeezing the little car between the pump and a massive blue tractor, which gave her the fright of her life as she turned to double back on herself. The engine started and a huge belch of thick smoke shot out before it made an alarming banging noise and cut out completely.

'Lucky escape,' muttered Meg to herself, turning the car right and slowly heading back onto the High Street. There had to be room for a little one in there somewhere…

She got right to the end of the street then spotted a side turning, nipping down and neatly parking in front of a huge and utterly filthy black pick-up truck. She climbed out, locking the door – discovering as she tried that Helen's little car had nothing as modern as central locking – and was barked at furiously by a very cute but incredibly vocal black cocker spaniel who was standing on the passenger seat of the truck.

Seeing it on foot, it was apparent how much Applemore had changed since her last visit. When she'd wandered along the main street with Helen back then, it had been faded and a bit sea-battered around the edges, the paint peeling on the railings that ran along the edge of the little harbour, and the hotel sign faded and tired.

Now the hotel had been freshly painted a sparkling white, and the sign was stylish and modern. Baskets tumbling with pretty spring flowers stood outside the entrance and filled the windows, which had recently been painted a dark slate grey. Old wooden whisky barrels had been painted, and were dotted along the pavements, stuffed with daffodils and nodding heads of tiny bright blue muscari. There was a café – that had definitely not been there before – with two little wooden tables outside, and a neatly painted blackboard announcing the bakes of the day. A little girl sat at the table by the window looking out and gave a shy wave, one hand holding tightly onto a sticky iced bun. Meg's stomach rumbled. Maybe she'd pick something nice up on the way back to the car. But first things first... the little supermarket. Helen had told her all about the drama there had been in the village when the tiny village shop had closed, leaving villagers with nowhere to go for their daily needs. There was a farm shop on the grounds of Applemore House itself, up the hill and out of the village on the other side of town, but that hadn't worked for the older villagers, or people who didn't drive.

The door slid open, and she stepped inside. It was exactly the same as her local branch back home in Heatherby, and she found it strangely comforting to potter along the aisles with a basket on her arm picking up bleach, and more washing up liquid, rhubarb scented cleaning spray and packs of fresh cloths and dusters. She threw in a pack of Eliza's favourite gravy bones, too, and a few bits and pieces to stock up the cupboards to keep her going until she made a trip to the bigger town ten miles away where there was a big super-market where she'd fill a trolley and get some cooking bits and pieces. For now, though, she grabbed a nice looking pizza covered with charred baby peppers and mozzarella, some milk for the all-important coffee to keep her going, and a bottle of red wine in case she fancied a glass after she'd finished clearing up that evening. Maybe if she really got down to it, she could get the sitting room sorted and put her feet up with a drink by the fire. She made a face at herself in the security mirror by the gin bottles. It would take some doing to get that sitting room sorted by this evening, espe-cially as it was already – she checked her phone to see the time – half-past one.

She was heading for the checkout when she dropped her phone. Bending to pick it up from under the shelf where it had slid out of reach, she straightened up awkwardly, and narrowly avoided crashing bodily into a tall, broad-shoul-dered man in a dark blue sweater.

'Sorry,' she said, flushing, because she realised as she looked at him his mouth was twisting into a half-smile and something in her had registered as they bumped into each other that he smelled very nice – of outside and fresh air and pine trees.

'My fault,' he said, surprising her with an English accent in the depths of the Scottish Highlands. 'I should have been looking out for people underfoot.'

Some part of Meg managed to process that along with dark hair flecked with steel grey, he had a strong jaw which hadn't seen a razor for a good few days, and dark blue eyes (which almost matched the sweater) with a kind twinkle to them. The same part of Meg that processed this information gave a tiny swoop of something in her chest that she hadn't felt in a very long time. If ever.

She laughed. 'I dropped my phone.'

*Obviously you dropped your phone, Meg, you idiot,* she heard herself thinking. *He hardly thinks you were crawling around on your hands and knees for fun.*

'Well, as long as you're okay,' he said, and she nodded.

'Yes, I'm fine.'

'Excellent.' His eyebrows lifted slightly. 'In which case,' he said, gesturing with his free hand towards the end of the aisle. 'I'll just –'

'Oh –' she stepped sideways.

'Not at all. After you,' he said, letting her past with a gentlemanly wave.

Fortunately, the shop didn't appear to have CCTV, so the shake of her head and roll of her eyes that Meg did to herself as she headed toward the checkout remained un-noticed by anyone.

'Did you get everything you needed?' A pink-cheeked girl with hair so blonde it was almost white smiled at her from the other side of the counter. Her nose was scattered with freckles, and she smiled at Meg cheerfully as she hefted the heavy basket up onto the counter.

Meg tried to gather herself.

'Yes, thanks so much.'

The girl reached behind her, gesturing to the stack of paper bags.

'Do you need a bag, or have you brought one?'

'Yes, please.' She hadn't even thought about bags when she'd rushed out of the house. Back in Heatherby she'd always kept them ready to go in the car, but they'd been folded and passed on to Janey when she was packing and tidying up.

'Righty-ho,' said the girl, humming to herself. She popped the groceries in one by one as she rang them through the till. Meg watched as a couple of older women rushed into the shop, exclaiming with surprise and brushing spots of rain off their shoulders. A clap of thunder boomed overhead, so loud that the floor almost seemed to shake.

'I had a feeling that we were about to get caught,' said one woman, who was short in stature with close-cropped grey hair and a cheery red raincoat. 'Is it alright if we put this up on the noticeboard, Holly?'

She unfurled a small, printed poster and waved it in their direction.

'Of course,' said the girl, nodding and smiling again. 'I had a feeling there was a storm on the way. I always get a headache beforehand, and I've been feeling weird all morning.'

Meg looked out of the door, eyes widening in surprise at the suddenly dark skies. 'It was sunny a moment ago.'

'Welcome to the Highlands,' laughed the girl. 'Give it five minutes and the weather'll have changed again.'

A crack of lightning lit up the sky and out of nowhere huge torrents of rain started falling.

Meg looked down at her shirt and blue jeans. 'I hope you're right about that. I'm parked at the far end of the street.'

# CHAPTER NINE

Gabe grabbed some lunch things for Ed, threw five packs of chocolate muffins into the basket, and headed back to the checkout with the maps tucked carefully under his arm.

'You can wait here until it stops,' he heard the girl at the checkout saying to the pretty dark-haired woman he'd almost fallen over a moment ago. She was standing, bags in both hands, looking out at the rain, which had been threatening all morning and had chosen exactly the wrong moment to materialise. The blue and white striped shirt she was wearing - sleeves rolled up to show the pale skin of her forearms – was going to be no match for the weather outside, even with the padded waistcoat as an extra layer.

He put his shopping down and the girl checked it through, noticing the maps under his arm and motioning to the bags hanging beside her with a raised eyebrow of query.

'Yeah, please. I've got my hands full as it is.'

He paid and walked over to the door, triggering the automatic sensor so it slid open. Raindrops were sheeting down from the sky, dripping down a gutter which clearly needed repair, and hammering onto the roofs of the cars parked opposite. He glanced at the dark-haired woman, who was biting her lower lip and frowning.

'It'll be over in a moment,' he said, to reassure her. 'Everyone says that here, but it really is true.'

'I hope so or I'm going to get soaked.' She raised her eyebrows and lifted the bags slightly in a gesture of surrender.

'You and me both.'

He watched her checking the notices on the board behind him and stepped to one side, in case she wanted to see the whole display.

Una would murder him if he got these maps wet. He looked out at the sky, trying to gauge what the chances were that the rain would stop in the next five minutes or so.

'Are you sure this is going to stop in a minute? It looks pretty permanent to me.'

She'd put her bags down on the ground. With her arms folded in an attempt to keep warm, she looked as if she'd rather be anywhere else but here.

'I hope so,' he said, indicating with a shrug of his shoulder the papers folded under his arm. 'I'm supposed to be halfway up the moor delivering these to my boss in the next ten minutes.'

'Are they important?' She looked at the papers folded under his arm.

'Relatively,' he said, frowning to himself as he thought on the hop. There had to be a way of dealing with this.

'That's not great,' she said, and smiled shyly, lifting a hand to push a strand of hair back from her face, tucking it behind her ear. She wore no jewellery – not even a wedding ring, some part of him noticed, inconsequentially.

'So –' he began, some part of him wondering why he was making conversation, when he'd basically kept himself to himself for the last six months.

'Are –' she said at the same time, making him smile.

'Go on.' He gestured slightly as he had earlier. Another huge rumble of thunder passed overhead, and the girl behind the checkout whistled in surprise.

'That's loud, right enough,' she said to anyone who was listening.

'Sorry,' he went on, 'I was going to say – are you visiting Applemore?'

'Something like that. I'm house-sitting for a friend for a couple of months.'

She looked up at him and he noticed her eyes, which were the colour of chocolate and fringed with long, dark lashes.

'And you're not from round here either, I'm guessing from the accent?'

He couldn't quite place *her* accent – it sounded very slightly northern. Yorkshire, perhaps?

'No,' he said, after a moment. 'I moved up from down south about six months ago.'

'I guess you're used to the weather by now.' She rubbed her arms in an attempt to warm herself.

'Well, I've learned to expect the unexpected. Let's put it that way.'

Ah, he'd had a brainwave. 'Sorry, I've had an idea to get these where they need to be without them dissolving into pulp. Excuse me.'

He headed to the aisle where all the household equipment was on sale and picked up a roll of black plastic bags, passing them over to the girl at the checkout.

'Would you mind if I borrowed the counter for a moment?'

'Course not,' said the girl cheerfully. 'Help yourself.'

The two older women looked on with interest as he unwrapped a couple of the bags, folded them over the maps and made sure that they were well and truly protected.

'Solved the problem,' he said, brandishing the now rain-proof papers at the girl by the exit. She shot him a smile and stepped back as he moved towards the sensor so the door slid open, a splatter of raindrops blowing in on the wind. 'Sorry about that,' he said, as the door slid closed again, and he headed back towards the truck, jogging along the now-empty street, head ducked to try and avoid the worst of the storm.

Stanley was curled up fast asleep on the passenger seat, completely unbothered by the weather. He tossed the maps on the back seat and opened the door, climbing in and turning on the engine with a groan of relief. He checked his phone – no messages wondering where he was, thank goodness – and started down the street.

On a whim, as he passed the supermarket he slowed, looking in to see if she was still waiting there at the door. She looked out at him through the glass, and he opened the passenger window, gesturing first at her then at the car, his eyebrows raised in query. Stanley helpfully hung his head out and barked with excitement.

'Do you want a lift somewhere?' he shouted through the rain, trying again to motion to the truck and then to her in the hope she'd get what he was saying.

She looked puzzled for a moment then shook her head, smiling, pointing back the way he'd just driven. She must be staying in the village, and happy to wait for the rain to go off.

It was funny, he thought as he headed back up the hill towards the moor, but he'd never have dreamt of offering a lift to a stranger back home in England. Even after six months living in Applemore he'd learned that there was a safety in the isolated way that they lived – nothing happened without it being noted by someone, and they spent so much time ferrying workers back and forth for one reason or another that it didn't seem unusual. She wasn't local, though, and so it wasn't really a surprise that she'd turned down his offer. He could be anyone, after all.

# CHAPTER TEN

*You are not very good at this*, Meg chided herself. She turned away from the door and studied the noticeboard, which was fastened to the wall, trying to distract herself from the strange pang of regret that she hadn't taken up his offer of a lift – but to where? Helen's little car was waiting for her only a few hundred yards away, and she could hardly ask him to turn around and take her back there. Plus – she scrutinised a poster about a fundraising bake sale with as much focus as she could muster – you just didn't hop into the passenger seat of random strangers, even if you were in the deepest depths of the Scottish Highlands. Even if – she wrinkled her nose and screwed her mouth to one side – they were *literally* tall, dark and handsome. Well, tall, dark grey and handsome.

It was funny really. In the same way that she still couldn't quite get her head around being forty-nine, she'd been surprised to discover that growing older meant you didn't notice that the movie stars and musician you'd swooned over as a student had aged in the same way you had. Now she watched actors in charming little Netflix romances and wondered why on earth she was watching people who looked young enough to be the same age as Phoebe, Helen's daughter, and therefore completely alien to her.

*Pilates, Yoga, Book Club, Village Improvement Meeting... English Classes available, (contact Rilla at Applemore House for a lift if needed).*

She carried on studying the signs, feeling increasingly uncomfortable that she'd been hovering in the store for so long, not that the girl behind the checkout seemed to mind. She'd been chatting away all this time to the two women who'd come in earlier, but now they'd finished up and were heading straight towards her. Meg tried to look as if she was particularly interested in the poster about *Pilates Classes starting this Thursday at 7pm*.

'The more the merrier,' said the smaller of the two women, tapping Meg on the arm so she turned and was greeted with a friendly smile. 'Will we be seeing you there?'

'Oh –' said Meg, automatically. 'Oh no, no, I don't think so. Thank you.'

'Oh, don't worry, you don't have to be any good,' said the other woman, in what Meg assumed was supposed to be a comforting manner.

The girl behind the checkout snorted with laughter. 'Aunty Dolina, for goodness' sake. For all you know she could be a world class Pilates instructor.'

The woman looked Meg up and down with one eyebrow raised and her mouth pursed. 'I think that's highly unlikely.'

Meg's mouth twitched with amusement.

'Pay no heed to her,' said the other woman, putting what she clearly thought was a comforting hand on Meg's arm and patting it again.

'Oh for goodness' sake Greta, I didn't mean the lassie wasn't the right *shape* to be doing Pilates –' (she pronounced it

Pilots, which made Meg want to burst into fits of giggles) '– I meant she's more than likely a newbie like the rest of us.'

Meg smiled at her and said, 'Well, I'm definitely that.'

She'd long ago accepted that she was in shape - as the saying went - because round was a shape. She was more amused by the fact that she'd been pronounced a lassie at the age of forty-nine.

Just as she was trying to work out what on earth she was supposed to say next, a woman of about thirty-five rushed into the shop, folding up an enormous dark green umbrella as the door closed behind her, dripping water all over the floor. She was carrying a little plastic envelope and had a worried look on her face, her brow furrowed.

'Greta, Dolina,' she said, giving them a quick nod of greeting. 'I'm looking for one of our lads, Gabe. You haven't seen him, have you? He's a big bloke.' She measured the air with her hand, looking at Meg hopefully. 'Bit o'stubble? Dark hair?'

'He was here a wee moment ago, Una,' said the girl behind the counter. 'He left with a load of what looked like maps wrapped up in some black bin bags.'

'Well, that's something,' said the girl, pursing her lips and looking heavenward as if for inspiration. 'At least they're no' going to get soaked in the rain. I forgot to give him something, and I was hoping I might still have caught him. Now I've come out in the rain for nothing.'

'Typical man, Una,' said the woman called Dolina, shaking her head in sympathy. 'They're never where you want them, are they?'

'Story of my life,' said Una, shaking her head. 'Trying to keep all these forestry lads in order will be the death of me.'

'You need some nice relaxing Pilates,' said Dolina cheerfully. 'That'll get your blood pressure down.'

Una, who was about to head back into the rain, looked confused.

'She means *Pilates*,' explained Greta.

'Whatever,' said Dolina, airily. 'Will we be seeing you on Thursday?'

'If I live that long,' said the girl, rolling her eyes. She brandished her umbrella as if it was a jousting sword and headed back outside.

'It looks like it's clearing up,' said Meg, to nobody in particular. 'I think I'll make a run for it.'

She grabbed the two heavy bags of shopping and set out into the rain. It had in fact lessened quite a bit and she was only soaked by the time she got back to the car, rather than drenched. That was some consolation, she decided, turning on the engine and heading back to the lighthouse cottage where hopefully Eliza would still be snoozing peacefully.

So he was called Gabe. She unpacked the shopping, dumping it all onto the space on the kitchen table she'd cleared that morning. Eliza pottered around the kitchen, sniffing chair legs and inspecting the inside of cupboards as Meg found spaces for everything.

By late afternoon, the weather had changed again, as everyone had said it would. A bright rainbow climbed from beyond the rocks on the shore up into a towering, still-grey cloud. The sunlight through the windows showed it had been quite some time since Helen's artistic mind had been focused on anything as pedestrian as window-cleaning.

She'd made a start on the sitting room, piling things into plastic crates as she cleared the table and the contents of the second sofa, which had evidently become a sort of storage unit at some point in the past. Boxes of things were piled up in one corner – she wasn't going to start going through Helen's online shopping orders – but she could sort books by genre and neatly stack craft projects and the innumerable balls of yarn in a crate and pile up the countless sweaters and cardigans which must have been discarded here and there with the intention of being taken upstairs.

*Books?* She'd sent a message to Helen, who was now at the airport waiting for her delayed flight.

*If they're fiction, they can go down to the library,* Helen replied.

*We're going to need a bigger library,* Meg messaged back, sending a photograph of the plastic crate which was stacked full.

*Yikes. All that from the sitting room?*

*No, that's the kitchen as well,* Meg replied. She didn't add that she'd already noticed several more towering heaps in other parts of the cottage.

*You are an angel to do this,* Helen wrote. *You don't have to,* she added a few moments later.

*I know. But I love you and I like doing it.* Simple, thought Meg, and true.

She carried on methodically, sorting and stacking and clearing and occasionally popping a log into the log burner more for the look of it than because she needed the heat. She'd changed when she got back and had discarded the sweatshirt she'd put on, hot from the hard work of bending up and down and going back and forth to the kitchen for cleaning cloths and black plastic bags for the random rubbish which seemed to have hidden itself behind sofa cushions.

She'd always loved order and keeping things tidy, a result of growing up in a chaotic house where she'd realised early on that if she wanted to get to school on time or have clean kit for PE she'd need to sort it herself. It had rolled over into her life with Michael – she'd been responsible for cooking and cleaning, and everything in the house as well as working, so she'd never found it particularly easy to stop and do nothing.

Helen would always insist on ordering a takeaway when she'd come to visit, something which Michael muttered about being a waste of money and which Meg suspected was another way for Helen to push back against his micro-managing of every aspect of life.

Anyway. She shook herself – that was enough ruminating on the past. She stood up, stretching out her back with a little groan. It was going to ache in the morning. Maybe she'd run a hot bath and have a soak while the frozen dinner she'd bought was heating in the oven.

'Yes, I'll feed you in a moment,' she said to Eliza, who was at the door in seconds, looking hopeful.

She'd never been a joiner-in. All the time she'd lived in Heatherby, she'd never taken a class or gone to the gym or anything like that. As she tipped some of Eliza's dog food into her bowl, Meg was lost in thought.

What *if* she went to the Pilates class? If Greta and Dolina were going, it clearly wasn't going to be some high-impact thing with loads of weights and an instructor barking at them… not that she'd even really mind that. But she'd never in her life signed up for so much as an evening class – it wasn't the sort of thing she did. Maybe now was the perfect opportunity to have a rehearsal. Nobody knew who she was up here. What's to say she wasn't the sort of person who turned up to a Pilates class because she happened to be house-sitting for a friend?

# CHAPTER ELEVEN

Gabe arrived back at the planting site about five minutes before Donald Grant was due.

'You timed that well,' grinned Pete, who emerged from the shelter of the driving seat of his truck, taking the bag of food that Gabe passed over with a nod of gratitude.

'Did they survive the rain?' Gabe looked down the moor, where his group of workers was busily planting. The air was fresh, a smell of damp earth rising as the sunlight warmed the ground after the storm.

'They all seem to be waterproof,' said Pete, unwrapping his sandwich. 'Thanks for this. Donald's on the way. Got the maps okay?'

'All sorted.' Gabe indicated the truck. 'And I'm pleased to report that they're bone dry and ready for the meeting.'

'Cool. Ah look, there's Donald coming now, and he's in the posh truck to impress the duke. You wait until you see the place, it's insane.'

They watched as their boss's matt grey Defender sped

along, the huge engine making nothing of the steep incline that led up to the top of the moor.

'Well, that was a bit of weather,' said Donald Grant, calling out of the window. 'That'll be trial by fire for the recruits.'

He climbed out of the car and shook their hands in greeting. Twinkly eyed, with untidy sandy red hair and the ruddy complexion of a Highlander, he wore his habitual brown cord trousers with a tattersall checked shirt under a hunter green fleece gilet.

'Luckily, it didn't happen on day one or the young lads would have been drenched. As it is, I expect they'll be heading straight back for a change of clothes before they take a trip to the pub for a drink this evening.' Pete grinned.

'Everyone warm enough?' Donald scanned the moor, hands in the pockets of his trousers. He was forthright and could be brisk when he needed to be, but Gabe had already worked out after six months on the job that he had a good heart and kept an eye on the wellbeing of his workers. He'd already invited Gabe round to dinner a couple of times, insisting that his wife Lucy liked to get to know the people working for the business. They lived in a rambling, comfortably untidy house outside Applemore with their two young children, and Lucy had turned out to be an excellent cook.

'Yeah, Una kitted the young lads with some waterproofs first thing this morning, so they were all set. Gabe's been in town getting the maps and picked them up some snacks for break time in a moment. I'll hand them out when you two head off.'

'Excellent. Una's a gem. I don't know what we'd do without her.'

'She's a tyrant,' snorted Pete, but with affection in his voice.

Donald looked at Gabe expectantly. 'Right, we'd better get this show on the road. Got the maps?'

'They're in the back of the truck. Give me two secs.'

'Chuck them in the back of mine then,' said Donald, 'and we'll get on our way. Don't want to be keeping the old boy waiting.'

Gabe opened the door of his truck and Stanley leapt out with excitement, tail wagging and his tongue lolling as he looked from one person to the other at the prospect of an adventure. He lifted his leg and peed extravagantly against the wheel of Donald's discreet but massively expensive Defender. Donald gave a bark of laughter.

'He can come along for the ride. Felix Lochbrannich loves dogs – it'll be an adventure for him. Stick him on the back seat with Bess.'

Once Stanley had hopped onto the leather seats and sniffed a hello to Bess, Donald's ancient yellow Labrador, Gabe put the maps safely out of reach and climbed into the passenger seat, belting himself in as Donald set off.

It wasn't a common or garden Defender like the other two, which were used for runabouts in the forestry business. This one was a custom Twisted model with sleek leather seats and all the mod cons you'd expect in a high-end vehicle, only the matt grey paintwork was already splattered with moorland mud despite having clearly had a valet clean, and the cup holder held an assortment of plastic toys and a My Little Pony patterned lunchbox.

Donald followed Gabe's gaze and smiled.

'Lottie left it this morning when I was dropping her and Jamie at school. I had to be somewhere else, or I'd have dropped it in to the school office. So she had an emergency school lunch, which no doubt she'll be delighted about, and I sneaked a bonus snack of Lucy's home-baked chocolate brownies and a cheese and ham bagel on the way back from my meeting. Everybody wins in this game.'

He chortled at his own joke.

'Anyway, sorry for hijacking you, but I thought it would be a good opportunity to have a word, plus I'd really like your thoughts on the Lochbrannich plans.'

Gabe felt his eyebrows lifting slightly, as if they were operating independently of him.

'You would?'

'Indeed. And I thought you'd like a chance to see what one of the bigger projects looks like.'

'That would be great.'

'You still enjoying it?' Donald glanced over at him briefly.

Gabe nodded. 'Loving it. I have to admit I was expecting to be a bit Billy-no-mates, turning up here on my own. But there's always something going on, whether it's the quiz night at the pub or stuff on at the outdoor centre. I'm keeping myself busy.'

'Glad to hear it. I keep meaning to go on one of those mountain bike rides with Jack, but I'm not sure my knees are up to it.'

'Never mind my knees,' Gabe laughed. 'My quads the next day after climbing the hill trails felt like lead.'

'Keeps you fit though,' Donald mused. 'You don't want to hit fifty and start falling apart.'

'Definitely not.'

'Look at the size of him!' Donald pointed to the far left and slowed the car right down, silent for a moment. A huge stag stood by the edge of the wood, frozen to the spot and watching them intently.

'You can't beat moments like that.' Donald shook his head in awe.

A moment later he looked down at his phone, which had been buzzing insistently.

'Really sorry,' he said, 'I hate to be rude, but I really need to make a quick call. Una's after my blood by the looks of it.'

'No problem at all.'

Gabe turned to look out at the moorland, lost in thought. The road snaked up towards the solid grey of the hills. As they drove higher, tiny waterfalls tumbled down, splashing white against the peaty brown of the water that gathered below.

It had been an unexpected sort of day already. He could still picture the look of surprise on the pretty woman's face in the supermarket when he'd almost tripped over her. Goodness knows why he'd offered her a lift – she must've thought he was a complete idiot, trying to pick up random strangers in the rain.

Donald was still talking into his headset, rattling off a list of instructions to Una, who would of course be taking them in her usual unflappable stride. Talking of Una... Gabe realised with a half-smile that he'd forgotten the sweatshirt she'd pressed on him so insistently. Something told him that Donald wouldn't be remotely concerned.

They whizzed along the empty road in the cushioned splendour of Donald's truck – his one indulgence, he'd called it, when Gabe had first arrived to take the job, showing it to him with a fond pat on the wing.

Gabe glanced at the clock on the dashboard, counting forwards and realising that it was one o'clock in the morning in New Zealand. He really needed to keep an eye on the time today and try to call him when Jacob got back and catch him before he set off for work. He'd sent Jacob a chatty message, with the news of what he'd been up to and a couple of photographs of Stanley on the beach, but in return had received an uncharacteristically brief reply simply saying 'give me a ring when you have a moment'. Finding a moment when you had an eleven-hour time difference wasn't as easy as one might imagine.

'So sorry,' said Donald, breaking into Gabe's thoughts. 'Here we are – well, here's the start of the estate, anyway.'

If you had been driving past, Gabe reflected, you'd barely have noticed anything to indicate that you were driving onto the Highland home of one of the richest men in the country. They rumbled over a cattle grid. A discreet dark green sign with white lettering announced that this was part of the Lochbrannich Estate. They drove on, along a well-kept road, through a long stretch of moorland and then up into a stand of thick mixed forest. The sunlight, which had broken through the clouds of the earlier storm, shone in pale rays through the trees, flickering on the window as they headed on, pausing for a moment to allow a couple of deer to dart in front of them before they leapt back into the darkness of the wood and disappeared.

'Wait for it,' said Donald.

They crested the hill, and Gabe's mouth fell open in surprise. Before them was a scene from a nature documentary. A storybook Highland glen stood before them, a picture of glassy blue-grey loch, flanked on either side by a patchwork of green fields, the familiar stone and heather of the moor, and deep green forest, all of which rose to meet the sky. The loch seemed to stretch out for miles, and in the distance the huge grey shoulders of distant mountains could be seen shrouded in a layer of pale white cloud.

'Wow.'

Donald grinned. 'Pretty amazing, isn't it? Wait until you see the house.'

They forked left, driving along the side of the loch with the water on one side and some well-kept pasture on the other, and then they turned a bend and Lochbrannich House came into view. Tall and turreted, it looked like someone had hewn a Disney castle out of solid grey granite.

# CHAPTER TWELVE

As they came to a halt a very tall, slightly stooping man with white hair emerged from behind a twisted yew tree, his hand held out in greeting.

'Donald, hello.'

'Your Grace,' said Donald, giving a brief nod, which seemed to be both a greeting and a very slight bow in recognition of his title. The man, however, rolled his eyes heavenward with a crooked half-smile, which immediately put Gabe at ease.

'Felix,' said the man, shaking Gabe's outstretched hand. 'Please don't stand on ceremony.'

After a brief chat about the weather, which Gabe had learned was even more of a pre-occupation here in the Highlands than it was anywhere else in the United Kingdom, the duke invited them inside for tea in the library.

'If we're going to have a look at these plans, we might as well do it comfortably.'

Donald grabbed the maps, and the duke spotted the dogs, insisting that they come inside and join them.

Gabe had never been inside a castle before. He'd have predicted suits of armour and huge tapestry hangings on the wall, along with ancient oil paintings of long-dead members of the family – and he was amused to discover that Lochbrannich House was everything he'd imagined, with the addition of countless stags' heads stuffed and hung from the wall. What he hadn't expected was for the place to look very much lived-in, with an untidy row of muddy wellington boots by the door, a pile of unopened post on a table in the huge hall, and coats and hats hung higgledy-piggledy on a wooden rack by the huge staircase.

'Come through, make yourselves at home.'

Stanley dashed around, sniffing everything, returning to look at Gabe with a slightly wild look in his eye. Even Bess had been roused from her habitual torpor and gave a bark, wagging her tail in greeting as a tiny rocket of a Jack Russell hurtled down the corridor barking and stopped dead in front of them, surprising everyone by rolling over in submission as Stanley sniffed hello.

'Moss,' explained the duke fondly. 'He's very sweet, but he's not all there, if you ask me. Terrible guard dog, even worse ratter.'

He waved them into a bright room filled with books and two huge sofas which sat on either side of an open fireplace where flames danced merrily. Moss hopped up onto one of the sofas and circled before collapsing with a happy groan. The other two dogs pottered around, getting their bearings.

'Have a seat,' said the duke. 'I'll be back in two ticks.'

He returned a few minutes later with a tray, surprising Gabe who'd expected him to have a butler or a maid at the very least. But the duke himself poured out three cups of tea, offered round a plate of shortbread biscuits, and then sat down on the armchair opposite.

'So as you know, Donald, my desire is to leave something of consequence when I pop off, whenever that might be. We've done more than enough damage to the environment, and if I can put something back before I go, and get the wheels in motion, then I'll be a happy man.'

'That sounds like a good idea,' said Donald, shaking his head and refusing a second piece of shortbread. 'That reminds me, we've left the maps out in the car.'

'I'll go and get them,' said Gabe, jumping to his feet. 'Wait,' he said, raising a finger in warning to Stanley, who had settled at his feet and raised a furry eyebrow in query. Stan hefted a sigh, but obediently didn't move an inch. 'Excuse me two moments.'

Gabe gave a sigh that was even bigger as he stepped out of the room.

'Everything alright?'

A tall woman with mouse-brown hair swept off her forehead with a velvet headband was standing in the hallway, watching him with amusement. She was dressed in riding clothes, her long legs clad in cream-coloured jodhpurs and a navy gilet, which was dusted with white horse hairs.

'Yes, just popping out to get some paperwork.' He tipped his head in the direction of the library door. 'I'm here with Donald Grant.'

'Ah, the forestry people. Arabella Roxburgh,' she said, extending a hand, expectantly.

Gabe, cursing himself inwardly for having probably committed some sort of faux pas by not bowing, shook her hand politely and then stood for a second, not sure if he was supposed to wait until she left the room before he did, or if he could carry on with his mission to collect the maps from the truck.

'I'll let you get on,' she said a moment later, her mouth twitching with amusement.

'Thanks.'

Gabe shot outside and grabbed the maps, returning to the library without incident to discover Donald and the duke were already studying an identical map which was framed and hanging on the wall behind his desk.

'Just explaining to Donald that what we want to do is fence here –' he pointed to an area near the loch – 'and plant a new forest of broadleaf trees, which hopefully won't be devoured by deer if we can get the fencing secure enough. And I want to try to repair the peatland where it's been destroyed, as well as creating some sort of volunteer planting scheme where people can come along and help us out, which of course is going to mean building a rather large bothy, as well.'

'That all sounds excellent,' said Donald.

'I've been reading about the rewilding projects, and the effect they're having on the countryside and on nature.' Gabe glanced for a moment out of the window at the still waters of the loch. 'I don't know if you've seen the research that they've done into the effects of returning wolves to the ecosystem in Yellowstone and how much of an impact it had.'

'Oh yes!' The duke looked delighted. 'This chap knows his stuff,' he added, giving a nod to Donald. 'Yes, it's excellent, isn't it? I think we're a way off bringing wolves to the Highlands – although it would solve our damn deer problem, mind you – but I think it illustrates the point perfectly. Shall we head out and have a look around?'

The duke took the lead, and Donald gave Gabe a fleeting thumbs up gesture as he followed him out of the room.

'Hop into my old jalopy,' said the duke, leading them around the side of the huge house to where an utterly filthy

Land Rover stood under the shade of another broad yew tree. 'Bring the dogs, they'll enjoy it. Moss, come on.' He whistled and the little Jack Russell appeared, jumping into his lap as he settled in the driving seat.

Gabe sat behind the two men with the dogs by his side as they set off down a track which led through the woods behind the house and up into a clearing.

'This is where I'm thinking we can start the planting, and then we can fence round here...' They drove on '... and put the wooden cabins up here, where they can look out over the glen when they wake up in the morning and have their cup of tea.'

A couple of hours later, having driven far into the vast Lochbrannich Estate, Gabe had a much better picture of the scale of the project they were looking at.

'So, as you can see, I have big plans.'

The duke pulled up the Land Rover outside Lochbrannich House and opened the door to let Moss out, climbing out himself and allowing himself a moment to stretch out his back.

'Age,' he said with a small smile, 'It comes to us all, unfortu- nately. Ah, Arabella.'

He looked across towards the door where the woman from earlier, now dressed in a sweater and jeans, was emerging.

'There you are, Daddy. We were beginning to think you'd been abducted by these two and thrown into a ravine.'

Gabe shot a look at Donald, who lifted an eyebrow.

'No, still here, unfortunately for you,' said her father, chuckling. 'Arabella's not a huge fan of my – I quote – *hair brained rewilding project* – are you, my dear?'

Arabella leaned back against the granite of Lochbrannich House and folded her arms, looking at her father with an expression of fond amusement.

'I'm mildly concerned that we're in danger of turning this

place into some sort of middle-class amusement park where well-meaning people trot back and forth every week so they can come and plant trees.'

'I think the answer is looking at rural re-population,' said Gabe, almost without thinking. 'It's about bringing money back into the local economy at a time when poverty in the Highlands is at an all-time high. If we create jobs, the young people won't leave, and people like Donald won't end up having to employ people like me.'

Donald gave a snort of amusement. 'He's got a good point, although I'd like to say for the record that I'm happy you're part of Grant Forestry.'

'He's got a good point indeed,' said the duke, clapping a hand on Gabe's shoulder. 'I have every intention of making a difference in whatever time I have left. Hopefully before I pop off I'll have changed your mind, my darling, and if not you can pull up all the fences and let the deer do their worst.'

'You know as well as I do there's more to it than that,' said Arabella, but she was laughing. 'I don't know if you can tell, but this is a conversation we've had over the dinner table on more than one occasion.'

Gabe laughed.

'I'm sure we'll have it a hundred times over. One lives in hope that she will come round,' the duke said, striding towards the house. 'Now I expect that you both have wives to get home to, and I've taken up far more of your time than intended with my rabbiting on.'

Gathering the dogs and saying goodbye, they headed back to Donald's truck, heading down the drive as the duke waved farewell in the rear-view mirror.

Once they'd turned the bend and the house was out of sight both Gabe and Donald let out massive sighs of relief.

'Sorry,' said Gabe, covering his face with his hands and groaning.

'What for?'

Gabe splayed his fingers slightly and looked at his boss sideways. 'I don't think Arabella Roxburgh wanted me siding with her father over his plans, do you?'

'Ach, her bark is a lot worse than her bite. More to the point, I had a feeling the old boy would like you, and I was right.'

'It's a great idea.' In his old life, he'd flown back and forth from London to New York to Dubai for meetings, not giving so much as a thought to environmental concerns or his carbon footprint. He'd learned so much from the diverse collection of people he'd met while tree planting, and soaked up as much knowledge as he could. He knew – as Arabella Roxburgh had said – that rewilding came with its own issues. But he'd also learned that there were ways to work with the community to create opportunities, not only for the current population but for future generations.

'A great idea, and it's going to make a massive difference to the business. Which is part of the reason I wanted to take you out here – one because I had a feeling you'd have something interesting to say, which you did, and two because I've got a proposition for you.' Donald slowed the truck as they bumped over a cattle grid and turned onto the road which headed towards Applemore.

Gabe turned to check the dogs were still snoozing contentedly on the back seat. Stanley was flat out, exhausted after a busy afternoon of chasing new scents and being admired by all and sundry.

'A proposition?'

Donald gave a brief nod. 'You came up here six months ago

and since then you've got your head down, worked hard, and soaked up information. We get a lot of people coming up to do planting work, but most of them are happy to make a quick buck and then head off. I don't know what your plans are, and I might be way off base but if you're interested in taking this further, I'd be delighted.'

'Taking it further?'

He sounded like a bloody parrot, echoing Donald like his brain was on half power.

'A promotion. Supervisor, more training, that sort of thing. You've taken it on the chin from the start and mucked in, taken responsibility for making sure the paperwork is sorted if there's nobody else to check it, all the stuff people tend to shy away from.'

Gabe shifted slightly in his chair, uncomfortable with praise. 'Only because if someone doesn't do it, it doesn't get done.'

It was true. He'd always been happy to step up, but mainly because they were chronically understaffed and mildly chaotic. It seemed easier to be the one who'd take down names or double check the first aid information was up to date than to wait around for someone else to do it. He'd been surprised by how much he'd liked the job and everything that had come with it. It had been something he'd signed up for on a whim, not a long-term plan. Now he was being offered a future when he wasn't really looking for one, and he wasn't sure how that felt.

Donald gestured with one hand, turning his hand upward. 'Anyway, have a think about it. I don't want to put you on the spot. In the meantime, we've got enough to be going on with the community projects coming up as well as the planting.'

'Community projects?'

For goodness' sake, there he was repeating words again.

'Yeah, we've got a couple coming up that I think would be a great opportunity for you to stretch your wings a bit, but I'll talk to you about that later. Come into the office on Friday. You can have a think about it, as I say.'

'Thanks.' Gabe looked at Donald thoughtfully. 'I will do.'

# CHAPTER THIRTEEN

The next morning, after a deliciously long sleep, Meg was making breakfast and thinking about her plans for the day ahead. Even after a year, it still felt quite alien to have her time completely to herself. Michael had always been keen to know what she was up to, eager to make sure she was working hard and keeping herself busy. She'd realised after his death, of course, that his desire to know her movements at all times was primarily because he had so many extracurricular activities – as Helen had once referred to as all the women he'd had on the side – to keep tabs on that it made life easier to know that his wife wouldn't cause problems.

So it was still strange to think that now she was free to do whatever she wanted, whenever she wanted. She filled Eliza's water bowl and put it down on the floor by the back door, gazing out of the window. After yesterday's mixed weather, the sky was almost clear, with only a few puffy white clouds over the islands in the distance. The sun had felt almost warm on her back when she'd let Eliza out for her morning potter around the garden, and she'd resolved to get out for a wander along the beach and stretch her legs with a decent walk. She had the whole of the Highlands on her doorstep, after all, and there was so much to explore - but that could wait until after breakfast.

She'd poured her coffee and was putting the milk back in the fridge when a movement in the distance caught her eye. Looking out, she saw a young woman with a baby carrier on her back walking down the path towards the little library. She walked slowly until she reached the wooden cabinet, then paused for a moment. Then she opened the door, looking left and right as if she was worried she might be seen. She closed the door then, turning away and walking a few strides as if she'd changed her mind, before turning back and opening the cupboard again. From a distance it was hard to make out, but Meg was almost certain that it wasn't a book but one of the boxes of eggs that she took out and tucked it inside her coat, holding it there with her arm crossed protectively over her chest as she walked quickly away, glancing over her shoulder to make sure nobody was looking at her. Meg ducked back out of view and watched as she disappeared, a tiny shape between the rocks, heading back – presumably – towards the beach path which led towards Applemore itself.

Meg sipped her coffee and headed back to the kitchen table, lost in thought. She'd received a cheerful message overnight from Helen who by now would be checked in or even in the air, well on the way to the other side of the world. Meanwhile, the cottage was looking slightly less chaotic. It hadn't been as bad as it first looked, and another day of sorting would mean she could settle in happily for the duration of her stay.

Later that afternoon, having promised herself a walk on the beach as a reward for a few hours of tidying, she picked up

Eliza's lead and the two of them set out to explore in the sunshine of a spring afternoon.

The cottages stood on the edge of a rocky outcrop which marked the entrance to the Applemore harbour. A stone wall had been built around the perimeter of the lighthouse and the cottages, and Meg let herself out of the gate, noticing for the first time the little KEEP OUT sign which stood to one side, half-obscured by a tangle of brambles.

The path was well worn, trodden by visitors and locals over many years. A hundred yards further along stood the white-painted wooden cabinet with Helen's neatly painted sign. Opening the doors, it was evident that the little library could do with a bit of a tidy-up as well. The books were jumbled, some turned the wrong way round, others stacked untidily. The eggs were – as Meg had suspected – gone. Her heart contracted in a squeeze of empathy at the thought of the girl, who'd looked so anxious and uncomfortable. Maybe she'd write a little sign and hang it inside, telling people they could help themselves.

She closed the door and headed down to the beach, following Eliza who was scampering along ahead of her, her fluffy white bottom bobbing up and down as she leapt over the tussocks of sea-grass.

The beach was beautiful, with pale white sand surrounded by the low, craggy dark rocks that gathered at the mouth of the Applemore harbour. By day, they looked scenic, but by night, without the aid of the lighthouse, it was clear how dangerous they could have been to fishing boats coming in with their catch. Meg wandered along the shore, watching as Eliza dodged the waves and listening to the gulls wheeling and calling overhead. It wasn't hard to see why Helen stayed here after her relationship had broken down. It was a beautiful place for her daughter Phoebe to grow up.

'Come on, Liza-Lou,' she called, her voice carried away by the wind. She clapped her hands together to get the corgi's attention and a moment later turned, making her way back up towards the sea path. A dark-haired man in outdoor gear was standing by one of the rock pools with a couple of young children, looking intently into the water. He glanced up, giving her a brief smile of greeting.

'We've seen two crabs and a baby starfish,' said the little girl, taking her father's hand.

'Jack,' said the boy, 'can we go and get cake from the café on the way back?'

'Conned again,' he said, grinning at Meg in complicity. Maybe an uncle or a stepfather, she realised. He held out his hand so the boy could pull himself up on the slippery rocks. 'Your mother will have words with me for giving you snacks before lunch.'

'That's okay,' said the boy cheerfully. 'We don't have to tell her.'

'You can't argue with that logic,' the man said, laughing. He had a strong Glasgow accent. 'Alright you two, you've got a deal. Edward, you've left your water bottle over there on the rocks. Lucy, you ready? Where's Archie?'

He whistled and an ancient, grizzly-looking brindle terrier appeared from the sea-grass, making his way over to say a brief hello to Eliza. The two dogs circled each other in greeting.

'You must be Helen's pal, Meg. I'm Jack McDonald.'

He extended a hand, and she shook it, slightly puzzled. 'Hello.'

'Ah, everyone knows everyone here. You'll find out soon enough. I've been living here for a few years now and I've learned to accept that you can't sneeze without rumours going round you're in bed with pneumonia. Right, come on you two, we've got a date with some chocolate brownies. If I bring some back to your mother, she'll forgive me for feeding you rubbish before lunch.'

'Nice to meet you,' said Meg, pushing her hair back from her face as a gust of wind blew in from the sea.

'I'll see you again, I'm sure,' said Jack, raising a finger in a half-salute as he set off for the village.

Meg was still mulling over what he'd said later that evening when she'd almost finished the big clear up. She polished the mirror that hung over the fireplace, sweating slightly as she stood too close to the wood-burner.

Did everyone really know everyone, or was that a figure of speech? Surely if that was the case, someone must know what was going on with the girl who'd looked so uncertain this morning. It didn't quite add up.

With the kitchen back under some semblance of control she could get to grips with cooking something from scratch rather than heating frozen pizza from the little supermarket – which would mean taking a trip to the bigger town to get some shopping, or investigating the farm shop up at Applemore House. Maybe she'd do that in the morning.

# CHAPTER FOURTEEN

'Hello there.'

Meg almost jumped out her skin the following afternoon. She'd taken a trip out of Applemore, heading to the bigger town ten miles away, where she filled a trolley of shopping and picked up a sack of the particular dog food Eliza liked. Not for nothing were corgis the chosen dogs of royalty. Eliza had very particular opinions about what she ate.

Closing the door of the car, she hoisted her bag onto her shoulder and turned, jumping in surprise when she saw a grey-haired woman standing on the gravel path.

'I'm sorry. I didn't mean to scare you.'

'Oh, you didn't,' said Meg, to a look of mild amusement. 'It's my fault. I don't know why; I always over-react.'

'I'm sure there's a perfectly logical reason for that,' said the woman. She was dressed smartly in a long grey woollen overcoat, with a red patterned scarf tied at her neck and a slash of red lipstick which contrasted perfectly with her silver-grey hair. Meg, who'd thrown a hoody over her top and headed to the shops in a pair of tired yoga pants, felt decidedly underdressed. She'd always made an effort when she lived in Heatherby, and it was Sod's Law that the moment she didn't, a random stranger turned up.

'I'm Kathleen. Helen might have mentioned I'd be popping by.'

Meg felt the corners of her mouth twitching in amusement. 'You have met Helen, yes?'

Kathleen gave a snort of laughter. 'She completely forgot, didn't she?'

She waggled the bag she was holding. 'Eggs,' she said, simply.

'Oh! Yes,' Meg said, smiling. 'Yes, she did mention you. In fact, I saw someone –' and then she stopped herself midsentence, realising that she didn't feel comfortable cheerfully announcing she'd seen the girl taking the eggs. Maybe it wasn't the case that everyone in Applemore knew everything.

'I'm just off to the village improvement meeting,' the woman continued, as if she hadn't noticed what Meg said, 'so I thought I'd drop these in – some for the library, and some for you as a welcome to Applemore gift. How are you finding it? Getting settled in for your house-sitting stint?'

'Oh yes.' Meg nodded. 'I've been sorting things out a bit in the house, and now I'm organised, I'm going to go to the Pilates class I saw advertised in the shop the other day.'

What on earth was she doing? It was as if her mouth had taken over and she had no control of it all of a sudden. It was Thursday. There was a new series of that thriller show she'd been watching on Netflix, and she'd already had this discussion with herself.

'Oh, that's a nice idea. I gather it's the first one tonight, so you'll all be beginners.'

'I hope so,' said Meg, still wondering who had taken control of her brain. 'I'm looking forward to it.'

Now this was getting ridiculous. Her peri-menopausal forty-nine-year-old body was perfectly comfortable sitting on a sofa reading a book or watching a movie.

'Well, in the meantime, I'll give you these,' said Kathleen, 'and I'll pop down and put these on the shelf.'

'I had a look earlier,' Meg said. 'I might tidy-up the books a little, and maybe put some of Helen's books in there as well?' She shifted from one foot to the other, wondering as she did if she was speaking out of turn.

'That's a marvellous idea. I think the plan was that everyone would keep an eye on the little library when it was installed, but you know how it goes – everyone thinks someone else will do it, so it doesn't get done. It is a bit untidy down there.'

'I'll give it a bit of a spruce up,' said Meg, relieved. 'Helen's given me free rein to put any of the books I've boxed up down there, so I'll swap them over and make sure there's nothing lurking.'

'I should have some copies of the village newsletter when I get back from the meeting as well. I'll pop a little stack down there for passers-by. It gets quite busy here as the weather picks up.'

'Really?' Meg had only seen the girl and a couple of others passing by.

'Oh yes, the sun comes out and there will be a regular stream of bodies coming past. You'll be fending them off,' Kathleen added with a chuckle. She looked at her watch. 'Anyway, I'd better get a move on or I'll be late for the meeting. Greta's in charge and she's a fierce woman indeed.'

She gave a cheerful wave and set off at a brisk pace down the path towards the library.

Thanks to daylight saving the clocks had gone forward, meaning it was still light when Meg set off for the class. She somehow took a wrong turn out of the village and found herself halfway up a farm track with no signal and the map on the screen refusing to load. She drove into a gateway and reversed carefully, trying not to land in a ditch. A moment later, seemingly out of nowhere, a red-haired young farmer in a set of muddy green overalls appeared on a quad bike.

He stopped and – painfully aware that she was at an awkward angle, with a herd of shaggy Highland cows peering at her from the other side of the fence – she opened the car window.

'Are you lost?'

'I was trying to find a Pilates class,' Meg admitted, realising how ridiculous she sounded.

One of his eyebrows shot up and he grinned. 'Well, these lassies are all about to calve, so I think they're a bit too pregnant to be getting all hot and bothered at an exercise class.'

Meg laughed. 'If you can give me some idea where I've gone wrong, I'd be very grateful. That's if I can get out of this gateway without turning the car upside down.'

He jumped down from the quad bike. 'Well, we can sort that jam for starters.'

He squeezed past her window and opened the gate, waving his arms widely so the cows backed off, snorting. 'Come forward a bit, then you'll have room to reverse back safely.'

A few moments later, facing back the way she came, Meg looked up at him with gratitude.

'Right. Take the road down to the bottom there, and you want to take the fork right as if you're going back to the village, and there's a sharp left after the hedge that you missed. Everyone does it.'

'Thanks so much.'

'No bother at all,' said the young man, touching his forehead in a salute. 'Enjoy your keep-fit class.'

Meg gave him a wave as she drove off, suppressing the urge to turn back down the lane and head for the lighthouse cottage as she did so.

Helen had mentioned that the new Laird and his girlfriend took over Applemore House, giving the whole place a new lease of life. The last time she'd been to visit they'd taken a walk up the drive – Helen cheerfully disregarding the sign which read PRIVATE NO ENTRY and taking her down a wooded path which led to a secluded beach, then back up through pines and huge masses of flowering rhododendron bushes to walk past the big house itself, which had been beautiful – more of a house than a castle – but clearly very dilapidated.

Now, a brand-new sign adorned the entrance to the drive, and someone had neatly trimmed the grass verge along the side. As she approached a group of whitewashed buildings, she could see cars already parked, and pulled in behind a tiny green Picanto which was even older than Helen's car.

A woman with long dark hair, dyed a bright mahogany tint, climbed out. She wore a pair of purple and green workout leggings with a rainbow-striped fleece on top. As she pulled up, she looked over at Meg and made a face that suggested she wasn't altogether enthralled with the idea of a Pilates class.

She picked up her bag and her bottle of water and slid out of the driver's seat.

'You look like I feel,' said the woman with a conspiratorial smile.

Hitching her bag onto her shoulder, Meg locked the car door and turned to see the woman still standing there, clearly expecting to have a conversation.

'You're not from round here,' said the woman, cocking her head slightly to one side.

Meg shook her head. 'No, I'm house-sitting for a friend.' Gosh she was out of practise with making small talk. That was what happened when you spent all day working online and only mixed with your closest friend and a neighbour.

'I guessed,' said the woman, falling into step beside Meg, 'because you locked the car.'

'Is that not normal?'

'Not in Applemore. We're so far from anywhere that nobody's likely to steal your car, and if they did the whole village would know about it before it had gone three miles down the road.'

Meg laughed. 'I never even thought of that.'

'Most of us don't even lock the doors, either.' She grinned. 'I'm Miranda, by the way.'

'Meg.'

'Nice to meet you, Meg. Shall we go inside and let the torture begin?'

Meg followed her up a neatly gravelled path towards an open courtyard full of huge containers filled with colourful spring blooms.

There was what looked like a converted barn with an enormous glass window where an arched door had once stood, and a huge sign announcing APPLEMORE FARM SHOP hung on the wall next to a doorway painted in a dark grey. Tiny spots of fairy lights danced in the windows, and outside the door a huge wooden rack – for flowers, perhaps, or something like that – was full of empty black buckets.

Opposite, there was a hanging sign which led through to the room where the class was taking place. Inside, a collection of women stood around chatting and at one end of the room a woman of about thirty with bright red hair tied back in a ponytail was tapping something onto the screen of an iPad.

'No sign of Beth yet?' Miranda looked around, searching for someone.

'She's not coming. Jack said one of the twins wasn't feeling well.' Meg turned to see a woman with dark hair pulled back from her face in a plait which hung over her shoulder. Curly tendrils had already started to escape and as she smiled a greeting she swiped at her forehead with the back of her arm.

'I'm boiling already. I had to run down because the bike had a puncture and Lachlan was in the middle of cooking dinner.'

Meg glanced around, not knowing anyone and feeling slightly like a spare part.

'Sorry,' said Miranda, a second later. 'This is – excuse my manners. I am terrible with names.'

'Meg,' said Meg, feeling shy.

'Ah,' said the dark-haired woman. 'You're the one who's house-sitting for Helen down at the lighthouse cottage. I'm Rilla.'

Meg gave a little smile of greeting. She was going to need a notepad to write all these names down if she was to remember them all. Maybe she could sneakily type them into the notes app on her phone when nobody was looking.

'Yeah, if I hadn't known you were Helen's house-sitter I would have guessed when you locked the car,' said Miranda, laughing. 'As it was, I explained it's a sure-fire way of working out the locals from the visitors. How long are you here?'

'Six weeks or so. Helen hasn't booked a return flight, because she wanted to wait and see how her daughter was doing after the birth.'

'Ahh, cute. I love babies,' said Miranda, 'especially when they're not my own.'

'I don't love babies,' said the dark-haired woman, 'not to say I don't love my daughter very much, I should add,' she said, lowering her voice slightly. 'But I was never one for fussing over prams. I don't think I held one until Kitty came along.'

'Oh, I'm the same,' agreed Miranda. 'Fortunately, mine is fully grown and off making his fortune in the big city. Have you left yours behind as well?'

Meg shook her head. 'I don't actually have any.'

It was the age-old question, and it always seemed to come up as soon as she met other women.

'Oh, my sister-in-law Charlotte is the same. She's off having the time of her life in South Africa with her husband. I'm not jealous at all,' said Rilla, laughing.

'Yeah, that's the joy of not having any. You can go off and do all the exciting things when you're not tied down for all those years.' Miranda gave a wistful sigh.

'Ah hello again,' said a voice, interrupting their conversation.

Meg turned and recognised Greta and the other woman, Dolina, who she'd met in the shop the other day.

'Nice to see you here,' said Greta, who was clearly ready to take on the challenge in a pair of grey cycle shorts and a loose lilac T-shirt over a matching vest.

'Hello again,' said the woman who she'd been with in the shop. 'Dolina,' she said, in case Meg had forgotten. 'And this is my daughter, Jenny.'

Jenny gave her a warm smile. 'Hi,' she said, giving a little wave.

'Rilla, Miranda.' Dolina gave them both a nod. 'I said to Greta I had a feeling you'd come along after we saw you in the shop. I said that lassie is definitely interested, because she was looking at the poster and –'

She was interrupted by the sound of a gong, which made them all jump slightly in surprise.

'Hello everyone, thank you so much for coming.'

The instructor was called Maisie, and looked nothing like Meg had expected. Small and round, with bright red hair and a face full of freckles, she announced that she'd recently moved to Applemore from the Island of Harris, and in her soft sing-song accent confessed that she was relieved that they'd all turned up.

'I was imagining standing here all by myself, trying not to be too upset.'

The class was unexpectedly fun. Dolina had them all in stitches when Maisie asked if they were familiar with their pelvic floor.

'We're not on speaking terms,' Dolina had said darkly. 'In fact, I'm no' sure that we're even living in the same part of the country.'

'Well, hopefully we can remedy that a little bit,' reassured Maisie, directing everyone down onto the mats on the floor.

During the relaxation session at the end, Meg lay on the mat, trying to clear her mind and allow her breath to reach the very bottom of her lungs as instructed. Miranda's passing comment had struck a chord with her – that one of the joys of being child-free was that it offered you the freedom to live adventurously. If there was one thing that her life had definitely *not* been, it was adventurous. Still, here she was taking a class and saying yes to something when she'd have said no in the past. That was a start, at least.

# CHAPTER FIFTEEN

She woke the next morning and realised as soon as she tried to climb out of bed that the gentle exercises had been deceptive. Everything ached, from her ankles all the way up to her neck. She tottered down the stairs in her pyjamas and opened the door, wincing slightly, to let Eliza outside for a quick pre-breakfast bathroom break.

'Morning,' she heard a man call in greeting.

Meg spun around with a muffled gasp of pain and saw with horror that there were two men in outdoor work gear standing by the lighthouse. One carrying a measuring wheel and the other – oh, you could not make this up – who turned as she watched to raise a hand in greeting was none other than the handsome man from the shop the other day. This village really was something else.

'Hi,' she said, giving a brief wave and stepping backwards, hoping they might mistake her tartan checked pyjama trousers for some sort of stylish Highland garb.

'Sorry if we woke you,' continued the other man, who was heading towards her. 'I'm Donald Grant.'

She opened her mouth to find an appropriate response.

'From Grant Forestry,' he added, gesturing to the neat lettering on the side of the pick-up truck parked on the grass.

'No, not at all,' she said, taking another step back. 'I was just – working. I didn't notice the time.'

She brushed an imaginary speck of dust off her pyjama trousers and tried to look casual.

The other man – Gabe – looked at her with the faintest hint of a smile twitching at one corner of his mouth. Coupled with the slightest hint of a raise of his brows, his expression made it clear that she wasn't doing a very good job of explaining her way out of the situation.

'Anyway, I had better get on.' She called Eliza, who with typical corgi contrariness had decided that there was something particularly intriguing under the rosebush by the gate.

'Eliza,' she said again. 'Come on, it's breakfast time.'

Eliza didn't budge. All Meg could see was the white and furry bottom and the wag of her tail.

Meg realised with a sinking feeling that Eliza was stuck.

'You okay?' The two men made as if to come over.

There was nothing for it. Pulling down the hem of her T-shirt and scuttling as quickly as she could with legs that seemed to be made of lead she scooted to the end of the garden path and unhooked Eliza, who shot off at double quick speed towards the kitchen in the hope of breakfast.

'You chose the wrong time to get hung up on a rosebush, madam,' said Meg, sliding the food onto the mat at Eliza's feet and grimacing at the thought of it.

'Now stay where you are until I get back. I'm going to get dressed before anything else goes wrong this morning.'

She clambered – slightly laboriously – up the stairs and headed for the bathroom. She'd showered when she got home from the class last night, and her hair had dried by the fire while she'd caught up on her tv show. At least it looked decent, even if she'd been caught – braless and barefoot – on the hop. She washed her face and put on some moisturiser, then brushed out her hair, leaning forward to inspect the threads of silver which were definitely multiplying. She pushed her hair back and put on some make-up. Just – she told herself – because it was good to make an effort, and because the woman she'd been following on looking gorgeous over fifty said that a little bit went a long way to making you feel good at a time when the world wanted you to feel invisible.

She could have done with being blooming invisible earlier. That would have solved a whole lot of problems.

Rubbing a splodge of concealer she'd missed, she peered at herself in the mirror for a moment. A smudge of chestnut shadow at the edges of her lids made her brown eyes look slightly more awake, and the ridiculously expensive mascara she'd treated herself to definitely made her lashes look better. She used a finger to apply some rose-coloured lip cream and then shook out her hair once more.

'You are being ridiculous,' she admonished herself, before heading for the bedroom where she pulled her favourite grey shirt and a pair of jeans out of the wardrobe.

Eliza was standing by the door, waiting to go out with a look that suggested that she didn't appreciate being kept waiting.

'Two seconds,' she said, putting on her shoes and grabbing the thick cream sweater she'd left by the door.

'Hello again,' said Gabe, as she opened the door of the cottage. 'We must stop meeting like this.'

She smiled despite herself.

'Taking a break from work?' The arch of his eyebrow suggested he hadn't believed her excuse for a second.

'Something like that.' She looped Eliza's lead around her palm, deciding on the spur of the moment to take a wander down to the library and check the contents.

'Sorry for the rude awakening,' he carried on. 'Donald seemed to think you knew we were coming today.'

Meg laughed, shaking her head in amazement. It was just as well she was used to Helen's disorganisation.

'Am I missing a joke?' Gabe cocked his head slightly and scratched his unshaven jaw with a curious look , a furrow forming between his dark brows. Meg felt that same unfamiliar swooping sensation and glanced downwards for a moment, looking down at her shoes before she glanced back up to meet his dark blue eyes.

'It's not you, it's my friend – it's her cottage. I'm housesitting, and she's got a memory like a sieve. Everywhere I turn there's something new popping up.'

'Did she have to leave unexpectedly?'

'Well, she's had almost nine months to get organised, so I would say no, on balance.'

'She's pregnant?' Gabe raised his brows in query.

'Not quite,' Meg laughed. 'She's a friend of mine from art school.'

Gabe made an open-handed gesture. 'You never know these days. You could be any age.'

Meg met his eyes with a shake of her head and a laugh. 'Definitely not pregnant. It's her daughter who is.'

'And she's left you in the lurch?'

'Oh no, not at all. She's just a bit – well, she's an artist.'

'Ah,' said Gabe, knowingly.

'Yes, exactly. So she's off to South America and I've turned up and basically spent the last few days firefighting but now I've got things under control.'

He looked at the garden, which was still very much in need of a good weeding and a clear out.

Meg wrinkled her nose and laughed. 'Well, almost under control, anyway.'

'Well, you were until we turned up. Sorry about that.' He gave a rueful grin. 'At least Donald's gone now, so there's only one of us left to worry about.'

'Should I be worrying?' Meg looked at him sideways. He was standing with a black folder in one hand and a large sheaf of papers in the other. He didn't look particularly alarming. More to the point, it wasn't exactly a hardship to have to stand here talking to him.

He shook his head, laughing again. 'Definitely not. I'm here to do some measuring for the planting and the fences they're putting up around the visitor centre.'

# CHAPTER SIXTEEN

'Visitor centre?'

Meg's eyes were wide and her rose pink lips were pursed as she looked at him.

'I... I'm getting the feeling that maybe you've missed a memo.'

She recoiled slightly, her brows arching upwards. She folded her arms and looked at him wordlessly.

'Sorry about this,' Gabe said, not quite sure what the procedure was when you turned up to a job and the client knew nothing about it.

She raised her chin slightly and hooked a strand of hair behind her ear with her free hand. 'Don't apologise,' she said, and smiled. 'I'm sure I've got the wrong end of the stick or something.'

He reached down to tickle the little corgi under the chin. 'She's very cute.'

'This is Eliza,' she said. 'Oh - and I'm Meg. We haven't actually been introduced.'

'Gabe,' he said, and for some reason he reached out and

shook her hand, which seemed weirdly formal under the circumstances.

'Hello.' She looked up at him and made a wry face. 'Well, here we are.'

'Yes. My boots seem to be very popular, anyway.' He looked down at the corgi who was conducting a detailed sniff-investigation of his feet. 'I suspect it'll be the scent of my spaniel. He's back at my place today, because I thought I'd better leave him as I was coming up here.'

'Does he normally come to work with you?'

'Always. When I'm planting trees, he likes to potter about sniffing out rabbit holes and trying to get into mischief.'

Meg reached down and unclipped Eliza's lead. 'Talking of which, I think she's probably unlikely to get into any trouble while we're standing here talking.'

'You're staying here looking after your scatter-brained friend's house while she's away. Are you working?'

She shook her head. 'Not just now, no. I'm – taking a break. So have you always worked up here?'

'No, I came up about six months ago on a – well, I suppose you could call it a break, too.' He shrugged. It was as good a way to describe it as any. 'I thought it would give me a chance to figure some things out, and it's surprising how peaceful it is out there on the moor planting trees in all weathers.'

'Must be freezing, though. You don't plant them in the winter?'

'That's the best time.' He pushed a hand through his hair as he spoke. 'You need to plant the trees when they're dormant, so it does as little damage to them as possible.'

'Oh, that makes sense. So were you out on the moors even in the snow and rain?'

He laughed. 'Even in the snow and rain. Especially in the snow and rain, it felt like. Now the weather's picking up and we're coming to the end of the season we're getting the fair-weather workers. But even they're likely to get soaked – you saw the weather the other day.'

'Oh about that,' she said, shaking her head and half-laughing. 'I couldn't really explain through hand gestures that my car was parked at the top of the street. But it was nice of you to offer me a lift, even if you were going in the opposite direction.'

'I don't offer lifts to just anyone,' he said, smiling.

'Well, I'm honoured. But I had a hot date with a load of cleaning equipment and some cardboard boxes.'

He cocked his head in query.

'My friend –'

'The chaotic friend.'

'Yes,' she went on. 'She's a bit more, um, artistically inclined than me. She said if I wanted to declutter the place in her absence she'd be more than grateful.'

'So you're house-sitting and decluttering and your friend's completely forgotten to tell you we're turning up to turn this place –' he thumbed in the direction of the building between the cottage and the lighthouse '– into a visitor centre.'

'Something like that, yes.'

'You must have the patience of a saint. I think I'd have serious words if a mate dropped me in it like that.'

She raised her palms up in a gesture of surrender and puffed out a breath.

'Not much you can do?'

'Literally nothing. I love her, but I have to admit I wasn't really expecting to be in the middle of a building site. Maybe this is my sign. I need to start asking more questions.'

'Well,' he said, holding up the clipboard as an offering, 'I've got the plans here, if it helps.'

'Can I have a look?'

'Of course. Come over to the truck and you can see them out of the wind.'

She followed him over the close-cut grass and he laid the clipboard out on the open back of the truck.

'So we're going to be putting a fence round there, and some hedging around the side of that, and a planting scheme here around the foot of the building.'

'I'm confused,' she said, looking at the plans. 'You said you plant trees, and the truck says Grant Forestry, and now you're talking about putting up fences and planting hedges?'

He laughed. 'Yeah, it was a bit of a steep learning curve for me, too. I came up here to plant baby fir trees. Next thing I know I find out that they also do fencing for the big country landowners, and then they also do things like this as part of their community offering.'

'Interesting. So you didn't work in forestry before this?'

He shook his head. 'Nope. I was a systems architect. This is all new.'

Gabe didn't mention that Donald handed him the project two hours ago over coffee at the forestry office, where Donald expressed his delight in having him on board. He had to admit that if he had known that his first project would come with a disconcerted – albeit very pretty – girl as part of the package, he would have put any residual doubts to one side.

# CHAPTER SEVENTEEN

Meg did a double take, realising that she was holding the leash, but there was no dog to be seen.

'Eliza?'

There was no sign of her. She must have headed to the beach.

'She's taken herself for a walk,' Gabe said, laughing.

'I'd better go find her,' Meg said, feeling torn. Half of her – a half she'd forgotten existed, it had been so long – wanted to stand there chatting to the handsome Gabe and ask him how he'd found himself up here working in Applemore. The other half, though, won.

'I'd better get on as well,' said Gabe, checking the time on his phone. 'I've got to get up the mountain and check everything is under control before lunch.'

Meg set off for the beach, the wind blowing her hair into her face until she pulled a band from the pocket of her jeans and looped it back in a ponytail.

When she returned, having discovered Eliza dancing with excitement at the edge of a rock pool where a tiny crab was lodged in some seaweed, she felt a bit deflated to come over the hill up from the beach and see that his truck had gone.

Back at the house she dusted sand off her jeans and headed inside, giving Eliza a snack and putting the kettle on for a coffee.

What on earth was Helen thinking, forgetting to mention that there was work planned up at the lighthouse? She couldn't feel angry at her, because years of friendship had taught her that Helen was just... Helen.

Her phone buzzed as the kettle came to a boil.

*Hope everything is going okay. My baby girl is enormous.*

There was a photo of Helen with her arms wrapped around a glowing Phoebe, who did indeed look as if she was about to pop.

*Everything is fine,* typed Meg. *Give P a kiss from me.*

She looked at the message then pressed send. A moment later, thinking about what the therapist would have said about allowing her feelings, she tapped another message.

*Woke up this morning to two random men noodling about outside... which was slightly unexpected?*

The therapist would have probably pointed out that she should be clearly expressing her dismay, but – Meg shrugged to herself as she scooped coffee into the pot and poured the hot water on top – nobody's perfect.

*Oh god, I knew there was something I meant to tell you,* came Helen's reply.

Meg's mouth curled up in a smile. Three little dots danced on the screen as her friend wrote a response from the other side of the world.

*There's a notebook on the mantelpiece with stuff I knew I'd forget written in it!*

*So you forgot to tell me you'd written a list of things you were going to forget to tell me?*

*That's pretty much it,* replied Helen, as Meg snorted with laughter. She carried her coffee and the phone through to the sitting room, Eliza trotting along behind her.

*I tidied it,* Meg said, shaking her head at the ridiculousness of the situation.

*Q.E.D.* Helen sent a row of laugh emojis. *If that doesn't sum us up, I don't know what does. Now, I better go. I've got a hot date with Phoebe's in-laws.*

Meg sat down on the sofa with the little green hard-backed notebook. Inside, in Helen's distinctive artistic writing, was a list of reminders. Bin collection, the number for the local health centre, where she'd find the fuse box and the water stop-cock.

She'd written down Kathleen's phone number **in case of emergencies... or if you fancy a coffee and a chat.**

She felt quite good seeing that. Knowing her of old, Helen had tried to bolster her in case she spent the whole time she was there house-sitting completely alone. Instead, she'd been out to Pilates, met Gabe – well, that wasn't exactly deliberate, but she was going to take it as a win – and had bumped into Kathleen as well. Not bad, she told herself, not bad. Maybe she really was making changes. She curled her feet up underneath her and pulled out her laptop, opening it up to search for information on free libraries, hoping for some inspiration.

She headed down later that afternoon, bringing Helen's wheelbarrow and one of the plastic storage crates. She'd loaded it with cleaning products, which she took out when she got to the little wooden structure, unloading them onto the grass and pulling out all the books along with a large quantity of sand and some dried sea-grass. Once she'd wiped down the four shelves and polished the little glass windows in the doors, she stood back, biting her lower lip and frowning, thoughtfully.

'Nice to see someone hard at work,' said a man in a flat cap with a grizzly little terrier trotting at his heels.

'Thanks,' said Meg, turning to say hello.

He gave her a nod and paused for a moment while she bent down to say hello to the dog. He had a kindly face, lined and weather-beaten under his cap.

'I'm giving it a bit of a clear out.'

'That's never a bad thing. I'll have to come by afterwards and see how it's looking once it's had a spruce up.' He glanced up towards the lighthouse. 'Settling in okay up there?'

Meg felt herself smiling. 'Yes, I am.'

'Glad to hear it. I'm sure I'll be seeing more of you in the next few weeks when we get going on the visitor centre.' He put out a hand. 'Murdo. My wife Greta said she met you at the keep-fit class the other day.'

'I'm Meg.'

'Nice to meet you, Meg. And welcome to Applemore.'

She wheeled the books back up to the house, having resolved to sort them out properly. Helen had so many books – not just fiction, but books on crafting and yoga, the history of the area, and lots more. She'd been quite insistent that Meg pass them on.

Meg put on some music and made some little stacks, sorting out any of the books from the shelves which looked too battered and worn to be of much interest to anyone. Then she got some old brown paper from Helen's art room, and copying the idea she'd seen online, decided to wrap up ten of them so their covers were hidden.

She wrote a brief one-line description on the spine of a thriller, then tied the book up in a parcel with some string, putting it to one side. For a romance, she wrote the first line of the book. Someone had donated a copy of Pride and Preju-dice. It would be far too obvious to write the famous first line on the brown paper, so she thought for a moment, tapping her pen on her chin.

She'd carefully written the words ***don't judge a book by its cover*** on the spine when a knock at the cottage door sent Eliza into a frenzy of excited yapping. She straightened up, brushing little pieces of brown paper onto the floor. This quiet life in the countryside she'd been expecting was proving to be anything but.

# CHAPTER EIGHTEEN

'Hello,' said Kathleen, standing at the door. 'You're not busy, are you?'

'Not at all,' said Meg, thinking it was the only British response to a question like that. If you were in the middle of conducting heart surgery and someone knocked at the door of the operating room, a British surgeon would probably stop everything, invite whoever it was inside, and put the kettle on.

'Would you like a cup of tea,' she heard herself saying, as she opened the door wider and gestured to Kathleen to come inside. Kathleen beckoned to someone outside and for a moment Meg wondered if she'd inadvertently invited half of Applemore to have a coffee. She was surprised and relieved a moment later when Miranda, the burgundy-haired woman she'd met at Pilates, appeared with a cheerful wave.

'We're not getting under your feet?'

'Absolutely not. I could do with a cup of tea, anyway.' She led them through to the kitchen.

'You *have* been busy,' said Kathleen. 'Helen's going to be delighted.'

'Or she's going to spend months wondering where I've put things,' laughed Meg as she made a cup of tea.

'How are your legs after Pilates?' asked Miranda.

'Oh, terrible. I could hardly move. I felt like I'd been frozen solid.'

'I'm still recovering. Looking forward to next week, though. I must be some kind of masochist.'

'Me too.' Meg fetched the jug of milk from the fridge and put three mugs down on the table.

'So you've met my niece Miranda, then,' said Kathleen, shaking her head no when offered sugar.

'Yes, she rescued me when I was contemplating doing a runner before I'd even made it into the class.'

Kathleen smiled. 'It's never easy, going somewhere new by yourself. And trying something new into the bargain – I think it's very impressive.'

Meg felt her cheeks going pink. 'Thank you.'

'I'd be terrified,' confided Miranda. 'But then I've never made it further than blooming Inverness.'

'Yes, we were saying how brave you are to come up here all by yourself. Not everyone would do it.'

Meg smiled. 'It didn't feel that scary because it's Helen's place.'

'Even so, landing up in a new village in the middle of nowhere takes some courage.' Miranda raised her mug in a gesture of salute. 'I agree.'

'So what brought you up here? I mean I know you're friends with Helen, but it's still a long trip. Have you left... anyone back home?'

Meg shook her head. 'No, nobody.'

'Ah, you're like me. I'm quite happy single with my little house and my job at the flower farm, and that's more than enough to be going on with. I don't have the energy to be dealing with men.'

'Meg didn't say she was single,' chuckled Kathleen. 'She might not have left someone back home, but she might have someone on the road. She's a traveller, after all.'

Meg grimaced. 'Not really a traveller. I only bought the van before I came up here, and only because I sold our house. I'm – well, I was – my husband died.'

'Oh gosh,' said Miranda, putting a hand out to squeeze her wrist. 'I'm so sorry.'

Meg put both hands up in a stop gesture. 'Don't be. We – it –' she still struggled to work out how to say it without sounding callous.

'It's complicated?' Kathleen raised her eyebrows gently.

'It was a bit, yes.'

Ah,' said Miranda with a sage nod. 'Say no more.'

But something in Meg wanted to get it out in the open, and to make it official. 'We weren't particularly happy,' she said, after a moment's thought.

It was Miranda's turn to grimace. 'Oh that's grim, I'm sorry.'

Meg sipped her tea. 'The thing is,' she said, surprising herself, 'it's hard because people expect a lot from widows, I've discovered. I had no idea that they were supposed to stay in their box and fulfil all the roles that society has mapped out for them.'

'I would say from my experience,' said Kathleen, 'that there are a lot of widows out there who *don't* fit into the box.'

'Certainly not from what I've read online.'

'Good on them,' said Miranda. 'I think women get enough flak for not fitting into the boxes we're expected to.'

'I'll drink to that,' said Kathleen, raising her mug and clinking it gently against theirs.

Meg smiled.

'Anyway,' Miranda said a moment later. 'We didn't come here to give you the third-degree. We came to pop in on the library, only when we got there the shelves were bare. I'm guessing this isn't some kind of avant-garde art installation?'

Meg shook her head. 'No, I'm in the middle of sorting the books, so if you want to borrow anything now is the perfect time. Helen appears to have bought half a bookshop in case of emergencies, and now she's decided she wants me to pass them on.'

'Ooh,' said Miranda, 'Can I have first dibs?'

'Of course. Do you want to come and see?'

Miranda was delighted by the piles of books scattered all over the carpet.

'I'll bring them back,' she said, beaming. 'Oh and look, the new Monty Don. Can I take that one too?'

'Of course!' Meg passed it over.

'Miranda works very hard up at the flower farm on the Applemore Estate,' said Kathleen, proudly.

'You need to come and see us. If you love flowers and gardening, you'll die on the spot. It's covered in tulips right now, and the blossom is almost here on the fruit trees.'

'I'd love that. Is it open for visitors?'

'Officially only at the weekend, but Beth never minds if it's locals. Pop in whenever.'

'I will.'

'So what's going on here with the wrapping?' Miranda picked up the newly covered copy of Pride and Prejudice.

Meg explained the idea.

'Oh I love that,' said Kathleen, turning over one of the other books in her hand. 'I bet people will pick up stories they'd never have even considered. I was worried when the bookshop closed and we lost the library service. Reading is such a lovely way to see inside someone else's way of thinking, isn't it?'

Meg beamed. 'Absolutely. I – when I was married, reading was my escape. I think people can be really snobbish about books like this.' She picked up a feel-good romance with a pretty flower-scattered cover. 'But it's so good to read something that you know is going to have a happy ending, especially when your life...'

She tailed off, trying to find the words.

'Especially when your life doesn't look like a storybook?' Miranda nodded. 'The last thing you need when you've got drama in your life is to sit down and read something stressful, I think. I love a good cosy romance so I might nab this one, actually. I love Holly Martin's books.'

Miranda picked up another couple of books and balanced them on the side of the sofa, turning over the one she'd chosen to read the back cover.

It was strange, Meg thought as she sipped her drink, that somehow it didn't feel particularly uncomfortable to have two women who were pretty much complete strangers sitting here chatting and drinking tea in the cottage. Back in Heatherby the only person who'd ever come into the house was Janey – Michael had never been a fan of people dropping by. Helen's cottage, however, seemed to be the sort of place where people turned up on the off chance someone might be around.

'It's good of you to get involved like this,' said Kathleen.

Meg smiled. 'Helen would be surprised to hear someone say that.'

'Not your usual style?' Kathleen looked at her thoughtfully. 'I might mention, come to think of it, that we could perhaps put a little book exchange in the mini supermarket. An extension, not a replacement. The little library is all very well, but it's not very helpful for people who have mobility challenges.'

'That's a good idea.' Miranda put the book down reluctantly, looking at it as if she'd quite like to curl up on the sofa and get stuck in. 'Hard to get down here with a buggy as well, if you've got small children.'

*Unless you've got a baby backpack,* thought Meg. She'd been thinking about the girl on and off ever since she'd first seen her, wondering if she was okay.

'I could bring a selection up to the village,' she heard herself saying. 'We've got a nice little pile of children's books.'

'Wonderful.' Kathleen put her cup down on the coffee table. 'We might even be able to find a little shelf somewhere. I've got a house full of old furniture.'

They said their goodbyes then and headed off for a walk along the beach in the spring sunshine. Meg – still achy and stiff from the Pilates class - trundled down to the library and back twice over with piles and piles of almost-new books. She returned, headed to Helen's craft room and made a brand-new little sign to hang inside.

**Help Yourself**, she wrote, wondering as she did if she was treading on toes. But the idea of that young girl sneaking up and taking the eggs as if she was terrified she'd be caught out had haunted her ever since she'd spotted her the other day. She knew all too well how it felt to creep about, looking over your shoulder and feeling anxious. If she was only here for a short while, she could at least make a difference in that time.

Kathleen obviously wasn't a woman who hung around once she had a plan in hand.

'Morning,' she said the next day, standing on the doorstep with a smile and arms full of a huge cardboard box. 'I thought it was worth chancing my arm that you'd be at home.'

Meg dusted down the flour that covered her top. 'Sorry, I was – well, I would say I was baking, but it feels more like a science experiment. Come in.'

Kathleen put the box down on the table in the hall and fished out a brown paper bag. 'I've brought you some cake, although if you're baking, perhaps it'll be surplus to requirements, but I was going to pop some into the library in any case. I painted a little bookshelf last night and sent a message to Michelle, the manager of the supermarket. She's more than happy to have a shelf by the door.'

'A library offshoot.' Meg smiled.

'Exactly.' Kathleen put the bag down on the kitchen table. Eliza, who had clearly decided that she was approved of, wandered over and allowed Kathleen to scratch her behind the ears. 'Ah, you're making sourdough.'

'Well, that's the intention. It turns out that Helen has left very detailed instructions in her little book, so I'm trying to revive the starter.'

She looked down at the dubious looking floury paste which she'd mixed in a Kilner jar. Apparently, this was going to come to life and turn into delicious bread by lunchtime tomorrow.

'It always seems like a lot of effort to make a loaf of bread,' remarked Kathleen, watching as Meg put it – as instructed – in the warmest part of the kitchen next to the hot-water pipes.

'I tend to agree. But I'm rather intrigued now.'

'I won't keep you,' said Kathleen. 'I wanted to pop this in and pick up some books and take them up to the village as I'm on my way. Might as well strike while the iron is hot, don't you agree?'

'Definitely.'

'And it's the weekend. Nice for people to pop in and have something new to read, as well. Not everyone has the luxury of being able to jump in the car and go out for a day trip somewhere, and weekends can be very long if you're at home with children.'

Meg smiled in what she hoped was a non-committal sort of way.

'I imagine,' added Kathleen. 'We didn't have any. My late husband and I – it simply didn't happen, and after a while I accepted that they weren't for me.'

Kathleen made her way down the sea path to the library. She was clearly well off, but it was clear that she could empathise with those who weren't so fortunate in life. She'd baked two fruit loaves and wrapped them carefully in paper, and deposited them on the shelf alongside three boxes of eggs. Having closed the library doors securely, she headed back up the path, collecting the mixed bag of books that Meg had sorted for her. With a cheerful wave, she climbed into her little red Fiat and set off for the village.

# CHAPTER NINETEEN

The sourdough was not a success. Helen's instructions were that all she had to do was "pop it in the basket overnight then turn it out and bake it in the Dutch oven". Meg had woken, flopped a sad looking doughy mass onto the worktop, and scraped it into the piping hot oven, burning her arm as she did so.

Forty minutes later the smoke alarm went off.

'Help,' she said, hopelessly flapping a tea-towel at the alarm, which seemed to be getting louder. She grimaced as she slammed the oven door closed to try to keep the smoke inside and tried to silence the alarm again, standing on the kitchen chair and waving her hands around. After a final angry blare, it gave up, and Meg climbed off the chair and headed to the oven.

'You,' she said to the bread, which she'd somehow managed to cremate, 'can go outside and cool off.'

She pulled open the back door of the cottage, walking down to the far end of the garden and plonking the red-hot Dutch oven on the top of the stone wall.

'Nice day for it,' said a now-familiar voice, and she looked across to the path to see Gabe striding towards her, a broad smile on his face.

He'd shaved, she noticed, and yet somehow his jaw was already darkened with a shadow of stubble. A black cocker spaniel was rushing back and forth in circles around his feet, nose to the ground and a flag of silky tail waving.

'Hello,' she said, feeling suddenly shy. She rubbed her nose to hide the smile which seemed to be curving across her lips without her bidding.

'Should I ask?' He tipped a curious head toward the metal pot, then as he got closer, his eyebrows shot upwards and he gave a chuckle of amusement.

'I was baking sourdough,' she said, laughing.

'Going well, I see.'

'I don't think it's one of my key skills, no.'

'Is this something you make a habit of?' Gabe leaned over, looking at the blackened object.

'Would it surprise you if I said no?'

'It's a relief, to be honest. If this was something you were doing regularly, I'd be concerned for your sanity. You know there's a perfectly good bakery in the village?'

'I do.' She shook her head, meeting his twinkling eyes with hers. 'My friend left me in charge of her sourdough starter and insisted that it wasn't rocket science.'

Gabe's mouth twitched again. 'It looks like it might be advanced bakery. How are you with cupcakes?'

'Oh I can make a mean cupcake,' said Meg, poking at the volcanic remains of the loaf.

'Well, that's something. I'll know where to come if I want one.' Gabe put a hand down on the wall, leaning against it as he looked at her with his ridiculously blue eyes. She liked the way the wrinkles fanned at the corners, as if he laughed a lot.

'I think if you're looking for bread, though, I might go elsewhere.'

'Luckily,' he reached into the back pocket of his jeans, 'I'm not looking for bread. I've come on a mission to find something to read.'

'You're in luck. I've just restocked the shelves.'

He was looking at her curiously, and after a moment, he leaned across.

'Sorry,' he said, lifting a finger to her face. He brushed her cheek gently.

Meg, whose knees seemed to have given way slightly, took hold of the stone wall with one hand and stepped backwards in surprise.

'Flour,' he explained. 'On your face.'

He had a slightly lopsided smile, which somehow made him look more handsome. She looked down at her shirt, which was covered in a dusting of flour all over, and swept a hand across her forehead.

'I expect I have it everywhere. And what do I have to show for it? A burnt missile.'

He grinned. 'You could start a munitions factory?'

'Not a bad idea.'

The spaniel jumped up at the wall in excitement as Eliza, clearly concerned she was missing out on some drama, scampered out of the back door and down towards them.

'Sorry Stanley,' he said, reaching down to pat the spaniel on the head. 'You'll have to take my word for it that there's a corgi on the other side of the wall.'

Eliza started yapping with excitement.

'Hello, little one,' said Gabe, leaning over to reach her as she stood with her front paws against the wall, desperately trying to look over. 'We're going for a walk if you want to join us.'

He looked up at Meg. 'The invitation is extended to you as well. Are you busy?'

Meg was about to make an excuse because she was covered in flour and he'd caught her on the hop and she needed a shower and... oh, a million other reasons, none of which made any sense at all and all of which added up to the fact that her heart was hammering in her chest in a way that was distinctly unfamiliar.

'No,' she said, before she could stop herself. 'Not busy at all. I mean apart from clearing up the munitions factory.'

He laughed. 'I'll head down and look for a book and you can meet us down by the library.'

Meg headed inside, rushing upstairs to the bathroom where she washed her face, brushed her teeth, and managed to swipe on some mascara and some cream blush and a bit of tinted lip balm in about three seconds flat. Then she looked at herself in the mirror and wondered if he'd notice she'd done herself up, and rubbed at her face with a towel before brushing her hair and tying it back in a ponytail so it didn't fly all over the place in the inevitable wind. She swapped her flour covered top for a grey and white striped fleece and pulled on her walking boots, whistling a startled Eliza from the sitting room where she'd already returned to the sofa.

Gabe was standing by the library cupboard, throwing a ball for Stanley. The spaniel seemed to have an inexhaustible supply of energy. He dashed up to her, pink tongue lolling, and then hurtled back towards his owner before screeching to a halt and waiting expectantly for the ball to be thrown again.

'Wait,' Gabe said, lifting a finger to steady him.

Eliza scuttled towards Stanley with her usual cheerful demeanour, her fluffy bottom waggling as he sniffed a greeting.

'I always thought corgis weren't very sociable.'

'It's a bit of a myth. Eliza loves people, because people mean snacks. And she loves snacks more than life itself.'

'Sounds like she's met her match in Stan, in that case. He's never met a food he doesn't like.'

Gabe looked over at the library cupboard. 'I found a book, thanks.'

'Oh good. What did you choose?'

'I don't know yet.'

'Oh you chose one of the surprises?'

There was something she really liked about that.

He nodded, giving her a half-smile. 'I liked the quote on the side, and I like the idea that you shouldn't always judge a book by its cover.'

Meg beamed and fell into step with him as they started to walk.

'So which one did you go for?'

He grinned and held out one of the brown paper wrapped copies. Meg immediately recognised it as the thriller which she'd read and loved a couple of months back. She'd written a cryptic quote on the side, based on the plot. It wasn't her usual sort of book – she often found thrillers left her double checking the doors were locked and that there wasn't anyone hiding under the bed before she got into it at night, but she'd loved this one despite herself.

'Watch your back,' he read aloud. 'Interesting, don't you think?'

Meg was torn between keeping quiet and letting him in on the secret.

'It's really good,' she said, watching his expression as she explained that she'd been the one to wrap it up.

'Oh, wow. I really like that idea. And now I know you've

enjoyed it, I'll look forward to reading it. We can compare notes afterwards.'

'Let's hope you don't hate it.' She grinned.

'I haven't walked this way,' Gabe said, taking a right as they reached the beach, 'but there's supposed to be a really nice path. It's just been opened up and takes you round towards the grounds of Applemore Estate.'

Meg watched the two dogs rushing around the beach, double checking they were heading in the right direction.

'Are we allowed on the estate?'

Gabe nodded. 'According to Donald, my boss, yeah. He pointed it out yesterday when we rudely interrupted your breakfast.'

'I wasn't eating breakfast,' she protested, laughing. 'I'd been up for hours working, actually.'

'In pyjamas?'

'Don't you ever work in pyjamas?'

Gabe laughed and shook his head. 'There's not a lot of call for pyjama clad forestry workers, in my limited experience.'

He stepped aside, letting her go ahead as the track wove up through a gap in the rocks and into the fresh smelling shade of a stand of pine trees. The air was cool and damp. They walked along for a few minutes in peace, the only sound the rustle of the needles underfoot and the panting of the dogs, who were still rushing around investigating their new surroundings.

'So I'm intrigued.' Meg slowed slightly as the path widened and he fell into stride beside her. 'How did you end up here in Applemore?'

'You're thinking it's a bit of a leap from industry to forestry?'

'It's not the most obvious career progression.'

'I was looking for a change. The pot plant on my desk was

getting tired of looking at me, and the idea of being outside for a while and not staring at a screen presented itself.'

'So you found yourself here.'

'I did.'

His arm brushed against her briefly as they walked on, and Meg decided she was glad she'd ignored the part of her that had wanted to say no to a walk with him.

'And now you're working on the visitor centre, which I knew nothing about.'

'Yeah.' He pushed a curl back from his forehead with a rueful look on his face. 'Sorry about that. I didn't mean to spring it on you.'

'Oh it turns out I should have known,' she said, stepping carefully over a tangle of tree roots. 'So it was my mistake.'

'I'm glad to hear it.' He laughed. 'I mean I'm not glad it's your mistake, but I'm glad you're not going to be camped out in the garden with a protest placard. It's the first community job I've been detailed with, so it'll make my life easier if you're on side.'

'It's not really my place to protest.' Meg shook her head. 'So what's the plan? What does a community job entail?'

'We – well, Grant Forestry – try to do a certain amount of work to put something back. It's one of the things I discovered about them once I got here. To be honest, when I arrived, I just wanted to get my hands dirty and do something that would clear my head.'

She glanced sideways at him. 'And then you realised you actually liked the job?'

'Well, the job and the people. Donald, who owns the company, is a decent bloke. Not surprisingly, he's got a group of good people working for him – it usually follows, doesn't it?'

'It does.' Meg thought about the staff of the company she'd

run with Michael. She'd been quite relieved to see the back of the staff who'd worked alongside him when she'd sold the business. None of them had ever quite been able to look her in the eye on the odd occasion when they met, and her discoveries after his death had made some sense of that.

'So what were you doing in your pjs then?' He looked at her with a mischievous expression.

# CHAPTER TWENTY

Her cheeks flushed, and she scrunched her eyes closed for a fleeting moment, laughing. Gabe watched as she bit her lip and looked at him with eyebrows quirking upwards.

'I wasn't working at all.'

'You don't say.'

She laughed.

'Next you're going to tell me you'd only just got out of bed.'

'Caught in the act.' She laughed.

He held back a long branch of pine which crossed the track, letting her walk ahead for a moment, noticing the bare skin of her neck where her hair was tied back in a loose pony-tail. A tendril of hair had come loose and curled on her neck like one of the early ferns that grew in the damp forest.

'So what do you do when you actually are working?'

She looked slightly uncomfortable, rubbing at her nose for a moment and frowning slightly as she spoke.

'I'm not working at all right now.'

'Nice.' He shot her a sideways look. 'You look about thirty years too young for early retirement.'

She laughed at that, rolling her eyes heavenward. 'It's closer than I'd like to think.'

'Tell me about it.' He grinned.

'I worked in design. Work in design?' She looked slightly confused. 'I'm not sure which, at the moment. I'm still trying to figure stuff out.'

'You sound like me six months ago.'

'Maybe I should get a job working in forestry.'

'We're always looking for new starters if you're interested,' he said, lifting an eyebrow.

'I don't think I'm the forestry type. I'd keel over after half a day planting trees.'

'We get all sorts, believe me. We've just agreed a deal with one of the big landowners up here to work on a project that's going to see people coming to volunteer alongside paid workers, planting a huge swathe of mixed leaf forest along the Glen of Lochbrannich, which is –'

He stopped himself mid-sentence. 'Sorry, listen to me going on. If you'd told me a year ago I'd be waxing lyrical about biodiversity and the positive impact of rewilding I'd have thought you'd lost your mind.'

But she was looking at him with what appeared to be genuine interest.

'That's amazing. Imagine coming here and finding something you're really passionate about.'

'You're right.' He'd never really considered it. 'It is pretty surprising.'

There was a wooden stile ahead that led into a field full of shaggy Highland cows.

'Better put these two on a lead while we go through here,' he said, catching Stan's collar and hooking on the leash. A moment later, he held the two dogs in one hand and offered the other as support as Meg navigated the winter-soaked wood of the stile.

'Thank you,' she said, taking his hand as she climbed over. The field was at a lower level, and she looked up at him with a smile that lit up her dark eyes. She was flushed from the walk and her hair windblown and untidy and he thought, as he passed the dogs through the gap in the fence, how pretty she looked in that moment, totally natural and at ease.

'So you're not working – at the moment – and you're house-sitting for your mate. I'm guessing that big campervan parked at the cottage is yours, yes?'

Stanley tugged impatiently at the lead as they made their way along the edge of the field. The cows gathered against the opposite fence, watching them with interest. Eliza, Meg's corgi, was wide-eyed.

'She's only seen about three cows in her life,' she explained, laughing. 'I think a whole herd has blown her mind. Yes, it's my van.'

She screwed up her nose again in the same expression as before.

'You say that like it's a bad thing. Most people would kill for something like that.'

Something about that seemed to tickle her, and she gave a snort of laughter.

'I would like to state for the record that I definitely didn't kill for it,' she said, shaking her head.

They circled back through the woods then, passing through a newly cleared path which took them past the edge of the grounds of Applemore House, which stood surrounded by trees with a huge sweeping gravel drive in front of it.

'It's nice of them to let people walk on their land,' said Meg, as they headed back downhill. The tip of the lighthouse was just coming into view, and Gabe felt a pang of regret that their walk was almost over.

'Yeah, it's been a real surprise to me to find that the landowners round here seem to be pretty friendly. I only realised I'd bumped into the woman who lives at the big house afterwards.'

'Rilla?' Meg pushed her hair back from her face.

'Have you met her?'

'She was at the Pilates class I went to the other night. That – for the record,' she added with a cheeky grin, '– is why I was still in my pyjamas. I couldn't move.'

'That explains everything.'

'I'll make sure I'm fully dressed the next time you turn up,' she added, as they reached the cottage.

Gabe tried to keep his tone casual as she opened the little wooden gate.

'Probably best,' he said, thinking as he headed back home that – despite his resolution that he had no interest in anything other than friendship up here in Applemore – the thoughts racing in his mind were focused in a different direction altogether.

# CHAPTER TWENTY-ONE

He checked his phone when he got home – three o'clock. If he nipped down to the supermarket and got some food, he could have a shower and then chill out for a couple of hours before ringing Jacob. Sunday morning had to be a good time to catch him before he headed out for a morning on the surf.

'Lovely day for it,' said Mrs Birnie, the elderly woman who lived in the cottage next door. 'I think we might be getting proper spring at last.'

She pulled off one of the gardening gloves she was wearing and scratched her nose with the back of her hand. 'My hay fever is on the way back, so that must be a sign.'

'I'm just heading up to the shop,' he said. 'Do you want anything while I'm there?'

'Oh you're an angel,' she said, beaming. 'I was going to head up there for a pint of milk when I'd finished gardening, but I'm worn out. Getting too old for this sort of thing.' She tipped her head toward the wooden planters that stood on either side of the stone step.

'I can always give you a hand with those, if you like.'

'Ach.' She smiled again. 'I complain about it, but it keeps me fit. I don't want to turn into one of those old ladies who just sits in front of the television all day long when I'm still energetic enough to get my garden sorted. But I won't say no to you picking up some messages for me if you're offering. Let me get my purse.'

'Not at all,' said Gabe. 'I think I can splash out on a pint of milk.'

'I was going to ask if you'd pick me up a packet of Penguin biscuits as well.'

'I can do that, too.'

He headed up the road on foot towards the little super-market. It was amazing to see how the village was coming to life with the beginning of spring and the change in the weather. All along the sea wall groups of tourists were gathered, chatting and eating ice cream or looking out to sea where in the distance the little boat which toured the waters showing visitors the sea life could be seen heading back to shore.

'Alright mate?' Gabe turned, hearing a familiar voice. The three young lads from his planting gang were sitting at one of the wooden tables outside the Applemore Hotel, and as he crossed to say hello a couple of other familiar faces returned from the bar with pints of beer and plates of chips. The smell made his stomach growl.

'Fancy joining us?'

'I'd love to,' he said, tipping his head in the direction of the store, 'but I'm on a mission for my neighbour. Promised her I'd pick up a couple of bits and pieces.'

'Come back afterwards,' said Ed, coming back from the bar with a bottle of expensive beer.

'I might just do that,' said Gabe, raising a hand in farewell.

He was just paying for the shopping when he heard the couple behind him pointing out the bookshelf which had appeared since his last visit.

'Look that's cute, isn't it? Dolina said they were putting a little shelf up here for people who can't make it down to the library.'

He smiled to himself, thinking about Meg. It had been nice – no, more than that – going out for a walk with her. He'd pretty much put relationships out of his mind when he'd left England, and for what seemed like a good reason.

He paid for the shopping and headed back to the cottage. It had clouded over and the tables outside the hotel had thinned out as people headed back into the warmth of the bar.

'Thanks so much for that,' said Mrs Birnie, beaming as he knocked on the door to deliver her shopping. 'How much do I owe you?'

She made to open her purse, but he shook his head.

'It's nothing, honestly.'

'Let me give you something as a thank you, then. Wait there.' She turned and made her way down the hall and opening the door into the little kitchen. The cottages were a mirror image of each other, but where his had been smartly decorated for letting purposes, Mrs Birnie's entrance hallway was wallpapered with an old-fashioned rose patterned paper and hung with countless framed photographs of her family.

'Here you are,' she said a moment later. 'Some scotch pancakes. You can take them for your lunch tomorrow if you don't eat them tonight.'

She passed him a paper bag, giving his forearm a squeeze with her free hand.

'You are very kind.'

'It's my pleasure,' he said, holding onto the bag of pancakes. They were still slightly warm and the smell of fresh baking rose to his nostrils. 'These smell good.'

'My grandsons love them,' she said, smiling. 'Whenever they come to visit with their families, they always insist I make a mountain of them so they can take them back when they go.'

'They're not local, then?'

She shook her head with a regretful smile. 'No, more's the pity. No, my children all went off down south in search of work. Their children did the same. It's sad, because it's such a lovely place to grow up, but it's the same story all the time in Applemore.'

'Hopefully things might start to change a little,' he said, thinking of the big Lochbrannich project. 'The forestry is always looking for people.'

'Och, yes, let's hope so. We need some young blood like you coming into the village to keep it going.'

Gabe grinned. 'I'm not sure I'd count myself as young blood.'

Mrs Birnie chucked at that. 'You're young in my eyes,' she said, shaking her head.

He had to admit that he'd felt like a teenager that afternoon, turning up at the lighthouse with butterflies in his stomach, hoping that he might just bump into Meg.

He unloaded the bag of shopping and made a cup of coffee, heading back into the sitting room and balancing his phone against a lamp on the table.

For a few moments, it rang out, and he was about to hang up.

'Hello!' A familiar face – older now, his hair sun-bleached and his skin tanned from a long summer spending every moment he could on the beach – grinned back at him.

'Gabe! Hi.'

Gabe felt the same complicated mixture of affection, pride, and something else he couldn't quite name whenever he spoke to Jacob. How you were meant to feel about an ex-stepchild who hadn't been a child when you came into their life wasn't something that the books or websites really talked about.

'Jacob.' He watched his face smiling broadly on the screen.

'How's it going?'

Jacob had developed a distinct New Zealand twang.

Gabe chatted to him, filling him in on the project plans, telling him about life in Applemore, asking how things were going on the other side of the world. Neither of them brought up the elephant in the room.

'Things are great.' Jacob looked happy. 'Really good. Rosie's due in a month. That's one of the reasons I was calling, actually,' he said, rubbing a hand over his face.

'Everything okay? I mean with the baby?'

'Oh yeah, so far so good. She's taking it all in her stride. She's out at a pregnancy yoga class this morning.'

'Interesting.'

Jacob grinned. 'It's not really your thing, is it?'

'I don't think I'm the yoga type, no.'

'We had the scan,' said Jacob, 'and it's a boy. And we wanted to give him your name as a middle name.'

It came out in a rush, Jacob suddenly sounding like the teenage boy he'd been when Gabe first met him. He felt a wave of affection for him.

'Jacob,' he said, his voice gruff with emotion. 'Are you serious?'

Jacob nodded. 'Yeah. We talked about it. I – I mean we kind of went through a lot together, one way or another. And I know I bailed at the first opportunity.'

Gabe shook his head. 'You didn't bail. You took the chance to start a new life somewhere amazing.'

'Somewhere my dad lived.' Jacob grimaced slightly.

Gabe looked at him through the screen, and for a moment wished more than anything that he could magic away the miles and be there to put an arm around the man who'd once been an angry, truculent young teenager.

'Somewhere,' Gabe said gently, 'where your mother wasn't.'

Jacob's lips were pressed firmly in a line as he nodded. There was a moment of silence.

'Sorry,' said Gabe, pushing both hands through his hair as he thought. 'That wasn't fair.'

'It was true, though. Living with an alcoholic wasn't much fun for anyone.'

'I think we can both agree on that.' Gabe lifted an eyebrow, and the understatement made Jacob laugh.

They talked for another half an hour, catching up on what they'd been doing and Jacob's plans for the house they were rebuilding. It had been tough for him, moving to the other side of the world only to lose his father a few brief years after they'd reconnected – but somehow the pressure, and meeting his easy-going girlfriend Rosie, had been the making of him.

'I'd better get going,' said Jacob, glancing over his shoulder. 'That's Rosie coming back, and I promised her I'd get started on painting the nursery this morning.'

'Sorry,' said Gabe. 'Didn't mean to hold you up.'

Jacob shook his head. 'Not at all. I'm glad you called – I didn't want to ask you by sending a message. It just seemed a bit impersonal.'

'I'm honoured, truly.' Gabe felt the lump rising in his throat again.

'You believed in me even when I was a complete pain in the ass.'

'You –' Gabe laughed.

'You going to try to deny it?'

Gabe gave a wry grin. 'No, you were a royal pain in the ass. But you grew out of it in the end. And now look at you.'

'Hey,' said a voice in the background. A moment later, a very pregnant Rosie joined Jacob, her long blonde hair tied back in a plait and a bump underneath her workout vest. 'Gabe, it's lovely to see you. You're looking great.' She gave a little wave and patted her stomach. 'Did Jake tell you about the name idea?'

'He did. I'm touched.'

She put an arm around Jacob's shoulders, and he looked up at her with affection.

'Did you mention your mother?'

Gabe sat back slightly in his chair, feeling the familiar sense of disquiet that entered him whenever his ex was mentioned.

Jacob shot Rosie a look, which even via FaceTime from the other side of the world clearly said *shut up*.

'What about her?'

Jacob shook his head. 'Oh, nothing. Nothing much. She's been – away.'

'Oh.' Gabe lifted his chin slightly in a nod of acknowledgement.

Jacob lifted his hands palms upward in a stop gesture. 'Anyway, I wasn't going to mention it. I wanted to talk to you about the baby, that was all.'

Rosie looked slightly pained. Gabe felt awkward that he'd been the one to make her feel uncomfortable.

Trying to smooth it over, he changed the subject, asking about the nursery renovation plans, and then once things were slightly less awkward, they said goodbye, with a promise they'd catch up sooner rather than later.

Gabe looked at Stanley, who was flat out and snoring on the sofa, worn out after his walk. Suddenly, an evening chilling at home in front of Netflix didn't feel that appealing. Grabbing his keys, he headed back out to join the lads for a game of pool at the Applemore Hotel.

# CHAPTER TWENTY-TWO

'Evening.' A tall man with fair hair and a black polo shirt was standing behind the bar. 'What can I get you?'

'I'll have a large Coke, please.'

Gabe heard his name being called and turned to see Pete and some of the others on the far side of the room, laughing and drinking. From the look of the table, there was more beer being drunk than pool being played.

'Anything else?' He turned back, used by now to the unspoken question that hung in the air whenever he asked for a non-alcoholic drink in a pub.

Gabe shook his head. 'That's it, thanks.'

'Didn't expect you to come back,' said Ed with a grin when he made his way across the room.

'A man can watch too much Netflix.' Gabe took a drink. 'And I had some good news from – from family.'

The words fell off his tongue and surprised him. It was the easiest way to describe it, but he'd always been slightly wary of inserting himself into a dynamic that was complicated at best. But there was no denying it – he was incredibly touched that Jacob wanted to give his unborn son his name.

'Cool,' said Pete, looking at his drink with a grin. 'Glad to hear it. But you're toasting it with a Coke?'

'As good as anything,' said Gabe, catching the pool cue as Leo, one of the gap year students tossed it his way.

'Your break,' said Leo.

He put his drink on the window ledge, looking out at the steely grey of the sea for a moment and wondering how Meg was doing over at the lighthouse. Then he turned, taking the chalk and rubbing it briefly on the end of the cue.

'Come on, boss,' said one of the other young lads, grinning at him from over his beer.

Gabe bent over the table.

'Five in a row?' Leo reached up, offering him his hand in a high-five.

'You're a dark horse,' said Pete, laughing.

'Mis-spent youth.' Gabe passed the cue to an eager Leo.

'I'll use that one. It must be lucky.'

'Or not,' said Pete a moment later, as Leo missed an easy ball and gave a groan of disappointment.

Five short minutes later the lads headed to the bar, laughing and joking about Leo's defeat at the hands of Gabe.

'You never told us you were a pool shark,' said Leo, shaking his hand with a good-natured grin.

'I'd hardly say that,' Gabe laughed. 'But yeah, I used to spend a lot of time playing pool when I was young.'

'Had they invented pool tables back then?' Leo ducked as Pete swiped at the side of his head. 'Same again?'

'I'm alright, thanks,' Gabe lifted his half-finished drink.

'You'd be wired on caffeine if you kept up with us pint for pint,' Pete said, finishing his beer and wiping his mouth with the back of his hand. He looked at Gabe with his head cocked slightly and a thoughtful expression. 'You don't drink at all?'

Gabe shook his head. 'Not really, no.'

'Sorry,' Pete shifted from one foot to the other. 'I didn't mean to – I mean...' He looked uncomfortable.

Gabe lifted his hands in an appeasing gesture.

'I'm not against people drinking alcohol... I've just seen enough of what it can do at close quarters. It was enough to put anyone off.'

Pete eyed his empty glass with a mock-guilty expression.

'Oh no.' Gabe shook his head again. 'I'm talking about a bit more than a couple of beers down the pub on a Sunday evening. I wouldn't begrudge anyone that. I ended up going off it because of everything it was tied up with.'

'Ah. Yeah. Say no more,' said Pete, lifting his head in an upward nod of understanding. 'Anyway, on a different subject altogether, I'm glad to hear you're on the books officially now.'

'You've spoken to Donald then.' Gabe felt himself relaxing slightly as the subject changed. No matter what happened, there was always a slightly awkward conversation about why he chose not to drink, but he'd worked out over time that if he just gritted his teeth and dealt with it once, it tended to be brushed over afterwards. Hopefully now that would be the alcohol conversation over and he could relax and enjoy the evening.

'Yeah.' Pete reached out a hand. 'I'm glad to have you on board. I mean not that you weren't already, but now you're not holding out on us.' He waggled his eyebrows as Gabe shook his hand.

'I wasn't holding out on you.' He laughed at Pete's expression.

'You're a good addition to the team,' said Pete, turning and taking a beer as Leo returned, putting a tray of drinks down on the table beside them.

'Thanks.' Gabe raised his glass slightly. 'Appreciate it.'

'You'll need to watch your back mind you,' added Pete, his eyebrows flashing upwards briefly.

'How so?'

'Well, Una's already been saying in the office that she's got a couple of nice single friends she knows that are on the look-out, and once she knows you've signed on the dotted line, she's going to redouble her efforts.'

Gabe groaned. 'Save me from matchmaking women.'

'Amen to that,' said Pete with a roll of his eyes. 'I'd get your excuses lined up and ready if I were you.'

'I'll bear it in mind.' Gabe found himself glancing out of the window again, his eyes drawn towards the far rocky shore of the little Applemore harbour. Typical that the first woman he'd wanted to get to know a little better wasn't planning on staying around.

'Come on then,' said Leo, breaking his reverie with a nudge of his elbow. 'Let's make it best of three. I reckon that was beginner's luck.'

# CHAPTER TWENTY-THREE

The next week and a half flew by as Meg found her feet, taking daily walks with Eliza and exploring the paths and trails around Applemore. They were both getting fitter with each daily hike, marching up the steep heather-clad hills and through the forest tracks that led down to secret coves and tiny white sand beaches. Eliza was delighted to discover that the seals seemed completely unconcerned by her existence, and would lie basking in the late spring sunlight as she stood beneath their rocks looking up at them, her little head cocked to one side in fascination.

Meg took a drive up one day to the farm shop where she met Gavin and Tom, the couple who owned it, and Eliza befriended their cute little sausage dogs.

'I gather from Dolina you didn't know anything about the plans for the visitor centre at the lighthouse,' Tom had said, chatting away quite happily as he operated the huge, sleek coffee machine behind the counter.

Meg had shaken her head, laughing. Dolina had appeared in the middle of a conversation between her and Miranda, inserting herself in comfortably and nodding along in sympathy. Afterwards, Miranda had said, with no rancour, that anything that Dolina overheard would be repeated and have spread round the village faster than you could spread the common cold.

'I didn't, no, but it was my own fault. I hadn't read Helen's list of things I was supposed to remember.'

'How is Helen getting on?' Tom passed over a beautifully decorated coffee, the froth on top swirled into the pattern of an oak leaf.

'Oh, she's having a lovely time.' She was still getting used to the fact that here in Applemore total strangers would strike up conversations with you as if they'd known you for years. 'Her daughter Phoebe only has a week to go now, so I think they're just getting everything organised. When I spoke to her the other day they were sorting out baby clothes.'

SOMEHOW IT WAS THURSDAY AGAIN – and time for Pilates class. Meg woke late and took Eliza for a quick run along the beach, promising herself a treat from the café afterwards as a bribe to get herself going. As she wandered back up the beach path with a panting Eliza, a fair-haired girl of about fifteen jogged past, her ponytail swinging jauntily.

'Morning,' said Meg, raising a hand in greeting.

The girl darted a quick glance at her and gave a shy half-smile. She was carrying a brown envelope, and when she reached the library cupboard she opened the door as if to look at the books, but then dashed off a moment later empty-handed.

*Strange,* thought Meg, wandering back up to the cottage. She was just filling her water bottle when she noticed a boy with a tangle of dark hair heading towards the little library, his trainers a flash of white as he strode purposefully. She'd seen a regular stream of people visiting the library in the time since she arrived – from curious tourists to locals out for their daily stroll. So far, though, there hadn't been many teenage boys taking an interest. Normally, from her limited experience, they were too busy playing Xbox or looking at their phones to be thinking about reading. She smiled as she watched him open the doors, and then close them again and turn back the way he'd come, walking more slowly this time. He wasn't carrying a book – but in one hand he held the brown envelope and in the other what she presumed must be a letter. He was grinning to himself as he read it, completely oblivious to the two men in high-visibility clothing who'd appeared out of nowhere and who were now measuring something on the grass by the beach path.

'Morning,' shouted one, as she locked the cottage – still not subscribing to Miranda's theory that everyone here left their place unsecured – and headed for the car.

She smiled and waved a greeting, realising as she did that the truck parked near the lighthouse was from Grant Forestry. She turned again, trying to look casual, wondering if Gabe was going to appear out of nowhere once again.

*No such luck,* Meg was surprised to find herself thinking as she climbed into the car and headed into the village. She'd left Eliza – tired from their walk along the beach – snoozing on the sofa.

It was funny that you could live in a place this small and not bump into the one person you'd quite like to see. She'd loved the walk with Gabe – because he was interesting, and interested in what she had to say, she'd tried to tell herself. But the truth was that for the first time in a very long time he was someone she'd like to spend time with, and she had no idea how that was supposed to happen.

Unless she just parked herself outside the cottage and waited for him to come back and get to work on the landscaping project, of course. That wouldn't look crazy at all.

She was still laughing at herself as she walked up the main street of Applemore village.

The sweet vanilla scent of the little bakery café was drifting through the air, catching Meg's nostrils and making her stomach rumble in anticipation before she'd even pushed open the door.

A little bell tinkled to signal her arrival and a woman in her early forties with dark curly hair appeared from underneath the counter.

'Ooh,' she said, straightening up with a little groan and a laugh. 'I think I need to do some stretches or something.'

'You should try the Pilates class tonight,' said Meg. 'I swear I feel better after only two classes.'

What on earth was happening to her? Back in Heatherby, she'd never so much as passed the time of day with someone in a shop, keeping herself to herself and dashing in and out as quickly as possible. Here she wasn't just chatting, she was volunteering information – and enjoying it.

'Maybe I will. I was helping make a load of sourdough loaves this morning and all that folding and stretching the dough has left me feeling like I need a hot bath.'

'Oh no,' said Meg, putting a hand to her mouth in horror.

'What's wrong?'

'I've just remembered that blooming sourdough starter. I shoved it in the fridge, and I was supposed to feed it. If my friend gets back and it's starved to death I'll feel terrible.'

'What are you doing in here if you've got a sourdough starter on the go?'

Meg looked at her with confusion.

'You could be making your own bread,' she went on, motioning to the beautifully shaped loaves which stood behind her on pretty wicker racks.

'I could,' admitted Meg, laughing, 'but my attempt at sourdough looked nothing like that. I think perhaps it's not my thing.'

'Well, in that case, that's probably good news for me. If everyone starts baking their own bread my husband Matt won't have a bakery business and this café will be up the spout as well.'

'Everybody wins,' said Meg, with another laugh. She scanned the shelves. 'Can I have one of those round ones, please, and a couple of sausage rolls as well?'

'Of course.'

She chose a sticky, old-fashioned iced bun and some cinnamon and raisin bagels to have the next day for breakfast, putting all the items into her reusable shopping bag and heading for the door with a wave of thanks.

'Oh, before you go,' said the woman, holding a blue cloth in one hand and a bottle of cleaning spray in the other. 'About that sourdough starter – you won't starve it to death if you leave it in the back of the fridge. It'll be fine until Helen gets back.'

Meg was shaking her head in amusement as she pulled the door closed behind her. It was the craziest thing to be living in a place where even when you *thought* people didn't know your business, they still seemed to have a pretty good idea who you were and what you were up to.

She went into the little supermarket, pleased to see that the lighthouse library offshoot seemed to be a hit. A woman in a red and blue striped fleece was browsing the shelves, a brown and white spaniel sitting patiently beside her wheelchair.

'Looking forward to Pilates tonight?'

Someone tapped her on the shoulder as she was scanning the shelves looking for olive oil. Meg turned to see Dolina beaming at her expectantly.

'I am,' she agreed. 'Although not looking forward to feeling so stiff that I can't get out of bed tomorrow morning.'

# CHAPTER TWENTY-FOUR

'How are you feeling?'

Miranda waved and strode across the farm shop court-yard. Meg had been admiring the masses of pretty floral bouquets wrapped in brown paper by the door outside the farm shop.

'Come and pick your own with me if you like. I'm just grabbing a morning snack for me and Beth and then I'm heading up to the flower farm.'

'Are you sure?'

'Of course. We're in the midst of chaos, as usual, but it'll be nice to have a distraction for half an hour or so.'

Meg hesitated. 'Oh, I should probably –' and then stopped mid-sentence.

'Are you meant to be somewhere?' Miranda raised a questioning brow.

'No. Nowhere at all.'

'Then come and have a look. I promise it's worth it.' Miranda held the door open and beckoned her inside. 'Have you got shopping to do?'

'I'll do it on the way back. I was going to grab a coffee and read my book for a while.'

They ordered coffees and some cake – Miranda recommending the chocolate-covered millionaire's shortbread – and then headed out together to the car park.

The weather was strangely warm, and Meg wound down the windows as she followed Miranda's little car up the farm track, past the front of Applemore House itself and down a slope to an unassuming pale green door, set in a wall which was faded with age and hung with ivy.

'I've brought cake,' called Miranda as they went through the doorway, 'And a visitor.'

'Oh hello,' said a tall woman in a blue and white striped Breton top and jeans.

'Meg, this is Beth, who still hasn't made it to Pilates, and is therefore not as limber and supple as us.'

'Watch it, you.' Beth grinned while taking the coffee Miranda offered her. 'Some of us have small children to think about.'

'Talking of Pilates,' said Miranda, biting into a piece of shortbread and dropping crumbs everywhere, 'I think I'm definitely getting fitter or something. I didn't actually want to cry when I got out of bed this morning.'

'Me too.' Meg laughed at Miranda's expression of surprise. 'I went for a walk before breakfast first thing.'

'You see,' said Miranda, waggling her eyebrows at Beth. 'Our bodies are temples, basically.'

'Temples full of sugar,' said Beth, breaking off a piece of chocolate and popping it into her mouth.

'That still counts. I said Meg could come and have a look around. She's staying down at the lighthouse while Helen is away.'

'Ah yes, Rilla told me. How's the work for the visitor centre going? Has it started yet?'

Meg shook her head. 'Someone turned up today to do some more measuring – well, I think that's what they were doing – for some fencing. Well, I assume it was for fencing.'

'You're going to have to work on your information gathering if you want to pass as an Applemore local,' said Miranda, laughing. 'If someone like Tom from the farm shop café or Dolina had been down there they'd have extracted all the info possible.'

'I'll bear it in mind.'

Miranda took her for a guided tour of the walled garden that made up the Applemore Flower Farm. There were neat rows of tulips and nodding blue muscari, structures of hazel wood and twine ready for sweet peas to grow up, and forget-me-nots massed together like tiny blue pinpricks.

'This is so beautiful. I can't believe all this is hiding behind that wall.'

'It's magic, isn't it? We're flat out at this time of year, of course.'

Meg put a hand to her chest as her heart seemed to swell behind her ribs. 'This makes me miss my garden.'

'Oh – are you a gardener too?' Miranda reached down to pull out a piece of chickweed, which was strangling a delphinium shoot.

'Not on this scale, but yes.'

'This place saved my sanity.' Miranda paused and looked across the rows of plants, a thoughtful expression on her face. 'Gardening is like therapy.'

'It really is. I wouldn't have survived my –' Meg stopped mid-sentence. 'Gardening kept me going.'

'Oh yes,' said Miranda. 'There's something about getting your hands dirty that just seems to clear your mind.'

'Someone else said that to me recently,' Meg said, thinking of Gabe.

'Someone?' Miranda cocked her head and narrowed her eyes.

Meg couldn't help smiling. 'Just someone I met.'

'Well, whoever it is, they seem to be making you smile, so that has to be a good thing, given everything.' Miranda started walking and Meg fell into step beside her as they strolled down towards an ancient, gnarled apple tree.

'I think you're probably right.' Meg said, putting a hand on the thick branch and feeling the undulations of the bark on her palm. 'I spent a long time being miserable.'

She surprised herself by saying it aloud. She instinctively liked Miranda, which is probably why the words had popped out of her mouth unbidden. Living by herself down in the lighthouse cottage she'd been surprised to find herself looking for connection and a chance to talk in a way that was completely alien to her. But there was something in Miranda's easy, laid-back humour that lent itself to the promise of friendship. Helen had told her on the phone the other day that Miranda, too, had experienced her fair share of hard times.

Miranda looked at her for a moment. 'Yeah, I've been there. You said the other day it was complicated?'

Meg hesitated for a moment.

'Sorry,' said Miranda, 'I didn't mean to pry.'

'You're not at all. It was complicated in some ways, and very simple, really in others. I think what it boils down to is that in an awful way Michael dying freed me, and that was hard to get my head around. It sounds so callous, doesn't it?'

She'd found an ancient album of photos on the shelf in Helen's sitting room the other day and opened it to discover pictures from more than twenty-five years ago. Photos of her wedding, where an anxious-faced young version of herself looked back at her. She'd looked at Michael for a moment, staring hard at the man in the suit who was smiling for Helen's camera, and felt unexpected compassion for him.

'Not really,' said Miranda, pushing a lock of hair back behind her ear. 'I mean it's a shame he's dead, but if he wasn't, do you think you'd have left him?'

Meg frowned. 'The person I am now would like to say yes?' She rubbed her forehead and thought for a moment. 'The man I married… he spent his whole life wanting more. I realised that afterwards. Nothing was ever enough. It was something missing in him, not something wrong with me. Once I figured that out, it was easy to let go of the past.'

'That makes a lot of sense.'

'The most complicated thing is dealing with people's expectations of what a widow should be.' Meg rubbed her chin.

'That's not your problem, though. Believe me.' Miranda motioned to her colourful, hippy-ish outfit. 'People will always find a reason to judge you for what you wear or what you do or how you behave.'

'I'm beginning to realise the secret is not to care.'

'It's the secret to living in a small town where everyone thinks they know everything, definitely.' Miranda raised an eyebrow. 'There's a lot more goes on that people don't notice, mind you.'

Meg thought of the young teenagers passing notes via the lighthouse library that morning, and the young girl furtively taking the eggs.

'I think you're probably right.'

'Oh,' Miranda grinned. 'Believe me, I am. There's all sorts of stuff going on around here and the gossips like Dolina –

who means well, but can't keep her mouth shut – don't have a clue about it. Saying that, I wouldn't put it past her to sign up for online dating in the area just so she could see who was on the market.'

Meg gave a gasp of horrified laughter. 'She would not?'

Miranda giggled. 'I hope not. But I can tell you that online dating in the Applemore area is not the most edifying experience.'

'Oh heavens.' Meg's eyes widened in horror. 'I couldn't do that in a million years.'

'Probably just as well. I tell you what, every time a half decent man turns up in Applemore they end up snapped up by one of the Fraser women. It's ridiculous.'

'What are you saying about us Frasers?' Beth, wielding a pair of secateurs, appeared.

'Nothing at all,' teased Miranda. 'Just telling Meg that now you lot are all paired up there might be half a chance for the other single women in the village.'

Beth snorted with amusement. 'Two of us,' she said, shaking her head as she spoke to Meg. 'I met Jack when he came to set up the outdoor centre, and Charlotte met Rob in Edinburgh. Lachlan already knew Rilla from when we were young.'

'Do you have to shoot holes in my theory?' Miranda rolled her eyes heavenward. 'Oh, she's got a point, though. Harry grew up in Applemore, so Polly didn't really take him off the market...'

'No, more that everyone else could see it and they couldn't. Anyway, now that I've disproved Miranda's mad theory that we are some sort of gaggle of man-stealing maniacs, I'm going to cut back the water shoots on this apple tree. It's far too late, but hopefully I won't kill it off.' Beth waved the secateurs at Miranda with a mock threatening expression.

'And I'd better let you get on with some work.' Meg realised she was keeping Miranda back from the never-ending list of things to be done in the garden in spring.

# CHAPTER TWENTY-FIVE

It was clearly one of those days. No sooner had she left Miranda than she'd bumped into Greta, who was standing outside the farm shop chatting to another tall, slender blonde woman.

'Ah, I was just talking about you, Meg.' Greta waved her over from the car park.

Meg dropped her keys into her bag and made her way over, trying to remember what it was she'd wanted to pick up in the shop. She had a memory like a sieve these days, it seemed. She'd spent half an hour the other morning searching for the coffee, only to discover she'd put it in the cupboard where Eliza's dog biscuits lived and left the dog biscuits in the fridge.

'Have you met Polly?'

The blonde woman was unmistakably Beth's sister. She was younger, with a smiling, freckled face, but her posture and build were identical.

'Hi,' said Polly, raising a hand. 'Nice to meet you properly.'

'I was just telling Polly that you used to do all that internet stuff.'

'That's the technical term for it, yes?' Polly looked at Meg with a mischievous smile.

'Ach, shush,' said Greta, batting Polly away with a good-natured laugh. 'I'm far too old to be getting on board with all these new-fangled terms. Internet stuff will do for me.'

'Internet stuff covers it pretty well,' agreed Meg.

'We need a website for the new visitor centre and I've been detailed with looking into it. I wouldn't have the first clue where to go to find someone who can make it, but I thought you might have some suggestions? We've got a bit of money to pay someone, but I've no idea what these things cost.'

'Oh, I can do it,' said Meg, without thinking. The words tumbled out of her mouth before she even realised.

'You can?' Greta beamed.

Polly crossed her arms and looked delighted. 'Well, that's a turn up for the books.'

'What sort of thing are you looking for?'

'Oh goodness knows,' said Greta, shaking her head. 'Matt who owns the bakery here said he'd take some photographs for it. Sandy, one of the village improvement society members, has done a little bit of writing about the history of the place. We're hoping we can just tag it on to the village website.'

Meg tried to keep her expression neutral. She'd seen the village website, which looked as if it was last updated in 2002, and which was in need of a serious overhaul. Her design sensibilities had been horrified when she'd clicked on the link.

'Perhaps it could have a little update as well,' Greta said thoughtfully. 'I don't suppose...'

'I'll do it,' said Meg, in an instant.

RACHAEL LUCAS

She got back to the house a couple of hours later, having sat down over a coffee and delicious toasted sandwiches, which Greta insisted on paying for. Her brain was fizzing in a way she had almost forgotten, the little cogs inside whirring into action as she thought about how best to convey the information in a way that would be easy for users to navigate but also look simple and stylish.

Eliza was waiting at the door looking unimpressed. Meg let her out, grabbing her lead and following at a brisk walk as the little corgi scampered towards the gate and out onto the grass.

'Sorry, darling,' she said, as Eliza peed on a tussock of grass with a disapproving expression. 'I didn't mean to leave you with your paws crossed for so long.'

It was strange how things happened. Miranda – out of the goodness of her heart – had offered her the chance to come and do some voluntary work up at the flower farm. The gardener in her should have leapt at the chance, but something inside her brain had jammed on the brakes. She might not have to worry about money, but the idea of a life of voluntary work and good deeds suddenly made her feel like she was about ninety. It was no wonder that the idea of getting her teeth into the work she'd spent her entire career doing had sparked something in the creative side of her brain.

She was just about to head back to the cottage when Eliza gave a startled bark and she turned to see the girl with the baby on her back heading towards the library. This time, though, Meg decided to wander over.

'Hi,' she said, smiling.

The girl had huge dark eyes and her hair was tangled and windblown from her walk along the beach path. The baby strapped on her back was wrapped up in a cosy blue and yellow coat, his pudgy hand clutching onto a loose strap. He beamed at Meg, showing two new teeth.

The girl, who had her hand on the door of the white-painted library cupboard, let go as if it was suddenly scalding hot.

'Sorry,' she said, stepping backwards. A blush rose in her cheeks and she ducked her head so her long hair half-covered her face.

'Not at all,' said Meg, kindly. 'I was just coming to check if we needed to stock up.'

She opened the door and saw that Kathleen had been down again, and there were two brown bags with some baked goods inside, and two boxes of eggs on the shelf below, next to a neat pile of village newsletters. She reached inside, taking the cakes and one of the boxes of eggs from Kathleen's hens.

'Would you like these? I would hate for them to go to waste.' Meg handed her the brown paper bags.

'Are you sure?' She looked dubious, but her eyes lit up.

'They won't last until tomorrow,' Meg lied, knowing perfectly well that they were freshly baked that morning. 'Kathleen likes to feel she's doing her bit but sometimes we end up overstocked with cake, so you'll be doing me a favour.'

*Sorry Kathleen,* she said to herself. Somehow she suspected Kathleen wouldn't mind being patronised for a worthwhile reason.

'Really?'

'Absolutely.' Meg smiled at her, and her heart warmed as she received a shy smile in return.

'I'm Meg, by the way.' She glanced up at the cottage for a moment, watching as Eliza bumbled about, sniffing tussocks of grass. 'I don't live here in Applemore.'

That seemed to instantly put the girl slightly more at ease.

'I'm just staying for a while, looking after my friend's cottage up there.'

'In the lighthouse?'

'Yeah. Amazing, isn't it? I can't quite believe it. Sometimes when I wake up in the morning I can see seals snoozing on the rocks, and at night time I hear the owls swooping around. I think they must live in the trees over there by the path that leads up towards Applemore House.'

'That's amazing. I love seals.' She smiled more confidently now. 'It's one of the reasons I walk down here most days. That and it keeps Kai happy. He loves being outside in the fresh air.'

'It looks like it,' said Meg, looking up at the baby's happy face. He was holding a fistful of his mother's hair and babbling cheerfully. 'And it must be nice for you, too. I always think it must be hard being at home with a baby all day.'

She shot Meg a relieved look and her whole body seemed to relax slightly. She was really very young – no more than twenty-one or two, perhaps.

'Oh it's nice most of the time, but Kai's been teething and he's been waking up a lot at night, so I've been exhausted for the last few days.'

The baby, seemingly aware he was the centre of attention, gave a delighted squeal and waved his hands in the air.

'Ouch! That's Mummy's hair!'

'And do you have anyone to help?' Meg said carefully, not wanting to pry.

'No, there's just me. I - well, we – moved here when I was pregnant. My boyfriend Calum got a job working over in Inverness, so he was supposed to be working away from Monday to Friday and coming home at the weekends, only he…'

She trailed off and her little face worked as she tried to compose herself.

'Sorry,' said Meg, 'I didn't mean to upset you.'

'Oh you didn't upset me,' the girl said, straightening her shoulders and lifting her pointed chin as if to gather herself for battle. 'He did. But I'm over that now. There's just me and Kai and that's fine.'

*Fine*, thought Meg, *except you're struggling to get by and too proud to admit it.*

The girl reached up, untangling her hair from the baby's hand with practised ease, letting his little fingers wrap around one of hers instead. He gurgled happily and pulled her hand up to his mouth, gnawing at her knuckle.

'I'm Laurel,' she said, after a moment. 'I forgot to tell you my name.'

'Looks like he's still teething,' laughed Meg. 'There are lots of new baby books down there on the shelf – I don't know if you saw them? We swapped over all the books the other day and someone donated a box.'

'Oh I didn't see.'

Meg stepped out of the way as Laurel looked inside, taking a couple of colourful board books and then looking at her with a questioning expression.

'Take them,' said Meg. 'It's all here so people can help themselves. The books, the eggs... all of it. We've got a little offshoot now in the shop in town. Have you seen it?'

'I did,' Laurel said, shifting the shoulder strap of the carrier and adjusting the sleeve of her hoody. 'I wasn't sure if we were allowed to take the books in there though, because it was in the shop.'

'Ah, that's a good point. I'll mention it to Greta. She's sort of in charge of – well, she seems to be one of those people who is in charge of everything.'

'My granny was like that.' Laurel smiled.

'I take it she's not here in Applemore?'

'No, I don't have any family here. Don't have anyone, actually. After Calum left…'

Meg remembered the village newsletter. She reached for the stack on the shelves and passed one over. 'Here you are. This might help a little bit.'

'What is it?' Laurel turned it over and read the front cover. 'Oh, right.'

'It's got a list of things like mother and toddler groups and stuff like that in the back. I thought it might be helpful. You might be going already of course.'

Laurel shook her head. 'No, the health visitor came once when we'd not long got home from the hospital but then Calum left and I was busy sort of getting to grips with everything, and –'

Meg's heart squeezed with empathy. 'Well, have a look and maybe go along to the village hall next time it's on?'

Laurel screwed her mouth sideways and raised her eyebrows slightly. 'Maybe.'

They were interrupted by Eliza shooting past, barking sharply. Meg turned to see what had caught her attention and saw a group of people standing by the lighthouse, one of whom pointed at her and then waved.

'Sorry, I'm keeping you from your visitors,' said Laurel. 'Thanks so much for the books and –' she gestured to the bag of cake.

'Oh don't thank me,' said Meg, 'but please drop by any time. And come and say hello,' she added as Laurel started walking away.

'I will.' Laurel turned, and a genuine smile spread across her face. 'I'd like that.'

'Me too.'

Meg walked briskly back up the hill. Goodness knows who these people were, but she was beginning to realise why Helen said she was never lonely living in the lighthouse cottage. It was like living in the middle of Piccadilly Circus out here.

'Hello,' said a short man in a green anorak and walking shorts. 'We've come to see the lighthouse, but we can't get in?'

'Oh, it's not actually open to the public,' Meg said, not for the first time. 'Well, not yet. It will be, later in the summer.'

He sighed and turned to beckon the rest of his group, who were milling about, peering over the wall into the cottage garden and trying to see inside the empty building which joined the cottage and the lighthouse.

'It's not open,' he called. 'I can't believe we've come all this way and we can't get in. I'm sure someone said on the forum that they'd gone inside.'

'Forum?' Meg said, faintly.

'Online.' He crossed his arms. 'It's a forum for people like us.'

Meg lifted her eyebrows in query.

'Pharologists,' he said cheerfully. 'Lighthouse baggers. You must've come across our kind before, out here?'

'Oh this isn't my house,' she said, gesturing to the cottage. 'It's my friend's place.'

'Lucky friend. Lucky you, more to the point.' He narrowed his eyes thoughtfully and gave a conspiratorial smile. 'You don't happen to have a key, do you?'

Meg shook her head, crossing her fingers behind her back and hoping that she wouldn't be struck down for telling a white lie. 'I'm afraid not, no.'

'I suspected not. They're all operated remotely nowadays, and the only people who can access it are the NLB.'

'Yes, that's right.' She nodded in what she hoped was a suitably knowledgeable manner. 'Sorry you've had a wasted journey.'

'Oh gosh no, we haven't. We've got some wonderful

photographs. And now we've troubled you enough, so we'll be on our merry way.'

He was very sweet, thought Meg, watching as the group marched off towards the sea path, heading off on a mission to find – or should she say bag – their next lighthouse.

'Come on, Eliza,' she called, opening the gate to the cottage. 'I think we've had more than enough excitement for one day.'

# CHAPTER TWENTY-SIX

Una believed an army marched on its stomach, so the table at the Grant Forestry office meeting was always laden with goodies from the café along the road, as well as countless cups of coffee and tea to keep everyone going while they ran over the figures and caught up on who was where for the following week.

By their nature, the forestry workers weren't inclined to appreciate sitting down for a meeting, preferring to be out and about. Una had clearly worked out that bribery through the medium of baked goods was the way forward. Gabe had been roped into joining the meetings not long after he'd started working, which probably should have been a sign to him that Donald was hoping he'd move into a more senior role. Now he'd agreed to take a promotion and would be salaried, rather than paid on a weekly basis, there would be no getting out of them.

Sitting on the edge of a table in a scruffy, relaxed old building in the Highlands was a far cry from his years of listening to corporate speak. That was probably why he didn't scarper out of the door at the first opportunity, staying behind long enough to pick up the leftovers for his gang up on the hill.

'Take these up for your tree planters,' Una said, tying a bag at the top and handing it to Gabe. She'd stuffed it full of the leftover pain au chocolat and flaky croissants, along with a couple of brown bags full of chocolate cookies which had been left untouched.

'Will do,' he said, grabbing the planting plan for the following week with his other hand. They had one more week on the moorland, and then they'd be getting started on the Lochbrannich Estate. The duke had been keen to get moving as soon as possible, and Donald had agreed, which had left Una chuntering with disapproval.

'The amount of money he's going to be sending our way,' Gabe's employer had said, thorough a mouthful of croissant, 'I'd get my two kids up there if it was going to make a difference.'

Everyone had laughed.

'I don't know what you're laughing about,' Donald had said with a chuckle. 'I'll have your kids as well. There's a decent bonus for everyone in the offing if we can get this job in the bag.'

'Right, I'm off,' said George in his Inverness accent. Short and wiry, he was one of their lead tree surgeons who'd recently been grounded due to injury and after years of working at height in the trees was reluctantly trying to keep himself busy. 'I've put the measurements for the lighthouse job on that email for you, Una, and I'm away to put those new trees in up at Midsummer House.'

He raised a hand in farewell and disappeared out of the door. A moment later, Una shot out of her seat and rushed after him.

'George, where's that measuring wheel you borrowed?'

She turned back a moment later, shaking her head in mock-disapproval.

'I don't know, you lot are a disgrace. He says he hasn't a clue what he's done with it. I wouldn't mind, but that's the third one we've misplaced this week. I bet he's left it up at the lighthouse.'

Gabe saw an opportunity and grabbed it. Meg had been on his mind since they'd been for that unexpected walk together, but he hadn't been able to think of a way to engineer a meeting. It was ridiculous, really, to be feeling this clueless at his age.

'I'll nip up and get it,' he said casually.

'Would you?' Una beamed at him, slipping back into her chair and frowning for a moment at the screen in front of her. 'I've got so much to do here, and I can guarantee George won't remember later.'

'No problem, I'll grab it. I could do with casting an eye over it before we start work next week in any case.'

He called Stanley, who'd been dozing on a dog bed under Una's desk.

'Bye darling,' said Una, reaching down and stroking the spaniel's ears. 'You be a good boy, now.'

'I will,' said Gabe, laughing.

'Not you,' Una said, rolling her eyes. 'Off you go. Out of my hair.'

Laughing, he headed to his truck. He threw the bag of pastries and cookies in the back, well out of reach of hungry spaniel jaws, and headed off towards the lighthouse.

He glanced at the clock. Nine in the morning. Meg didn't have any reason to be up early... he'd probably get there and find she was still fast asleep.

It was another gorgeous day. Everyone in Applemore had

promised that early spring was the nicest time of year up in the Highlands, but the weather seemed to be pulling out all the stops. The sky was blue and the sun unseasonably warm, so much so that he rolled down the window as he drove along the narrow road that led to the lighthouse. Stanley leaned out of the window, his ears flapping and his tongue lolling as he took in the sights and the scents of the countryside.

Cow parsley had suddenly appeared out of nowhere along the hedgerows. The trees and bushes seemed to be covered with green shadow as their leaves burst into life. In the fields, the farmers were busying themselves with the lambs. Daffodils gathered around a wooden stile that led to a footpath through the woods. He pulled the truck to a halt as a red-haired young farmer on a quad bike appeared from a gateway and raised a hand in warning.

'Won't be long,' he shouted to Gabe, giving a friendly wave.

A moment later, one shaggy-coated Highland cow appeared, stepping out onto the road as if she wasn't quite sure she was in the right place. She looked from left to right, peering in the direction of Gabe's truck. He leaned over and put a hand on Stan's collar.

'No leaping out of the window,' he said, warningly. Stan was stock still, his eyes wide. Even after six months of living in the countryside all the wild – and not so wild – life was a novelty to him.

A moment later, another two cows appeared, nostrils flaring as they bunched together with the leader.

'Come on lassies, get a move on,' called the young farmer.

About twenty more cows came through the gate, jostling each other and mooing as they were guided by the young farmer towards the gateway which was already open just up the lane. The young farmer gave a wave and shouted his thanks as he scooted off on his quad bike. An older farmer, identical in the same dark green boiler suit and red hair, appeared from the original field with a long walking stick in his hand.

'Morning,' he said with a nod. 'Sorry to keep you.'

'No problem,' said Gabe, lifting a hand in acknowledgement.

He bumped over the cattle grid that led onto the road down to the lighthouse, and was surprised to find the gate already open but nobody about.

He pulled up, closing the gate behind him out of habit, and made his way down the track towards the lighthouse, pulling up on the grass verge by the path.

His heart jumped as he noticed Meg walking back up from the lighthouse library. He climbed out of the truck and stood leaning against it, watching as she made her way towards him.

Stanley hurtled towards Eliza with undisguised delight, bouncing around her with his feathery tail wagging furiously.

'I'm sorry, he's got no chill whatsoever.'

'Nor does Eliza, it would seem.' Meg joined him, laughing as her little corgi rolled upside down on the grass.

'Fortunately, I'm much cooler.' He grinned. 'Although it's a low bar.'

'Fortunately, I'm too old to be impressed by people pretending to be cool.'

'Touché.' He grinned. 'I shall stop trying, in that case.'

'Were you trying?' Meg said innocently.

'You're very sharp for this time of day.' He looked at her dress, which was pale green and patterned with flowers. 'And not in pyjamas, I see.'

Meg laughed. 'No, I've taken to sleeping in my clothes so I don't get caught out by random men turning up at all times of the day and night.'

'Is that a problem around here?'

The sea wind was blowing up the path from the beach, and she caught her hair in a ponytail in her hand, twisting it over her shoulder as she spoke.

'No, it's mainly you.' Her eyes sparkled mischievously.

'I'm glad to hear it.'

'Actually,' she continued. 'I say that, but there's an ever-increasing number of tourists turning up to look at the light-house. In fact, I did have a random man who appeared yester-day. A pharologist, no less.'

Gabe rubbed his jaw. 'A what?'

'I'm glad you said that. I felt very ill educated when he announced himself. Turns out it's the proper name for a light-house enthusiast.'

'A lighthouse enthusiast.'

'Not just a person who quite likes lighthouse,' Meg went on. 'A full-on enthusiast.'

'Who knew that was a thing.'

'Exactly. Well, you learn something new every day. And now it's only – what time is it? Nine? And you've learned a thing already. That means you can take the rest of the day off.'

Gabe laughed. 'That would be nice.'

It would be nice, particularly if it meant he could stand here chatting to Meg in the sunshine all morning. He'd wondered since their walk if he'd imagined the spark between them as they spoke, but it was definitely there. There was something in the air – something he hadn't felt for a very long time.

'I was just putting some stuff down in the library cupboard. It's definitely getting busier since the weather has improved.'

'Ah, that makes sense.' They started walking down towards the lighthouse. 'I came to see if one of the fencers left a measuring wheel down here yesterday.'

'It's by the side of the lighthouse door. I haven't seen one of those since school. Do you remember when they used to give us one and make us measure the football field?'

Gabe laughed. 'I'd forgotten that. Do you think it was just an excuse for the teachers to get us out of their hair for half an hour?'

'Oh, definitely. I wouldn't want to be in charge of a class of ten-year-olds, would you?'

Gabe picked up the wheel and turned it, resetting the counter to zero. 'Absolutely not. So did your pharologist get what he wanted?'

'Nope. I had to disappoint him.' A smile curled on her lips. She really was pretty.

He lifted an eyebrow in query as he looked up at the lighthouse.

'He wanted to look inside. I had to tell a small white lie when he asked if it was open.'

'So it's unlocked?'

She nodded. 'I don't think we're meant to have the key – but there's a spare one hanging up in the building that's being turned into the visitor centre.'

'I've never been to the top of a lighthouse.'

'I hadn't either,' she said, and then put a hand to her mouth. 'Uh-huh?'

'I sneaked up. The door was open, and I figured the chances of being caught were fairly slim.' She stole a glance up at him and her eyes danced with mischief.

'So now I know where to come if I want to break in.'

'Yep. I'm here for all your lighthouse needs.'

He looked at the dogs, gambolling happily around in the long sea-grass. Stanley didn't have any reservations – he just leapt straight in feet first, grabbing the opportunity for fun whenever it arose.

'How about now? I'm game if you are.'

She bit her bottom lip and her brow furrowed for a brief moment, then she nodded.

'You only live once. What are they going to do – kick me out?'

'That's a good point.' He called Stanley, who hurtled over and skidded to a halt at his feet.

'He's so well behaved.'

'Most of the time.' He took the truck keys out of his back pocket. 'I'll stick him in there out of trouble.'

'You can leave him in the cottage with Eliza if you like. I'm sure they'll be fine.'

He followed her into the little cottage, ducking his head to avoid a low beam as they stepped down into the cosy sitting room. Eliza hopped up onto the sofa while Stanley rushed around, sniffing the furniture.

'Stanley, lie down and try to look like you're at least halfway to house trained.'

After a moment, Stanley joined Eliza on the sofa.

'There you are,' Meg said, laughing. 'They look like they're about to watch something on Netflix. They just need some popcorn and a Coke each.'

'It's quite a long way up,' she added a few minutes later as they sneaked through the door that led into the lighthouse itself.

Meg went in front, which left him no choice but to admire the dip of her waist in the pretty dress as she climbed the stairs in front of him. She stopped midway for a rest, bending over at the window ledge to catch her breath.

'Sorry,' she said, puffing. 'I'm not quite at forestry fitness level.'

'Don't apologise,' said Gabe, who'd been admiring her

curves. He averted his gaze as she straightened up. 'I expect if you did this every day, you'd soon get used to it.'

'I don't know,' Meg said as they started climbing again, '– for all we know the rocks could be littered with the bodies of exhausted lighthouse keepers who keeled over from overwork.'

He shook his head, laughing. 'It's a possibility, I suppose.'

They reached the top and he gave a low whistle.

'It is amazing, isn't it?'

'Imagine being up here every day, in all weathers.'

He ran a hand along the rail that stood around the lamp.

'It's a scary thought, isn't it?' She put her hand alongside his. 'Imagine being up here in the middle of winter in a storm. It's so high.'

'I suspect they were so busy keeping safe that they didn't have time to think about anything else.'

Meg turned and gazed out to sea. 'Apparently you can see the light from here for five nautical miles. And did you know that every lighthouse has a different sequence? I didn't have a clue about any of that stuff.'

'Careful,' he said, looking at her profile. 'Your disguise is slipping. You look like a perfectly nice girl, but you're actually an undercover pharologist, aren't you?'

She put her hands over her face and turned to look at him, pulling them away with a silly expression on her face. 'Exposed!'

'I knew it.'

'There is a perfectly logical explanation,' she went on. 'I've been reading up a load of information that was sent to me for the website.'

He stood looking out to sea alongside her as Meg explained how she'd volunteered to help out.

'That's really kind of you.'

She tipped her head to one side, frowning. 'It is, but I've also realised I miss the creative side of my work.'

'Funny to think we were both working in the same field and here we are now, on top of a lighthouse, miles away from civilisation.'

'I think the residents of Applemore might object to that remark.' Meg laughed.

He gave a vague, open-handed gesture of apology. 'I guess I'm officially a resident now I've signed on the dotted line, so I think I'll give us a pass for that one.'

'Ooh.' She turned to look at him. 'So it's official?'

'It is. Contract signed, and somehow my attempt at running away from reality has ended up with me finding a whole new career in forestry.'

'Not sure what it says about me that I ran away from reality and ended up building a website, which is exactly what I spent the last twenty years doing, more or less.'

'I suspect it means you've got a good handle on what your skills are.'

'Or I'm really very boring and have no sense of adventure.' She wrinkled her nose and made a funny face, which made him laugh.

'I don't think anyone could accuse you of that. You sold everything, bought a camper van, and drove to the frozen north.'

'True, I suppose. Anyway, so now you're officially on the payroll, what happens now? Are you going to be off chopping down trees all over the Highlands?'

He shook his head and tapped the glass, pointing down towards the sea path below them. 'I'll be back next week, getting a crash course in fencing from George, the guy who left the measuring wheel here. Talking of which, I really ought to get back. I've got a mountain of snacks for my tree planters in the back of the truck and they get tetchy if they're not fed regularly.'

'I don't want you getting sacked for sloping off to climb lighthouses when you've just officially started working,' Meg said as she walked ahead of him out of the light room, 'Although it would be a pretty good story to tell at dinner parties.'

'I've found that my dinner party opportunities are a bit thin on the ground up here,' Gabe said, his voice echoing in the narrow stairwell.

He picked up Stanley from the cottage and headed back to the truck, giving Meg a wave and a sound of the horn as he left.

*You are such an idiot,* he berated himself as he drove back along the street past the harbour, catching a glimpse of the lighthouse in the mirror. That would have been the perfect opportunity to ask her out for a drink or something to eat one night. The only consolation was that he'd be back there the following week. Maybe he'd actually get his act together by then.

# CHAPTER TWENTY-SEVEN

Meg flopped down onto the sofa beside Eliza, who'd been pacing back and forth looking at the door since Stanley left.

'You and me both,' she said to her, laughing.

Eliza circled around and collapsed on the crochet cushion with a sigh.

This was ridiculous. She was swooning like a teenager over a boy, except she was forty-nine and should be far too old for that sort of thing. Her phone buzzed and she picked it up, smiling to herself as she saw Helen was sending photos – probably more beautiful shots from her exploration of Santiago.

But no, the photos were of an exhilarated, damp haired Phoebe holding a tiny, scrunched up little pink bundle.

*Look at my amazing girl!*

Meg felt tears rising in her eyes, surprising her. Tiny Phoebe, with her My Little Pony obsession and her stripy tights and love of jumping in puddles, was a mother.

*Proudest granny in the world,* said the next message, accompanied by a picture of Helen with her arm around Matteo,

Phoebe's partner. Matteo was holding the baby, and Helen looked as if she might burst with joy. The baby looked – as babies tended to – like a small cross thing who'd rather be somewhere else, but everyone was so full of happiness that it didn't seem to matter.

*Huge congratulations,* wrote Meg. *She's beautiful. And you all look so happy!*

*Oh – I forgot,* another message came through from Helen, *she's called Rosa.*

*What a gorgeous name! Give them all my love.*

*I will! Huge love and hope everything is going well!*

Meg put down the phone and looked out of the window. The sun was shining, and she was sitting on the sofa looking at web design ideas and reading about the history of the lighthouse in Britain. She could be doing that in the evening instead of watching something on television, and taking advantage of the lovely weather to get Helen's garden into some sort of order.

All of Helen's gardening things were stacked in the disused building next door. Given that it was about to be turned into a visitor centre imminently, she decided that maybe clearing out the bits and pieces – old easels and boxes of art equipment, canvases which had been stacked against the wall and goodness knows what else – would have to go on her things-to-do list for the following week. If that meant she happened to be floating about casually while Gabe was busy working on the fencing, well, that was just a happy coincidence.

She rolled up her sleeves, pulled on a pair of gardening gloves, and got to work.

The soil was sandy and easy to work, which made weeding a pleasure. She worked methodically, pulling out dandelions and chickweed, giving the perennial plants in the border space to grow and breathe. The roses were already coming up, so she dead headed the dried-up hips which were hanging on from last autumn, throwing everything into the compost bin in the garden at the back of the cottage. By the time she'd finished one long bed which ran parallel to the wall she was ravenous, not to mention baking hot. The unseasonal weather was promised to last another week, and everyone in the Highlands was soaking it up. She stopped for a lunch break, taking off her shoes and popping upstairs to change into an old, faded T-shirt she'd had for years.

Taking her sandwich out into the garden, she sat down on the step and surveyed the work she'd done so far.

There had been a fair few walkers passing by that morning, most waving a hello or calling across as she worked, and as she ate she saw the teenager from the other day hurrying past. Intrigued – and wondering why she wasn't at school – Meg stood up, casually strolling into the back garden as if putting something else into the compost bin, and watching as the girl looked left and right then popped another letter into the library.

After she'd gone, Meg took a stroll down to the library to have a look. Sure enough, tucked between a rather dry looking literary novel which had remained untouched for the last few weeks and one of her brown paper-covered books was an envelope. Meg smiled to herself. Whatever was going on, it was very sweet. She hadn't expected being the keeper of the library would come with so much more than books.

By the end of the day, she'd finished the garden. Stiff as a board, her knees grumbling, she straightened up and assessed her handiwork. The garden had good bones, and Helen had worked hard to make it pretty over the years. All it had needed was a bit of a spruce up to reveal the beauty that was hiding underneath a layer of overgrowth and weeds.

It all sounded horribly familiar. Meg made a face as she

looked at her reflection in the sitting-room window. She was filthy, her hair had come loose from the ponytail she'd tied it back in earlier, and she had dirt on her nose. Meg brushed it off, remembering with a jolt of longing in her stomach how she'd felt when Gabe had brushed a smudge of flour off her cheek. She turned away, shaking her head. This was – no, *she was* – being completely ridiculous.

She ran a hot bath and sank into the lavender scented bubbles, thinking back to the day she'd handed over the last of the furniture to the removal men. Back then she'd picked a piece of her own lavender and thought how long it had been since she'd had a decent night of sleep. Now, hiking miles every morning on the footpaths around the coast with Eliza, she was sleeping eight hours every night without fail and waking feeling completely rested. It was funny how things had changed. She hadn't heard from Janey in a while – she really ought to send her a message and see how things were going back there. It was strange, though – she still wasn't sure where she was going next, but the one thing that was certain was that she missed nothing about Heatherby.

"Shining a light into the darkness, the lighthouse is a beacon of hope that brings a feeling of safety to sailors at the point when they need it most," she read, curled up on the sofa beside Eliza later that evening.

That was a lovely thought. It was funny how this place had given her something like that – a feeling of hope where she'd had none.

There was something magical about the lighthouse. She got up and wandered through to the kitchen, looking out of the window and far across the inky black sea. Night had fallen, but the last pale streaks of light still lingered like a halo across the shoulders of the far-away islands. When she'd visited Helen years before, it had been in midsummer, and it had been as bright as day at eleven o'clock, darkness only falling for a few short hours before daylight returned. Those were the easy months for the fishermen who worked out of the harbour.

In winter, though, when the nights were long and stormy, the lighthouse guided them home, warning them to beware of the rocks which curved around the natural harbour of Applemore. She'd been delighted to discover the history of the lighthouse. In the last days of the nineteenth century a tiny croft house had stood on the land, occupied by another Meg – wife of a fisherman called John, who had been lost at sea. After he died, every night she lit a lamp and set it at the window to act as a guide to his fellow fishermen.

Meg closed her eyes, imagining how it would have felt to go to bed every night longing for your love to return. Her chest rose and fell with a heavy sigh of longing. In all her married life, she'd never felt that sort of passion. She'd married Michael because he'd been a route to escape from a lonely family life where she'd never felt good enough. Her mother had been angry and critical, so it hadn't really seemed unusual that her husband had treated her in the same way.

Meg looked at her reflection in the window. Objectively speaking she wasn't bad looking. She had a nice, open sort of face and eyes that crinkled when she smiled. She had – perhaps, if she was lucky – another fifty years. Meg could live her life all over again. Not everyone got that chance.

Tucked up on the sofa again with a hot chocolate in hand and Eliza snoozing on the rug by her feet, she stayed up far too late typing up the information she'd been given and making it as interesting as she could for the website. Greta – true to form – had emailed through the notes, and a striking set of photographs which had been taken of the exterior of the lighthouse, as well as some scans of faded black and white pictures of the workers when they'd lived in the cottage. It was such a strange feeling to sit in this spot, knowing a century ago there would have been the lighthouse keeper and his family in her place.

Somehow she found herself down a rabbit hole on the internet, trying to search for some facts and figures about the Applemore area and the population over the years. The next thing she knew she was reading a report into the increasing problem of rural poverty in the Highlands, and then staring into a long-dead fire as she tapped a pen against her teeth. It was clear there were things being missed in Applemore – and important ones, at that. The chance that Laurel was the only person in the village who was struggling to get by for one reason or another seemed unlikely.

There had to be something she could do to make a difference while she was there – but how?

# CHAPTER TWENTY-EIGHT

'What d'you think?'

Meg turned the laptop around to show Kathleen, who'd popped by a couple of days later on her way back from her regular delivery of eggs to the library. Kathleen put down the novel she'd chosen and leaned across, looking closely at the screen.

'I've come out without my reading glasses,' she said, 'but it looks very nice. Very clear.'

Meg rubbed her forehead. She'd done her usual and worked herself into a headache, staring at the screen without a break and forgetting to get outside. Poor Eliza, who'd been given cursory leg-stretches on the beach path, was in dire need of a decent walk.

'Hopefully it'll meet with the village community society whatsit's approval.'

Kathleen chuckled. 'The Applemore Village Improvement Society,' she said in mock serious tones.

'That's what I meant.' Meg grinned. 'I'll send the link to

Greta, grab a shower, and get this poor neglected corgi out for a nice walk.'

'I'm very impressed,' said Kathleen, looking at the screen again.

'Thank you. It's nothing, really.' Meg felt her cheeks going pink and cleared her throat, bending to stroke Eliza's rough fur.

'Don't belittle your achievements.'

Meg straightened up and Kathleen was looking at her steadily, head cocked slightly to one side.

'I bet you studied for a long time to learn how to do that sort of thing. Helen said you studied together?'

'We did. She realised she wanted to focus on painting, and I liked the design side of things. I taught myself the web stuff for the – for our – business.'

'Hmm,' Kathleen's elegant brows lifted slightly.

Meg shifted from one foot to the other in the silence.

'I think,' said Kathleen, after a long moment, 'that it's probably time you acknowledged your achievements.'

'You sound like Helen.'

'Well, I'm glad you've got her in your corner. And you've got me, now, as well.'

Kathleen reached over, putting a hand on Meg's arm and squeezing it gently.

'Have a think while you're out for a walk with Eliza. Mull it over. Look where you are.'

And with that, she patted Eliza on the head, picked up the novel from the table, and headed off with a cheerful wave.

The sunshine had brought out lots of walkers, and Meg passed several as she wandered along the path towards the village. The locals – whose faces she was beginning to recognise – smiled and nodded a hello. You could tell the tourists by their walking gear – or lack of it. They were almost always dressed from head to toe in sensible clothes to suit all weathers, but the day-trippers taking advantage of a sunny day were in t-shirts and jeans, clambering the rocks and startling the seals who were basking in the heat.

'How's it going?' Anna in the bakery café looked up and smiled a greeting when Meg arrived. 'Hello, little one.' She leaned over the counter, beaming at Eliza. 'I love corgis.'

'Good, thanks.' Meg lifted her hair off the back of her neck. It was warm outside, but the café was deliciously cool. She took a cold can of lemonade from the fridge. 'Tell your husband thank you so much for the photographs. Greta sent them through, and they look great.'

Anna beamed. 'Oh, he'll be chuffed to hear that. He's been getting to grips with a new lens – he took those just before you arrived in Applemore.'

'They're amazing. They could be done by a pro photographer – it's made a real difference to the look of the website.'

'I can't wait to see it.' Anna rang up the drink on the cash register. 'Anything else?'

'No, that's great, thanks.' Meg had suddenly remembered something she'd read last night. She waved goodbye and headed for the little supermarket, leaving Eliza outside clipped to the dog ring on the wall and picking up a basket.

The bookshelf had been a hit by the looks of things. Greta had hung a sign saying "FREE – HELP YOURSELF" on the wall above it and judging by the gaps on the shelves people had taken her at her word. That felt like a sign, somehow.

She zoomed up the aisle, not wanting to leave Eliza alone for long, and threw in a selection of bits and pieces – some pasta, a couple of packs of noodles, cookies, tins of baked beans – the sort of thing that didn't need to be kept in the fridge. That would do, as a start.

When she got back to the cottage, she took the little

wooden chest with a lid she'd discovered when she'd been rummaging around in the lighthouse building and brought it inside. It didn't take long to find some offcuts of sturdy fabric and a staple gun upstairs in Helen's studio.

She'd thought a lot about Kathleen's words as she'd walked into the village. For years – no, for the whole of her life, in fact – she'd always looked to someone else to give her permission to do things. When she'd had ideas for the business, she'd offered them hesitantly, then sat back while Michael took all the credit as the company grew.

She worked quickly – muscle memory was an amazing thing, really. She hadn't made anything like this for so long, and yet it was as if she was back at design school, knocking something together for her final assessment, fuelled by coffee and a sense of purpose.

Once she'd finished, she sat back and looked at it and – smiling to herself, thinking of Kathleen's words – felt a sense of pride in her work. It wasn't bad at all.

Outside the Applemore weather – unpredictable as ever – clearly hadn't read the forecast. The promised week of glorious sunshine seemed to have come to a very sudden end, but Meg was undeterred. Ignoring the threatening grey clouds that were gathering over the sea, she lifted the box into her arms and set off for the little library cupboard.

It was heavy, and she had to stop several times and put it down to catch her breath. But she made it, puffing and panting, and set it down on the circle of gravel at the foot of the library. Then she turned, wiping sweat from her forehead with the back of her arm, and started walking briskly back up the hill to the lighthouse cottage.

Then she collected the bag of shopping and a few other bits and pieces from the kitchen cupboard and was about to set out again when she realised she really ought to make a sign.

She dashed back upstairs, finding some tape, a piece of white card and some of Helen's brush pens. Then – shoving the sign in the shopping bag – she marched back down the beach path again.

She'd taped the sign to the inside of the library cupboard window and was just arranging the things inside the box when a familiar voice made her jump.

'Hello again.'

Startled, she leapt to her feet, bashing her head on the edge of the cupboard door.

'Ow!'

'I'm so sorry,' said Gabe, looking concerned. 'I came to say hi and now you've got a head injury.'

She rubbed the back of her head, frowning slightly. 'I think I'll live.'

'Now I've given you a head injury, it seems like a really bad time to ask you if you wanted to go for a –' He pushed a hand through his hair and matched her frown, but his expression was half-amused, half-concerned.

Something in Meg's chest leapt and her heart started hammering rapidly.

'I saw you when I got out of the truck and thought I'd grab the chance to ask if you'd like to go for a coffee sometime, but now you've had a bump to the head I'll be wondering if you're only saying yes because you've got concussion.'

'I don't have concussion,' she said, shaking her head vigorously from side to side. 'Look.'

Gabe's eyebrows quirked upwards. 'I'm not sure that's a diagnostic criteria.'

'I'd love to,' said Meg, wondering if he could see her heart thumping through her T-shirt. She raked a hand through her hair, suddenly conscious that she was sweaty and windswept from her walk.

Gabe grinned. 'Excellent. I'd like that a lot.' He looked at her through slightly narrowed eyes. 'Now, are you certain that you're okay? That was a bit of a bump.'

She put her palm flat on her head and checked. 'I think I'm fine. It probably sounded worse than it was.'

A movement caught her eye, and she turned to see another man clad in work clothes standing at the top of the hill.

'Someone's waving to you. I mean I assume he's waving at you?'

'It's George,' said Gabe, lifting a hand in acknowledgement. 'I better get to work.'

She walked alongside him, aware that she was taking one and a half steps to each of his long ones as he strode along in his heavy work boots.

'So what's the box? Have you run out of shelf space for your books?'

Meg shook her head. 'It's a – I don't know what you'd call it.'

Apparently the bang on the head – or more likely the fact that she was feeling ridiculously giddy, like a teenage girl – had rendered her incapable of forming proper sentences.

'I tell you what, you can tell me over a coffee. If you give me your number, I'll send you a message and we can work out a time and a day.'

He passed over his phone, and she looked at it for a moment as if she couldn't quite work out what she was supposed to do with it.

'It would help if I unlocked the screen,' he said, laughing. 'Here, put your number in and I'll ring you.'

A moment later, her phone vibrated in her back pocket and out of habit Meg pulled it out, looking at the screen.

'That should be me,' said Gabe, wryly. 'Unless I'm just one of any number of men asking you for coffee right now.'

Meg scrunched her face up, laughing and cringing at herself in equal measure.

'Well, I've managed to make myself look spectacularly uncool.'

'All the best people are, I think.' Gabe tipped a head in George's direction. 'Now I really better get to work.'

She watched him striding off to meet his co-worker and suppressed a smile at the sight of the two of them. George was as small and wiry as Gabe was tall and broad. Together they unloaded a truck full of wooden stakes and got to work.

She didn't want to get under their feet, and realising that the campervan had been sitting outside the cottage for the last few weeks without being turned over, she decided to grab the keys and take it for a quick drive around the quiet roads. The last thing she needed was a flat battery.

She headed along the coast, surprised at how many other vans there were on the little roads. Applemore was off the main North Coast 500 route, but a steady stream of visitors seemed to take a detour and come to visit. She drove up into the hills, slowing to look at a group of people dotted on the moorland. A truck with the same livery as Gabe's was parked on a wide strip of grass verge, a heap of white sacks piled in the back. These must be the tree planting gang. Some of them were moving quickly, bobbing up and down as they made their way through the moorland. It looked like back-breaking work.

She pulled over onto the side of the road, realising that she had no idea how on earth to turn the van around. It was so huge, and the road was so narrow. She checked her phone and worked out that there was a junction a mile or so ahead where she could double back and follow the road that passed behind

Applemore and up towards the farm shop. Maybe she'd pop in and have a coffee at the café and stay out of the way while Gabe and George were working. The alternative – which was trying very hard not to look out of the window and appreciate him in his work gear – was tempting, but probably not a great idea.

Of course she hadn't factored in parking at the farm shop, either. As she approached, she realised with a sinking feeling that cars were lined on either side of the drive – there must be something on in the studio, or else everyone in the Highlands had come out for a day trip.

She spotted Rilla, her dark curls pulled back off her face with a clip, as she was moving slowly towards the entrance with an increasingly anxious sensation in the pit of her stomach.

Rilla waved and jogged over to her, a wide smile on her freckled face. 'Wow, this is pretty snazzy.'

Meg made a face. 'Snazzy, and impossible to park.'

'Ah, come round the back. There's loads of room behind the building where the buses park when we have tours come in.'

She guided her past the side of the café, past packed tables of visitors enjoying what looked like being the last of the spring heatwave. There was a huge parking spot next to a stack of wooden crates.

'Stick her in there,' shouted Rilla, beckoning her forward and then making a stop motion.

'Thanks so much.' Meg climbed out, relieved.

'Bit of a contrast to our old van,' said Rilla, putting a hand on the bonnet. 'I don't suppose I could have a peek inside?'

'Of course you can.' Meg slid open the side door.

'Oh this is heaven. Look at the little kitchen – and you've got an oven, and everything. I miss escaping in ours so much.'

Rilla climbed inside and ran an appreciative hand along the worktop. 'And look, you've got a spare bed up there. That's so cute!'

'I'm not sure what I was thinking there,' admitted Meg.

'Kitty would love it. I keep promising her we'll go away, but…'

'I imagine you're really busy with –' Meg waved her hand in the general direction of Applemore House and left the sentence unfinished.

Rilla scratched her head. 'Oh, the wild camping and stuff? Yeah. Not as much as you'd think.'

'I forgot you had the camping places here.'

Meg had seen the hand-drawn map of the Applemore Estate that hung in the entrance to the shop. Hidden in the trees were little clearings with compost loos and little gas-powered showers where van owners or campers could come and stay, with the luxury of the shop and café just a wander through the woods away.

'Yeah, we started it when we first got together. But now our poor old van – it was my dad's project before he died – has given up the ghost, and I keep meaning to do something about it. Kitty is desperate to get away on an adventure in the summer holidays and I'm determined to take some time off, but I keep getting caught up in stuff.'

'I've noticed that seems to be part and parcel of living here.'

Rilla unclipped her hair and shook it out before tying it back again. 'Yeah, you've noticed? I only came here a few years ago to clear out my dad's old cottage – it's there, in fact.' She pointed to one of the whitewashed stone buildings. 'And the next thing you know, here I am.'

'I can see why Helen is so busy. There's always something to do.'

'Yeah, I've just gone back to my first love as well, although it means late evenings two nights a week.'

'What do you do?'

'I teach adults who don't speak English as a first language. Before I met – well, re-met – Lachlan, I used to travel the world teaching. Now I'm here, but I meet people from all over the world. The language school is a charity, so we don't turn anyone away.'

Rilla's eyes lit up with passion as she spoke. 'It's really important to me that we can do something for people who need help, especially when we're living in a place like this.'

'It's funny, isn't it? Scratch the surface of Applemore and there's more going on than you realise.'

'And not all good.'

Meg shook her head. 'Funnily enough, I've just done something… maybe I should have checked with someone.'

Rilla looked at her curiously. 'Now I'm intrigued.'

'I don't know if you know but Miranda's aunt Kathleen has been leaving eggs and – well, bits and bobs like cake and things – down at the library.'

Rilla nodded, catching her bottom lip in her teeth as she listened.

'Well, there's a –' Meg stopped herself, not wanting to give anything away 'I think that there are people who need a bit of help. So I saw a thing online about a community cupboard, where people put things –'

'Oh this is amazing.' Rilla's eyes welled up with tears and she wiped them away with an impatient finger. 'Sorry, I am hopeless. I cry at nice things all the time.'

'Don't apologise. I think it's lovely. Anyway, I've been watching people come and go while I've been staying at the cottage, and I've popped a little chest down there beside the library and left some bits and pieces in it.'

Rilla put a hand to her heart. 'That's such a gorgeous idea.'

'I probably should have checked with someone.'

Rilla shrugged. 'And waited for three weeks until the village improvement society had a meeting, and everyone agreed it was a good idea and then debated what kind of box it should be, or what colour you should paint it?'

Meg giggled. 'I've gathered from the process of renovating the old building into a visitor centre that there's quite a lot of that going on.'

'It drives me bonkers.' Rilla jumped down from inside the van. 'I think it's a brilliant idea, and I have definitely got your back. We'll just tell Kathleen and she'll deal with the committee lot. She doesn't take any nonsense.'

'I've gathered that,' said Meg, thinking of her little pep-talk.

'Are you going to the shop? Sorry, I've been standing here holding you back.'

'I'm staying out of the way while they do some fencing for the lighthouse visitor centre.' Meg's stomach did a little flip of anticipation, remembering her encounter with Gabe earlier.

'I was supposed to be putting up a notice on the board. We're looking for someone to do some admin stuff for the Applemore Brewery.' She waited while Meg closed the door and locked the van, making a rueful face as she did so.

'It's a habit,' Meg explained.

'Oh, don't worry, I still do it without thinking. I think it's probably the signifier that divides the Applemore born and bred from us incomers.'

As they reached the courtyard, the first spots of rain started to fall.

'I knew it,' said Rilla, laughing. 'I hung washing out this morning, and I knew that would bring the rain.'

Meg followed her into the farm shop, still surprised –

despite having chatted to her at Pilates, and met her in town on a couple of other occasions – how down to earth Rilla was.

'You don't really think of someone living in a castle hanging out washing.'

Rilla raised her eyebrows. 'I didn't really think of myself as someone who'd be living in a castle. Weird how life turns out, isn't it? It's something in the air up here. You turn up in Applemore and the next thing you know it's caught you in its clutches.'

'I think you might be right.' Meg watched as Rilla pinned a notice on the board and stood back to survey her handiwork.

'Now all I have to do is wait for the perfect person to appear.'

She raised her crossed fingers. 'I better get back to the house and rescue my laundry.'

# CHAPTER TWENTY-NINE

George worked like a dervish. Gabe, who'd seen him in action numerous times since he'd been grounded from his favourite occupation of climbing and felling trees, had stood to one side while he'd explained what they were going to do, talking at a hundred miles an hour and gesticulating at the same rate.

'We'll get a fence up here round the side, and a wee gate that'll lead into the visitor centre place, and run it up the side o' the path to stop people from thinking they can park their cars on the grass. Then we'll mark out this spot up here where they can park, and hopefully we'll keep them out o' trouble. And then we'll put a ramp over there so people can get in if they're using a wheelchair. Simple enough.'

It was going to be a fencing trial by fire. George was a surprisingly good teacher, and by midway through the afternoon they were working together at a decent pace. Gabe suspected privately that if George had been left to his own devices he'd have the whole job done in about two hours, but if that was the case he didn't let it show.

'Who's that nice looking lassie you were talking to when I arrived?'

They'd stopped for a coffee and something to eat and were sitting on the tailgate of the truck under gathering clouds.

Gabe cleared his throat and tried to sound casual. 'Oh, that's Meg. She's staying here looking after the cottage while her friend is away.'

George gave an upward nod. 'Oh, aye.'

'I just went to see if she needed a hand.'

George took a slurp of the coffee from his flask and looked at Gabe sideways. 'Oh, aye,' he repeated.

Gabe's mouth twitched in amusement. He liked George, who was a man of few words who didn't miss a trick.

'And would that have been you giving her your number?'

'That would have been me taking hers, to be precise.'

'Good man.' George gave one of his rare grins. 'Now you're on the books up here you'll be looking to settle down, maybe.'

If only it was that simple. Meg was the first woman he'd met who had made him wonder if his resolution to stay single was flawed. She made him laugh, he liked her company, and he couldn't take his eyes off her whenever she was near. It was a perfect combination, except for the minor detail that she was a temporary fixture and he'd just signed a full-time contract for a job he'd discovered he loved. Gabe screwed the lid back on his coffee flask and straightened up, looking at the sky. 'Looks like rain.'

'Aye. We'll no' melt, right enough,' said George. He chucked the dregs of his coffee onto the grass and stood up, signifying the end of their break.

A couple of hours later, they were about a quarter of the way through the job. A white van with neat lettering on the side rattled over the cattle grid, making them both look up.

Gabe's heart leapt for a moment, thinking it was Meg returning from wherever she'd gone in the van.

'Afternoon, boys.'

'Kenny, how's it going?'

It was Kenny, the local builder, who seemed to have a monopoly on any jobs going in the Applemore area. Everywhere work was being done Gabe had noticed his van, privately wondering if he'd cloned himself. It was either that, or he didn't sleep.

'Just here to do a wee recce before we get going on this visitor centre business. Do you know if the lassie's in the cottage?'

'Ask this one here,' said George with a mischievous grin.

'Oh aye?' Kenny looked at Gabe expectantly.

Gabe shook his head with a laugh. Honestly, it was no wonder that news spread through this village like wildfire. He could place a bet now on how long it would take before Una was asking questions in the office.

'Sorry to disappoint but I haven't a clue.'

'Fingers crossed the key's still under the rock, in that case.' Kenny strode off towards the lighthouse, whistling as he went.

The key must have been there, because a moment later he returned, taking a laser level and some other kit out of his van and heading back to get to work.

'It'll be a race to the finish with Kenny on the job,' said George, picking up his mallet and taking a handful of nails out of his work belt. 'We better get moving.'

The weather, however, had other ideas. They worked through the rain when it started, narrowing their eyes to focus as the clouds overhead darkened the skies so it felt like dusk. But half an hour later the heavens opened, and they were just packing up the last of the things onto the back of the truck when Meg's campervan appeared through the gateway, the expensive suspension making short work of the cattle grid.

'I'll leave you to it,' said George with a wink, tossing his truck keys in the air. 'See you back here first thing in the morning, unless you get a better offer.'

Gabe shook his head in mock dismay.

'Have a good one,' shouted George out of the window, his arm waving as he set off for home.

Feeling slightly discomfited, he watched as Meg pulled the van up onto the gravel parking in front of the cottage wall. She jumped out and looked over at him, shading her eyes against the rain.

'Nice afternoon!'

His desire to talk to Meg fought for a fleeting moment with a desire to avoid being a grist for the village gossip mill.

Laughing at himself for being an idiot, he headed across the grass towards the cottage.

'I'm guessing you're packing up in this?'

The rain was coming down in sheets. A rivulet ran from a strand of hair on her shoulder down her chest and disappeared into the valley between her breasts. Gabe pulled his gaze away, looking at her face. There was a smudge of black mascara on her cheek, and she lifted a hand, pushing her wet hair back from her face.

'Yeah, we're all done.'

'Do you want a coffee?' She motioned to the cottage. 'Or at least come in out of the rain for a minute.'

He followed her down the garden path and waited as she unlocked the door to the cottage. Inside, Eliza was waiting with her stumpy tail wagging in delight to be met by not one, but two humans ready to give her attention.

'Hello,' he said, bending to give her a pat. 'Yes, we are soaking wet.'

'Let me grab a towel. I can't believe you've been working in this.'

She ran up the little wooden steps and he heard her footsteps above him as she found a couple of towels, returning a moment later in a dry T-shirt, rubbing at her hair.

If he'd been offered a preference, he had to admit that he'd preferred the way the soaking T-shirt had clung to her body, revealing delicious curves beneath the wet cotton, but –

'Thanks,' he said as she passed him a towel. He rubbed his hair and tried to get a bloody grip of himself.

'I'll make a cup of tea,' Meg said, leading him into the kitchen. 'You must be soaked right through.'

He was, but it was pretty far from his mind right now.

'I haven't had a chance to message you about coffee,' he said, pulling his phone out of the back pocket of his work trousers.

'I did wonder,' teased Meg, getting two mugs out of the cupboard. 'Although it'd be a bit awkward if you'd only mentioned it out of politeness given that you're going to be working right outside the cottage for the next few days.'

He shook his head, laughing. 'No, definitely wasn't planning on leaving you hanging.'

He typed a message and a moment later Meg turned back from the fridge, milk in hand, and picked up her phone from the table.

'Yes, I'd love to go for a walk and some lunch on Saturday.' Her eyes were sparkling as she spoke. 'How do you take your tea – or would you rather coffee?'

'Tea's fine. Just milk, please.'

'The fence is looking good already.' Meg slid the mug across to him.

'That's mainly George's work. I'm very much a newbie at this business.'

'You must be doing a decent job of it.'

He ducked his head. 'I guess. It's quite humbling to go from being at the top of your game to the very bottom of the ladder and making your way back up.'

'I read somewhere that it's good for your brain to be learning new things. I'm supposed to be learning French on Duolingo, but I'm hopeless. I get passive-aggressive emails from an angry owl every time I forget to do my daily lesson.'

'I think it probably is. I like the fact we're doing something different every day here, which I suspect sounds insane to anyone else. I'd rather be visiting a different forestry site than waking up in another country for another meeting.'

'It makes sense to me.' Meg's eyes met his and there was a moment of silence.

A second later it was broken by a sharp knock at the door of the cottage.

'Hello,' called a woman's voice. 'Meg, are you in?'

Meg widened her eyes and looked at him with amusement. 'Considering I'm living in a cottage in the middle of nowhere, there is a surprising lack of privacy around here.'

She got up and headed into the hallway. A second later, she returned with a vaguely familiar looking woman in her seventies with close-cropped grey hair and a friendly, pixie-like face.

'Ah, sorry to interrupt,' she said, smiling at him. 'I just happened to be passing.'

Gabe had to suppress a grin at that, given that the lighthouse was situated a distance out of the village on a twisting road to nowhere, unless by some chance she'd come the quick way along the beach path. Considering she was neatly dressed, bone dry, and with not a hair out of place, that seemed unlikely.

'I was speaking to Rilla up at the big house, and she

mentioned your idea, which is absolutely wonderful. I bumped into Kathleen and said you're such a good addition to the village community. It's just a pity you're not staying. We'll have to work on that,' said the woman, waggling a jokey finger.

Get in line, thought Gabe. I don't want her going anywhere either.

Meg was looking nonplussed, her face pink and her brows gathered together so a little furrowed line settled between them.

'The little goodwill cupboard. Food chest. I don't know why anyone didn't think of it already,' said the woman.

'Oh yes,' said Meg, faintly. 'I was a bit worried I was jumping the gun.'

'Not at all. I think it's wonderful.' The woman put her hand on top of Meg's and squeezed it fondly. 'We need more people like you. If you were staying put, I'd be recruiting you for the village improvement society.'

Meg seemed to gather herself. 'I'm so sorry,' she said, turning to the cupboard. 'I don't mean to be rude. Would you like a cup of tea? We're just drying off, which is why –'

'No, no,' the woman raised a hand, stopping her mid-sentence. 'I was going to have a little chat with you about the website, which looks wonderful, but I don't want to keep you if you're busy.'

'Oh, don't worry, Greta, it's fine,' Meg began, but the woman shook her head with a little smile.

'I'll leave you two young ones to your tea and chat,' she said with an impish smile.

And with that, like a whirlwind, she said her goodbyes and was gone.

Meg collapsed back onto the kitchen chair after seeing Greta out. She rolled her eyes and made a comical face.

'Oof.'

He looked across at her, shaking his head in amusement. 'Exactly.'

# CHAPTER THIRTY

Meg looked at Gabe, who was gazing at her intently from the opposite side of the table, his chin resting in his hand. 'Okay, so can we rewind a bit? What was she talking about?'

'Which part? The website?'

'The... food chest? Goodwill cupboard? Are they the same thing?'

Meg cupped her mug in both hands, looking at him over the rim for a moment as she thought.

'There's a girl... I'm sure she's not the only one, but she's the only one I've seen. She's clearly struggling for money, and she's on her own with a baby. I know Applemore is very pretty and looks like a picture postcard, but I hate to think of...' she tailed off for a moment, putting her mug back down and looking away, conscious of his intense gaze.

'Go on.' His voice was gentle.

'We didn't have a lot of money when I was growing up. I remember that feeling of being hungry between meals, and never quite feeling like there was enough to eat in the school holidays.'

'So you don't want someone else to feel the same way.'

She nodded. 'The weird thing is that when I realised that the food that was being left on the library shelf was disappearing pretty much every day, I worked out there was a need for it. It's hard to ask for help, especially if you're too proud to admit you're struggling.'

He was looking at her steadily, a kind expression in his dark blue eyes which made her feel safe to keep on talking. She adjusted the handle of the mug so it lined up with the ridge on the table.

'The person I was before – I think I'd have felt bad about it, but too scared to step out of line and do something. I don't know if it's something to do with being here where I don't know anyone...'

Gabe raised an eyebrow at her. 'Apart from random women who turn up on your doorstep on a rainy afternoon?'

'Okay, apart from...' Meg stopped for a moment and thought. 'The strange thing is – I know more people here than I ever knew back in Yorkshire, even counting people who worked for us.'

He tipped his head slightly in acknowledgement. 'Maybe that's a sign of something.'

'Perhaps?' She turned her hands palm up, looking at them for a moment as if they might hold the answer. 'Anyway, I'd read an article online about community larders where people left food – an extension of the library, really, where you can pick up what you need, no questions asked.'

'It's a really good idea. So you thought you'd just take the initiative?'

'Goodness knows what I was thinking. If I was sensible I'd probably be trying to help her find some way of making some money. Her boyfriend seems to have upped and left when the baby arrived, and she doesn't know anyone around here.'

'Well, your friend – Greta, wasn't it? She seemed pretty impressed. And doing something nice for someone who needs help is never a bad idea.'

'Like your community projects.' Meg pushed her hair back from her face. It would be drying all crinkly in the warmth of the kitchen. Goodness knows what she looked like.

'Exactly. If you ask Donald Grant, he'll make light of it, but the materials for stuff like the fencing outside aren't cheap. Not to mention the day rate for the work. He doesn't take a penny for it.'

'And you're doing the community orchard and the play area at the school, as well.' Meg raked a hand through her hair in the hope of making it look halfway decent. It was ironic that Gabe, who'd been soaked through, was sitting there looking handsome and unruffled in a grey T-shirt, having peeled off his soaked work coat and hung it on the back of the chair.

'You've been reading the village newsletter, I take it?' He grinned. 'Una in the office was telling everyone she'd written a bit of a PR piece telling everyone what we were up to.'

'I've got a whole *stack* of village newsletters in the front porch,' Meg said, laughing. 'I've been given the job of making sure they don't run out down at the library.'

'I know where to come if I want to catch up on the Applemore gossip, then.' He surveyed her over the top of his mug, the lines at the edge of his eyes matching their twinkle of amusement.

'And PR puff pieces, apparently.' She felt her mouth twitch sideways in a teasing smile.

'Ouch.' Gabe grinned. 'To be fair to Grant Forestry, they put their money where their mouth is. It's a refreshing change from the corporate flannel I used to hear when I was working in industry.'

'I can imagine. It must be good to be working for someone with integrity.'

'Yeah, he's a good bloke,' agreed Gabe. 'He can afford to give something back, mind you - there's a hell of a lot of money flying around at the moment. He's just signed that contract for the Lochbrannich Estate that'll bring in a fortune.'

'The rewilding thing you were talking about when we were out walking?'

'Yeah. I think it'll be a really interesting project. Talking of which, she mentioned the website – is it all done?'

'Pretty much. I forgot how much I missed doing stuff like that.'

'Do you think you'll do more? You could set up on your own – I bet you'd get loads of business.'

She'd been thinking on the way back from the farm shop earlier. Bumping into Rilla had set off a thought process which was still crystallising in her mind. She tapped a finger on her lips, musing for a moment.

'I'd like to do work for charities, that sort of thing. I don't need the money – it sounds ridiculous, but it's true. I could make a difference by offering my skills.'

'I get the money thing.' He cleared his throat. 'When I walked away I got a package. Took a sort of voluntary redundancy when they offshored everything.'

'And of course now you're making the big bucks,' Meg said, indicating his work coat hanging on the back of the chair.

'Oh yeah, raking it in.' He pushed a hand back through his hair, leaving it standing up in untidy salt-and-pepper spikes. 'The cost of living up here isn't really comparable to down south.'

'So, do you think you'll buy somewhere up here?'

He glanced away for a moment, then returned to meet her

gaze. 'Possibly? I still own a place down south, but its… complicated.'

'Ah. Is it rented out?'

He shook his head. 'No, my ex is still living there. It's one of those things that needs to be sorted, but –'

'It's complicated.' She finished his sentence for him and he gave a brief nod before rubbing his hands over his face for a moment and then looking straight at her.

'We met through work. It was the kind of environment where you worked hard and played hard at the end of the day, and I'd sort of missed the boat as far as marriage and kids were concerned, not that I was that worried. She worked in the same department, so we were thrown together a lot of the time, – ended up on work trips, that sort of thing. She was fun. Liked a drink after work, but everyone did – it was how we decompressed.'

It was Meg's turn to rest her chin in her hands. She looked across at Gabe as he continued.

'I felt for her, because her ex-husband had moved to New Zealand, leaving her in the lurch with a high-pressure job and a teenager to look after.'

'And the inevitable happened.'

'Yeah.' Gabe's thick brows furrowed at the memory. 'We got together. It was fun, until it wasn't. We got together, bought a place – and the wheels started coming off almost straight away. A few drinks after work to relax is one thing, but this was another.'

'That sounds really tough to deal with.' Meg's heart contracted.

'It wasn't great. I tried to make things easier for Jacob – her son – but I didn't know how much of a difference I was making. Then he decided he wanted to move to New Zealand to be with his dad, and that was the beginning of the end, really. We limped on for a few more years, but it wasn't fun for anyone. By the end, we were living separate lives in the same building.'

'That sounds familiar,' Meg said, softly. 'Same idea, different story with me.'

'You're divorced?'

She shook her head and braced herself. 'No, he died.' She paused for a moment. 'I got the house, the business, the life insurance... and a large portion of guilt about that to work through.'

Gabe winced, giving a look of empathy.

'Luckily I had enough money for expensive therapy,' she said drily.

He gave a snort of laughter. 'Sorry, I shouldn't laugh.'

'It wasn't the best marriage in the world. Still...' she tailed off.

'Oh, I'm sorry.' Gabe cocked his head slightly. 'Maybe that's not the right thing to say?'

Meg made an open-handed gesture. 'Sorry for him. It's sad when anyone dies young, isn't it? But the thing I've worked out – thanks to the aforementioned expensive therapy – is we shouldn't ever have been together.'

'Ah. Yeah, that sounds familiar too.'

'I guess we've got lots to compare notes about.' Meg looked down at Eliza, who had appeared at her feet and was pawing at her leg with impatience. 'Sorry, I'm being summoned. Do you need to go out?'

Gabe glanced up at the clock on the kitchen wall. 'I better get going. I hadn't realised the time. Stan's back at the cottage and he'll be waiting at the front door with his paws crossed.'

Meg felt a pang of regret as they headed for the door. Talking to Gabe felt – right. Like she could sit across the table from him and never run out of things to say. But it was half-past six already.

'Saturday, then?' Gabe said, pausing with a hand on the doorframe.

'I'd love that.' Eliza shot through his legs and headed for the garden. Gabe turned, laughing.

'Hopefully the weather will be more like this than this afternoon's performance.'

'Fingers crossed.' Meg lifted a hand, the gesture echoing her words.

'See you tomorrow, then.'

With the crooked smile that made her heart flip, he gave a wave and headed back towards his truck.

# CHAPTER THIRTY-ONE

*Morning! Change of plan,* said the message from Una the next morning. *Can you come up to the office? Donald wants you up at Lochbrannich.*

Gabe stood in the steam-filled bathroom looking down at his phone, cursing Una and her chirpy messages. He wiped steam from the window and looked at his face in the mirror, rubbing the week-old growth on his jaw. It was tidy enough to pass as a conscious attempt at a beard rather than what it was – the laid-back approach to grooming that came hand-in-hand with a job spent outdoors in all weathers. He ran a hand through his hair and started towelling himself dry. Back in the day he was clean shaven and dressed in a tailored suit every day, a row of freshly laundered shirts hanging in a line in the dressing room off the bedroom he'd shared with his ex. Now he pulled on a faded T-shirt under a sweater and covered up with weatherproof gear to protect him from the elements out on the hills.

He headed into the bedroom, pulling on a pair of work trousers, but compromising with a new grey shirt with the

Grant Forestry logo embroidered on the pocket. He'd pull a sweater over the top for the meeting, then hopefully head out to the lighthouse to get on with the fencing job. Gabe had left Meg's cottage reluctantly last night, wishing he could have stayed and talked into the night. The sun had come out when they were inside, and he'd waved a goodbye to her from the truck, watching her standing by the cottage gate, the early evening light shining low across the grass as Eliza cavorted around.

He brushed his teeth and headed to the office, knowing he'd be able to grab a coffee from the machine before setting off to Lochbrannich that morning.

Una was just filling the filter when he walked in.

'Perfect timing,' she said, turning to him with a smile. 'You can fill me in on all your news while we wait for that to brew.'

'My news?' Gabe looked at her, nonplussed.

'A little bird tells me you were late in leaving the site last night.'

'George,' groaned Gabe, laughing. 'For goodness' sake.'

'I haven't spoken to George,' said Una, rifling in her desk drawer and pulling out a birthday card, which she proceeded to unwrap. 'Kenny was working on the lighthouse visitor building and apparently you were spotted heading into Helen's cottage with her pretty friend who's house-sitting.'

Gabe raised his eyes heavenward. 'This village is something else.'

'Strike while the iron's hot, and all that,' said Una, uncapping a pen and looking at the card thoughtfully. 'We don't know how long Helen's away for.'

'I think Meg said two months,' he said unthinkingly.

'Aha,' said Una, pen poised over the card. She looked up at him. 'Plenty of time for you to make your move.'

'Making moves is not really my style,' Gabe said, feeling his phone vibrate in his back pocket and pulling it out to check who was messaging him.

'Well, it should be,' said Una with an owlish look. 'We've only got one life. You might as well grab happiness if it's standing there for the taking.'

'I'll get those coffees,' said Gabe firmly. He headed across to the cupboard and took out a couple of forest green mugs with the forestry logo on the side. 'I swear if I stand still too long, someone's going to stamp Grant Forestry on my forehead.'

Una gave a snort of laughter. 'It's important to have a strong corporate identity,' she said, as he passed her a coffee a moment later.

'There's no way anyone could accuse us of anything but that,' said Gabe, relieved he'd managed to change the subject. 'Anyway,' he added for good measure, 'what's the deal with the Lochbrannich site today? Has anyone told George I'm going to be elsewhere?'

'We're sending Jamie up there instead.'

Jamie was one of the new tree planters who'd been working with them for a month or so. He'd arrived in a beaten-up old truck and had proved a hard worker, eager to learn and progress.

'Oh, he'll be pleased about that.'

'Yeah, we're trying to get some of the planters who are keen to stick around on the books – we've got work coming out of our ears right now. Talking of which, sorry – you asked about Lochbrannich. Apparently you were a bit of a hit with the duke – I reckon it's the posh English accent – so Donald's keen to get you up there.'

'My accent's not posh,' he protested, laughing.

'Sounds it to me,' said Una, now licking the envelope for the card she'd written. 'I must get that posted today.'

'I'll take it on my way if you like. Am I waiting for Donald?'

Una shook her head. 'No, it's just you going up. Here, I've printed you off the plans with the planting schedule now we've got it sorted. I think he just wants to run through the ideas with you, from what I can gather.'

'Fair enough.' Gabe took the plans, relieved that this time it wasn't pouring with rain so they were at risk of turning to pulp before he got them to the duke's office.

'I am going to go bananas if I don't find someone to give me a hand with all this admin soon.' Una put her hands on her head, pushing her hair back in a gesture of stress.

'You're not meant to be as stressed as this at this hour of the morning,' Gabe said, something in the back of his mind slotting into place. 'What kind of help are you looking for?'

'Anything. It's so blooming hard to get people up here. I don't mind someone doing it from home – in fact I'd probably prefer it.' She looked around the office territorially. 'This place is my domain.'

Gabe raised a finger. 'Leave it with me,' he said.

Una narrowed her eyes and looked at him. 'If you can solve my problems, I'll love you forever.'

'I wouldn't go that far,' said Gabe, laughing as he headed for the door. 'But let me see what I can do.'

He sat in the driver's seat of the truck, looking at his phone for a moment. Stanley, eager to get going, was sitting on the passenger seat panting enthusiastically.

'Two secs, Stan,' he said, typing.

*I think I might have a solution to your problem,* he wrote.

A moment later, he saw she'd read the message. Three little dots meant a reply was on the way, and then a moment later they disappeared.

*Oh and by the way, I won't be up at the lighthouse today. I've got a meeting at Lochbrannich I wasn't expecting.*

He hit send before he second guessed himself. It was possible that Meg couldn't care less if he was there or not, but he'd felt an unexpected wave of disappointment when he'd realised he wouldn't bump into her while he was working today.

*That'll keep the Applemore gossip mill at bay,* Meg replied a second later.

*Too late for that,* he replied, laughing to himself.

*Seriously?*

*Oh yes. Kenny the builder must've hot-footed back with the news I had a cup of tea with you.*

*Or Greta,* Meg replied. *The Applemore News Network has eyes everywhere.*

He turned on the ignition. Much as he'd like to chat to her all morning, he had work to do.

*Forgot to ask – what's the solution to my problem?* (*More to the point,* she added, *what's my problem?*)

*The girl you were looking out for. I think I might've found her a job, if it helps.*

*Seriously? Oh, wow. That's amazing. Thank you!*

*I'll tell you more later,* he typed, before tossing the phone to one side and pulling out onto the road. *Better get to work.*

Lochbrannich had burst into life since his last visit. The trees which had been in bud were now shaded with acid green as the new leaves danced in the sunlight, and the forest floor was carpeted with a sea of bluebells. The colours of the glen had changed completely, as if someone had taken a water-soaked brush to one of those Magic Colour pictures. Deep blue water sparkled in the sunlight, and the foliage of climbing roses twined round the gate posts.

'Ah, we meet again.' The duke was waiting for him as he pulled up, standing in the shade of one of the stone pillars that flanked the heavy door at the entrance to Lochbrannich

House. He held out his hand and shook Gabe's with a warm smile.

'Coffee first, I think, don't you?'

Gabe got the impression as they sat chatting in the duke's study that he was happy to have someone to talk with that supported his plans.

'Jennifer, my wife, would have been all for it. Sadly, she's not quite well enough at the moment to listen to me rabbiting on, which is where you come in.' The duke chuckled wheezily.

'Oh, I'm sorry to hear that.' She hadn't been around the last time he'd been there, either. He was just wondering what the protocol was regarding asking after her health when the duke cleared his throat and stood up, wandering across to the other side of the room.

'Nothing serious,' he said, picking up a framed photograph and looking at it fondly for a moment. 'A little bit of a problem with her heart, but I think we've got it under control now, thank goodness. I'm going to collect her from the hospital tomorrow. It's a bit of a drive,' he said with another chuckle, 'but she's worth it.'

Gabe smiled, watching as he put down the photograph.

'My daughter thinks I'm stark raving mad, of course. She's more old school than me. As I mentioned before, she'd have a fence around the estate to keep people out, but that's not the way forward, in my opinion.'

The duke smiled. 'Shall we?'

Gabe got the impression that the duke was mainly looking for a sympathetic ear.

Driving along in his battered old Land Rover, the duke chatted away, pointing out the wild garlic in flower and discussing the plans he had to clear out rampaging rhododendron bushes making their way up the hillside.

'This place has given me such a lot of pleasure over the years. I feel it's one's duty to give something back.'

'I think that's a great way of looking at it.'

'Fortunately, Jennifer agrees.' The duke pulled up at the entrance to a little wood, turning to look at Gabe for a moment, his bushy brows questing upwards.

'And are you married?'

Gabe shook his head. 'No, I –'

'Ah, divorced. Yes, we've all been there.'

'Not divorced, no, but I – well, no, I'm single. At the moment,' Gabe added, crossing his fingers mentally and thinking of Meg.

'It sounds like you have a young lady in mind.' The duke gave a nod of approval. 'I met Jennifer when we were in our late forties. Best decision I ever made, marrying her. We've had forty years together and I couldn't be happier.'

'Forty years?' Gabe couldn't hide his surprise.

'I shall take that as a compliment,' said the duke, his shoulders shaking as he laughed. 'Yes, the happiest years of my life. Goodness knows it made up for the first forty. My first wife was a terrible mistake.'

Gabe snorted with amusement.

'One shouldn't speak ill of the dead, but really. It was a blessing in disguise when she popped her clogs.'

'I know someone else who might say the same thing,' Gabe said as they climbed out of the Land Rover. Possibly in rather more delicate terms, he added to himself, trying not to laugh.

'I won't suggest we walk up there right now, but if you have a moment sometime, take your little spaniel and have a wander up to the top of the hill. Once you get through the woods there's a pretty little bothy. I'm thinking we might turn that into extra sleeping quarters for staff. Just wanted to point it out to you.'

'Ah, I misunderstood. I thought you were planning to mostly have volunteers doing the work?'

'Oh not at all, no. I'm hoping we can get some bodies in here on a full-time basis. I want to give something back to the community. It's all very well getting keen beans up here to do some planting, but we have to think about the local economy, don't you think?'

Gabe nodded, thinking once again about Meg. He got the feeling that she and the duke would get on well.

'This young lady you have in mind,' said the duke, looking at Gabe with a thoughtful expression. 'Does she know how you feel?'

Gabe looked at the sunlight dappling the forest floor for a moment, listening to the sound of Stanley and Moss hurtling around following scents.

'I don't know,' he said, after a long moment. 'It's complicated.'

'Well, I should let her know,' said the duke. 'Love has a way of ironing out complications, I've found.'

Gabe didn't say anything, but watched the dogs as they barrelled down the hill towards them before screeching to a halt in a shower of dead leaves and mud splashes.

The duke put an arm on his shoulder for a moment, surprising him.

'Forgive me. I'm being an interfering old duffer.' He patted Gabe. 'But I was given the same advice forty years ago, and I'm very glad of it.'

# CHAPTER THIRTY-TWO

Meg – trying not to look as if she was hovering in the hope of bumping into Gabe – was hovering, in the hope of bumping into Laurel. It was a difficult process, because she didn't want to appear to be gate-keeping the library, or for that matter the contents of the little chest.

Greta had appeared again first thing, along with another couple of women from the village improvement society.

'Such a brilliant idea, isn't it?' Greta had patted Meg on the shoulder and beamed at the women proudly.

'I read about it online,' Meg had explained, feeling like she needed to make it clear that she hadn't just come up with the idea by herself. 'Lots of places have them – people swap seeds and baby plants, leave surplus food and all sorts of things.'

'I don't know why we didn't think of it before,' said Greta. 'We're all trying to do our bit to reduce food waste, and recycling is such a problem up here in the Highlands.'

'I feel a wee bit guilty that we've not thought about young people needing support,' said one of the other women. 'Right under our noses, as well.'

'Well, we can do our bit now,' said Greta, looking inside the chest and frowning. 'In fact I think we might be able to do something quite clever up at the village hall.'

Meg had watched as the three women had bustled off back to chat to Kenny, who along with a carpenter colleague was now busy putting some framing up along the walls of the lighthouse building next to the cottage, getting ready to board it out.

She'd given him a wave hello, feeling self-conscious as he'd shouted a greeting with a wink as she passed.

It was almost lunchtime now, and the two men from Grant Forestry who were hard at work fencing looked up as she slipped out of the gate for the third time that morning.

'You're going to wear that wee dog's legs down to stumps if you keep walking her,' shouted the smaller, older man. The young lad alongside him grinned.

Meg gave a shy smile.

'Only kidding you,' he said. 'We're not disturbing you with the banging?'

Meg shook her head. 'Not at all, no.'

'Glad to hear it.' He gave her a broad grin and got back to work.

The noise of the initial work going on in the visitor centre to be was far louder, but she'd been far too distracted to notice. She wandered down towards the library, straightening the books on the shelves for the umpteenth time that morning, rearranging the selection she'd recently wrapped and labelled in brown paper before carefully pulling the door closed and sliding the catch to make sure it didn't blow open in the breeze.

It felt like everyone from the village had come for a walk that day – everyone except the one person she hoped to bump into. If she'd thought about it, she'd have taken the initiative and got Laurel's number. Now instead she had no idea where she lived, and no idea how to get a hold of her – short of leaving a note up at the village hall where the mother and toddler group was held. Actually, that wasn't a bad idea at all. She headed back up the hill with Eliza, who was definitely less enthusiastic about her fourth walk of the morning than she had been her first. She was just about at the back gate when she heard a shout carried on the wind and turned.

'Hello,' said Laurel, waving as she strode up the hill towards her.

'I was just looking for you,' said Meg, realising as she did how ridiculous it sounded.

'You said I should come and visit,' Laurel said, smiling shyly, '– and I spoke to one of my friends back in Bathgate and she said you wouldn't have said it if you didn't mean it, so –'

Meg felt a smile spreading across her face. 'I did mean it. I'm glad you came. Come in. I was just going to make some lunch.'

Laurel followed her into the cottage.

'Do you need a hand to get that off?' Meg put a hand to her mouth, laughing as she realised what she'd said. 'Obviously not, or you wouldn't be able to manage at home.'

Laurel unclipped the strap around her waist, somehow managing to reach back and hold on to baby Kai as she wriggled her arms out of the straps. A moment later she was holding him – round and jolly, in a blue padded coat covered in dinosaurs – in her arms.

'Is he walking?'

Laurel giggled. 'No, he's only five months old.'

'Sorry, I'm not very up on babies,' Meg said. 'I mean my friend Helen – whose house this is – had one, but she's currently in South America with a newborn of her own.'

'You didn't have any?' Laurel looked at her in surprise.

Meg shook her head. 'Not one. Just a very opinionated corgi.'

'She's so cute.' Laurel looked at the armchair by the fire where Eliza had flopped down, exhausted after her multiple walks. 'Can I put him down here on the sofa?'

'Of course. Have a seat and I'll make us some sandwiches. Ham? Cheese? Cheese and ham?'

'Cheese and ham would be lovely, thank you.' Laurel settled Kai down against some cushions where he sat, looking around quite happily.

Meg wasn't sure what age babies started eating food, so she made an extra round of sandwiches and brought through a jug of orange juice and some glasses.

Laurel was sitting up with the baby tucked up under her sweatshirt when she returned with some plates.

'I don't know why, but he always seems to be hungry whenever I try and eat. I fed him just before we came out for a walk.'

'Let me pass you some sandwiches over.'

Laurel looked at the three plates. 'He's not quite ready for cheese sandwiches.'

Somehow this made them both start laughing, and then a startled baby Kai coughed and spluttered so Laurel had to sit him up and pat him on the back. A moment later, he gave an enormous burp, which made them both laugh.

'Well, I think we've established my knowledge of small humans is pretty limited,' Meg said after taking a sip of orange juice. 'Fortunately, I have other talents.'

'I didn't know much about them until I had one,' admitted Laurel. She reached into her pocket and pulled out a little wooden rattle, which Kai took from her with a squeal of delight. 'I went to the baby group, like you said. It was really nice. I was worried I wouldn't know anyone, but there was a girl there who'd just had a baby as well – she's called Alina.'

'Pretty name.' It was such a surprise to see how much happier Laurel looked.

'She's Polish. Her boyfriend Marek is working up at the tree planting place.'

'Oh, I've got a –' Meg felt a flutter of butterflies in her stomach as she thought of Gabe and the message he'd sent her earlier, making her smile. 'Someone I know works there, too. Funnily enough, that's why I was looking out for you.'

Laurel looked at her expectantly.

'My friend – he says he thinks he might have found a job for you. Something you can do from home around Kai.'

Laurel's eyes widened, and for a moment Meg wondered if she'd spoken out of turn. She watched as the young girl looked down at her baby, fiddling for a moment with the sleeve of his little cardigan, then looking up with her mouth pursed together and her brows knitted tightly as if holding herself together. Her eyes were bright with tears that threatened to spill over.

'That's really kind.'

Meg felt a wave of fondness for this brave, proud young girl who'd crossed her path completely by accident.

'It's nothing.'

'It's not nothing,' said Laurel, shaking her head fiercely. 'It's – it's the sort of thing my grandma would have done if she was still alive. It makes me feel like there's someone who notices we're here.'

'I do.' Meg reached across from the armchair by the sofa, putting a hand out so Kai reached his little starfish fingers out and caught one of her fingers.

Laurel looked at his hand and then up into Meg's face.

'I really appreciate it. Thank you.'

Kai released Meg's finger, and she sat back against the heap of Helen's crochet covered cushions. Framed photographs of Phoebe at all ages lined the wooden mantel and she gazed at them for a moment.

'Is that your friend's daughter?'

Meg looked back at Laurel.

'Yes. She's just had a baby, which is why I'm here house-sitting. My friend went to South America to be with her.'

Laurel looked at the photographs for a moment, then back at Kai.

'I didn't have anyone looking out for me,' explained Meg. 'My family life wasn't – well, it wasn't really like that. I suspect you know what I mean.'

Laurel nodded, straightening the crochet blanket which was folded over the edge of the sofa. 'Yeah. I wanted it to be different for Kai, and we moved here and I thought we'd have a nice life. Seaside for him to play in, a nice little house, all that stuff. And now it's just the two of us. It's not...'

'Not easy. I know. You've done an amazing job so far, though. Look how happy he is.'

'If I can get this job, it would make all the difference. I can't believe you thought of me.'

'Leave it with me.' Meg picked up her phone. 'Give me your number. I'll speak to my friend and we can take it from there.'

# CHAPTER THIRTY-THREE

It was funny how the Pilates class had somehow given a shape to her weeks. It was Thursday again, and Miranda was leaning on the side of her car with her arms folded when Meg pulled up alongside the farm shop centre.

'You're looking very perky,' said Miranda with a knowing expression.

Meg reached into the back of the car, hiding the blush she knew would be rising on her cheeks. She grabbed her mat and her bag and straightened to see Miranda hadn't moved. Her brows lifted in query.

'What?' Meg couldn't help smiling.

'Oh, nothing.' Miranda shook her head.

'Ready for our weekly torture session?'

'I think I'm getting slightly fitter.' Miranda flexed her right arm. 'That might just be all the digging I've been doing, mind you. You must come and have a coffee up at the flower farm and see what we've been up to.'

'I'd love that.'

They headed inside, where half the class members were

already rolling out their mats and getting ready, standing around in groups and chatting.

Meg felt a tap on her shoulder and turned to find Dolina, lips pursed and eyes wide in mock amusement, looking at her.

'What's this I'm hearing,' she said, cocking her head to one side as if she was a robin who'd spotted a particularly tasty morsel.

Meg couldn't help smiling. 'Hearing about what?'

Miranda looked at Dolina and then back at her, waggling her eyebrows.

'Oh for goodness' sake.' Meg shook out her mat and laid it down on the ground.

'I said she was looking happy,' said Miranda.

'That'll be because she's been on a hot date with that silver fox that's working up in the forest.'

'I haven't been on a date,' Meg protested.

'Hmm,' said Miranda.

'I tell you what, I wouldn't say no,' said Dolina, with a cackle of laughter. 'I saw him in the shop the other day and Greta was telling me he'd been seen up at the cottage. You're a fast worker, my girl. I'm impressed.'

'I haven't done anything!' Meg shook her head and started laughing.

'Yet,' said Miranda with a grin.

'I'm saying nothing,' Meg conceded. 'This place is ridiculous.'

Dolina clasped her forearm with a warm smile. 'Och, we're only having you on. We like a wee bit of romance here.'

'She's right.' Miranda nodded. 'It's nice to see people looking happy – there's enough blooming misery in the world. And you are definitely looking happy.'

Meg pressed two fingers to her lips, realising that she was smiling again.

'Right, everyone,' said Maisie, the instructor. 'Did you do those follow-up exercises during the week?'

Afterwards, as always, people gathered in little groups outside in the courtyard, laughing and chatting. The sky was still bright and the air crisp, but not cold. Meg pulled down the hem of her sweatshirt and hitched her bag up onto her shoulder, listening as Rilla told everyone about a strange group of campers who'd turned up that week to stay at the estate.

'We had to tell them that no, we weren't really the right setting for a full moon naked dance ceremony.'

'I don't know,' Jenny, Dolina's daughter had said, laughing, 'we could have all come and watched.'

'I would have thought you see enough wrinkly sausages on the butchery counter in the farm shop,' her mother said, snorting with amusement at her own joke.

Meg looked around at the now-familiar setting. The planters which Miranda and Beth had filled were now coming into bloom, and the windows of the art gallery next to the studio was hung with paintings done by the children's art class that took place once a week. Across the courtyard, solar powered fairy lights danced in the breeze, hanging around the entrance to the shop and café.

'So you'll have to report back,' Miranda said, giving Meg a nudge and bringing her back into the conversation.

'Sorry?'

'About your hot date.'

'Ooh yes,' said Rilla, laughing. 'The old Applemore magic is working on you, I hear.'

'Welcome to Applemore,' said Miranda, in mock-prophetic tones. 'You can visit, but you'll never leave...'

Meg mused on it as she was driving home in Helen's battered little car. She'd taken some cuttings from a geranium on the windowsill and set them in a glass of water a week or so ago, thinking she'd grow them on and pop them outside in the planter by the door. For a few days, every time she'd checked it seemed to be doing nothing at all, and she wondered if she'd lost her touch. Then one day, as if by magic, the tiniest roots had appeared, pale and almost translucent, curling through the water. Was she taking root in Applemore?

She'd half wondered, half hoped that Gabe might reappear the next morning. The fencing was almost complete, and as she dressed she glanced out of the window, realising with disappointment that it was George and his young helper, Leo, once again.

*Morning,* she read on her phone, her heart giving a little skip of excitement at seeing Gabe's name pop up. *I passed Laurel's number on to Una and I've just been in the office - apparently they're having a chat today. Thought you'd want to know asap.*

*That's amazing. Thanks so much.*

*Una doesn't mess about,* Gabe typed. *I had a feeling she'd be straight on it.*

*I think Laurel will be keen to get started as soon as she can, so that's good.* Meg felt a wave of anticipatory nerves as she continued tapping a message. *What are you up to today?*

*I was hoping I'd be working with George, but I'm heading up the coast with Donald to look at a deer fencing job.*

Well, that answered that question. Still, it was sweet of him to let her know straight away. She'd text a good luck message to Laurel later.

# CHAPTER THIRTY-FOUR

Gabe had a suspicion it was one of those days before he'd even had his first cup of coffee. He'd turned up at the office only to discover that he wasn't up at the lighthouse site as he'd hoped, and then managed to lock his keys in the cottage when Stanley unexpectedly bolted out the front door after a cat which happened to be walking past. His phone had rung three times with missed calls from a number he hadn't recognised, and whoever it was hadn't left a message.

'Penny for them?' Donald looked across at him as they headed back towards Applemore after taking a look at the deer fencing site.

'Just thinking I must be on one of those junk call lists. I've had three dropped calls today.'

'You should do what I do,' chuckled Donald. 'I let 'em rabbit on, then start singing down the phone to them. They soon hang up and leave me alone.'

Gabe grinned. 'Maybe I'll try it if they call back.'

They drove on in comfortable silence, Gabe looking out of

the window as the Highland scenery whizzed past. It was strange how it contrasted to his old life – back then he hadn't noticed the change in the seasons at all. Summer had, of course, meant a holiday in some exotic location, and winter a week or two skiing from a chalet, but he couldn't remember a time in his life when he'd watched the leaves growing day by day from the tiniest buds on the trees, or seen the vivid green of ferns as they appeared – the first tiny spirals in the undergrowth, unfurling to reveal themselves along the verges of the single track roads that wound through the hills. He'd come to Applemore to escape, and somehow here he was with a whole new life ahead of him. The only challenge he was facing was -

'That didn't take as long as I was thinking.' Donald broke into his thoughts. 'I think I'll nip off early and get the kids from school as a surprise.'

His phone rang once more. The same unfamiliar number appeared on the screen. Donald grinned wickedly.

'Now's your chance. Do you want me to join in with the chorus?'

Gabe lifted an eyebrow in amusement and accepted the call.

'Hello?'

'Gabe.' The voice was immediately familiar. He felt a lurch in his stomach.

'Don't hang up.'

Donald raised a finger, and Gabe widened his eyes slightly, shaking his head. Realising something was up, his boss gave the briefest of nods.

'I can't talk now.' His voice was terse.

'I need to talk to you. Can you call me on this number?'

He gritted his teeth, closing his eyes and exhaling through his nostrils as he tried to gather his thoughts.

'Fine,' he said after a moment. 'I'll call you in half an hour.'

'Everything alright?' Donald turned his Defender onto the road that led down towards Applemore. A young deer stood on the edge of the moor, stock still, watching them as they passed.

'Yeah.' He turned the phone over in his hands, staring at it as if it was an unexploded bomb. 'I hope so, anyway.'

When they got back to the office, Donald dropped a hand on his shoulder in the yard.

'Let me know if there's anything you need, alright? I'm on the end of the phone if you need me.'

'Thanks.' Gabe watched as he headed out of the yard and climbed into his car to collect the children.

He crossed the yard and popped his head into the office, where Una was standing with a baby in her arms, talking to a skinny young girl in black jeans and a cardigan.

'Gabe,' Una said, looking at the baby with delight. 'Look at our new office colleague. Isn't he a cutie?'

The baby grabbed the beads Una was wearing round her neck and stuffed them into his mouth, covering them – and Una – with drool. She looked at him starry-eyed.

'Very cute,' said Gabe more grimly than he intended to. He shot the young girl a smile to make up for it. This must be Laurel. Meg would be delighted at the news that things seemed to be working out.

'Just got to make a call,' he said to Una, who wasn't paying attention. He walked back from the yard to his cottage, giving Mrs Birnie next door a quick wave hello as he passed. He opened the door to find Stanley had dismembered his favourite stuffed toy and the rug in the hallway was covered in fluff.

'Come on, you,' he said, clipping on Stan's leash, 'I'll take you over to the grass for a quick pee.'

He sat on the wooden picnic bench that looked out across

the bay, Stanley whizzing around at the full extent of his lead. The phone felt like a lead weight.

Across the harbour, tall in the distance, stood the light-house. He turned away, letting out a sigh of resignation, and pulled the phone out of his pocket.

'Thanks for calling back,' said Rebecca.

He'd blocked her number when they split – not out of spite, but out of self-preservation. Whenever she'd had too much to drink, which was every night, she'd call and leave long, angry messages on his voicemail, speaking until the time ran out, calling again an hour later, apologising for being unpleasant, calling again as she opened another bottle of wine and her temper rose. Then the next day he'd get a stream of long, sometimes apologetic messages. And then the whole thing would start all over again.

'Look, I'll keep it quick,' she said, into the silence. 'It's about the house. I need to talk to you.'

'I don't think we have anything to say to each other.' He stared out to sea, watching as a fishing boat set off from the harbour.

'I understand. And I know why you feel that way.' Her tone was conciliatory, but it was nothing he hadn't heard before.

'I don't know where you are,' she continued. 'I spoke to Jake the other day, and he said he'd spoken to you, but...'

He hadn't explicitly stated to Jacob that he didn't want his mother knowing where he was, but the agreement had hung in the air, unspoken. They'd both been through enough.

'I'd like to meet up. I can come to you –'

'No,' Gabe snapped the word out, stopping her mid-sentence. It was the last thing he wanted. Applemore was his escape.

'It's about the house,' she repeated.

'Fine.' He'd compromised enough for her in the past – she could do the same for him. 'I can be free this weekend.'

He swallowed back the immediate feeling of bitter regret that rose in his throat. How – even now, even after all this time and moving to the other end of the country – was she still disrupting his plans for happiness?

'Oh –' her voice was quiet. 'Thank you. I mean it, Gabe. Thanks.'

'It's fine,' he said, aware his jaw was rigid with tension as he spoke. 'I'll be there tomorrow afternoon.'

'Do you want to come to the house?'

He shook his head silently. 'No, I do not. I'll meet you in Thursby's on the High Street at three.'

'Oh, that's great. Good idea. I'll see you then.'

He watched as the fishing boat moved across the water, heading out to sea.

'Gabe?' Rebecca's voice said, bringing him back.

'Sorry. Right. See you tomorrow.'

He hung up without saying goodbye, putting the phone down on the table and staring at it for a moment as if it was an unexploded bomb. It had been a long time before he'd lost that feeling of dread when it rang, and now here he was again.

He sent a quick message to Donald, explaining that he'd some business to attend to back in England, but that he'd be back to work on Monday all being well.

*You'll be worn out from the drive,* Donald replied swiftly, *take Monday off. That's an order.*

That was work dealt with. Whatever the hell was going on with Rebecca, the truth was he needed it dealt with. He'd brushed the issue of the house under the carpet, knowing that at some point he'd have to address it, and it looked like the time was now.

More importantly – and he was only realising now how much more important it felt to him – he had Meg to deal with.

He called Stanley and started walking down the path to the beach. Perhaps a walk would give him time to work out what to say to her.

'I'm really sorry.'

He'd found her in the garden in a pair of pale blue jeans which were grass-streaked and muddy at the knees. She'd looked up to see him walking towards the garden gate, her pretty face open and smiling as she straightened up and came towards him, unaware he was about to blow out her date in favour of... of what? That was the trouble. He had no idea.

'I'm sorry, something's come up. I'm going to have to take a rain check on tomorrow.'

Meg was standing on the opposite side of the garden wall, hands leaning on the stone, her hair blowing in the wind. She looked up at him, frowning at the sun in her eyes.

'It's fine,' she said. Her voice was a little too bright.

He swallowed. 'I need to go down south. I told you about the house situation.'

She nodded and brushed her hair back from her face. 'Oh yes, of course.'

'Believe me, if there was any way I could avoid this, I would. I've been putting it off for long enough.'

She pressed her lips together and gave a little nod of acknowledgement.

'It's fine,' she said again. 'We can do it another time.'

'I'd like that,' he said. 'Let me just get this ironed out.'

They chatted briefly. He made her laugh, telling her about Una starry-eyed with the baby in the office, and she said that Laurel had messaged to say thank you and that she was going in on Monday to sign a contract. But his mind was elsewhere, and after a few minutes he whistled Stanley and said his goodbyes, heading back down the path towards the library and back to the cottage to throw some things in an overnight bag.

Rebecca was unpredictable, and he had no idea what he was walking into – but if he was to have any chance of a future, he needed to face up to the past.

# CHAPTER THIRTY-FIVE

*You are being ridiculous*, Meg told herself, washing her hands in the kitchen sink.

It was a lunch date, for one thing, not a proposal of marriage. But the trouble with Applemore was that now she'd have Miranda, and Greta, and goodness knows who else all wondering how her mythical date went, and she'd have to tell them it hadn't happened.

She glanced out of the window and saw a man in work overalls with a ladder passing by the back of the lighthouse. Drying her hands and wandering through to the sitting room, she saw the builders had returned. A second later, there was a knock at the door.

'Hi love,' said Kenny, the builder. 'Just wanted to let you know that we're going to be working over the weekend. I'm a bit behind on my jobs, so we're trying to catch up.'

'Oh,' said Meg, trying to arrange her face into a suitably cheerful expression. 'Okay, that's fine.'

'Hopefully it won't mean too much noise.' He chuckled.

'I've got some noise-cancelling earmuffs in the van, if that helps.'

He waved an arm toward his van, where the man who she'd seen with a ladder a moment ago was now unloading some sort of scaffolding contraption.

'I'm sure it'll be fine,' she said politely. 'Actually, I'm going to be away for a few days, so you can make as much noise as you like.'

She frowned at the words that had fallen out of her mouth, which had seemingly become disconnected from her brain in the last few minutes.

'Oh, that's good news. I won't feel guilty in that case.' Kenny chuckled. 'Going away in your big van, are you?'

'Yes,' said Meg. 'Yes, I am.'

'Looks like you'll have a bonny weekend for it. I better get on,' said Kenny, turning and heading back down the garden path. 'Have a good one.'

There was nothing to stop her going on a van trip. The library shelves were tidy and stocked, the house was organised, and the whole weekend was now a massive yawning gap of… nothing.

She ran up the stairs, grabbed a few things and a wash-bag, and threw them into an overnight bag. Swiping a selection of food from the fridge and cupboards, she packed them all into the van. How hard could it be? People did wild camping all the time. She'd seen them on the way to Applemore, tucked into little parking spots and on verges.

Eliza, who had been whisked from a comfortable snooze on the sofa and into the van before she knew what was going on, was sitting on the passenger seat looking at her every once in a while with a slightly suspicious expression.

'It's called having an adventure,' Meg told her firmly.

What it was, she reflected as she drove north, trundling along behind a row of cars who were tailgating a tractor and trailer, was a hair trigger reaction to Gabe's announcement he couldn't make their date. She'd been excited and nervous all week, but there was something about the idea of opening up that made her feel a little bit… exposed, was probably the word she'd choose. And with what felt like half of Applemore knowing what was going on, it all felt a bit like she was opening herself up to be made to look like a fool. Especially now she'd have to turn around and say no, as it happened, she hadn't gone for lunch with him. Meg grimaced at the thought of it.

She'd searched on her phone for one of the campervan parking apps and spotted a pretty little beach with white sand ninety minutes up the coast. It felt like a good place to start.

What she didn't expect was to discover that on a sunny Friday evening she wasn't the only one who'd had the same idea. The little parking space by the beach was packed with campervans. A group of five lads in their early twenties were sitting at the only picnic bench on the grass, a disposable barbecue burning on top of some stacked up bricks. A huge dog was tied to the bumper of one of the other vans, and it lunged and barked at her when she looked out of her window.

Meg gritted her teeth. She'd just have to get on with it. This was all part of the adventure, she told herself.

Eliza clearly felt much the same. She glued herself to Meg's ankle as they walked down through the little path to the beach, not even stopping to sniff the sea-grass or any of the turf covered sand dunes.

The beach itself was breathtakingly beautiful – a long stretch of sand which wouldn't have looked out of place on a Caribbean postcard. A couple were walking hand-in-hand along the shoreline, and in the distance, Meg spotted another group putting up a tent. It was hardly the deserted escape she'd been imagining.

She got back to the van and got things organised, switching on the gas hob and boiling the kettle for a cup of tea. Eliza had perked up after being fed and was curled up like an ammonite on her little fluffy bed under the table.

At least the mobile reception was as decent as promised. Meg sat down at the table and opened her iPad, ready to find somewhere slightly less crowded for the next day.

She was trying to navigate the app, peering at the screen with her new reading glasses, when a message from Helen appeared.

*Hello darling, sorry for the radio silence. It's all go here with the new little one.*

*Don't worry,* Meg typed, *I can imagine. All good here.*

*Glad to hear it. I was going to call but we've just got her off to sleep... now I don't want you to feel you have to say yes, but I've been contemplating staying longer.*

Meg looked at the words on the screen. Helen had lived in Applemore so long that it was hard to imagine her anywhere else for any length of time. When she'd left, she'd lingered for a while in the studio, looking out of the window at the beautiful view Meg had grown to love, and said how much she'd miss it.

*I had a funny feeling you'd like being in grandma mode... how long are you thinking?*

It wasn't surprising Helen would want to stay on a few weeks longer, really.

*I'm not sure. A few months. Maybe longer? I love being here – it turns out I could rent a little place really cheaply.*

Rent a place? Meg stared at the words on the screen with amazement. A few months?

*I've been stuck for so long,* Helen typed. *I hadn't realised until I got here – obviously it's heaven being here with Phoebe and her little family, but it's more than that. There's so much here. I feel like my creativity has just blossomed...*

Meg's eyes were saucer-like. Everything Helen treasured – her art equipment, her books, her paintings... it was all sitting there waiting for her to come back.

*Sorry for rambling,* came another message a moment later. *I feel like I've had a whole new lease of life.*

*What about all your art stuff?* Meg typed, and then deleted it, realising that she didn't want to sound like she was raining on her friend's parade.

*That's amazing,* she wrote, instead.

*I don't want you to feel you have to hang about... but on the other hand you're welcome to stay as long as you like. It's completely up to you. I know you're having a nice time but you might be ready to move on and have some adventures in your little house on wheels.*

Meg made a face. So far, not so good on that front.

*Hrmm,* she typed. *The jury's still out on that one.*

*Oh really???* Helen typed.

*Maybe I'm just having some teething problems...*

*Uh oh, baby crying. I'll try to call you tomorrow. You can fill me in. Grandma duty calling xoxo*

Months. Meg put the phone down on the table and pressed her palms flat downward, as if to ground herself somehow. She'd been thinking as she drove about how to move forward with her plans to offer her skills to charities. If she stayed in Applemore for a while, maybe she could have a chat with Rilla and see if she had any contacts in the charity sector. It would be good to do something that made a difference.

She picked up her mug and opened the door of her van, looking out across the field that ran alongside the parking space. Even in her current state where she was crammed like a sardine into an accidental van gathering, she'd still take this over life back in Heatherby a million times over.

Meg woke early the next morning after a fitful sleep. Giving Eliza a quick leg stretch, she decided the best thing to do was make her escape before the rest of the vans came to life. She'd found a little campsite attached to a farm by a loch which was a couple of hours away, near Beauly, and set off with a strong coffee in her travel mug.

She stopped en route at a farm shop – noting that it wasn't a patch on Applemore – and picked up some bits and pieces to keep her going for a couple of nights.

'Hello there,' said the woman who owned the campsite, smiling as she held open the gate for Meg to drive through.

'I'm Lilian,' she said, bending to pat Eliza once Meg had parked in a little tree-lined spot by a stream. 'We've got a little shed over there with some eggs and things you might need, but I won't trouble you unless you need anything.'

She had a sweet, welcoming face and light grey hair twisted up in a bun.

'I think I'll be okay,' said Meg. 'I've got some thinking to do, and this looks like a good place to do it.'

'You've chosen a good spot. We've got a couple of other vans coming later, but they'll be parked out of your way so you can come and go as you please. That little path there takes you through to the woodland walk. It's my favourite.'

'Thanks,' said Meg.

The woman gave her a warm smile. 'Sometimes it's nice to get away for a wee break, isn't it?'

It was, reflected Meg, later that afternoon, but maybe solitude was alright in short doses. She wondered what was happening back at the library, and if anyone had chosen the books she'd wrapped and neatly labelled with what she hoped were intriguing descriptions. She even wondered how the building work was going – although she was quite glad not to be listening to the repetitive thud thud thud of hammering and the clatter of metal scaffolding being assembled.

She checked her phone, telling herself she was looking for a message from Helen, but the truth was she was wondering what was happening with Gabe. Whatever was going on, he'd looked tense and uncomfortable when he'd turned up at the cottage.

There was a message from Miranda, though, asking if she wanted to come up and see the flower farm on Tuesday afternoon, and another from Laurel, saying how amazed and excited she was that she'd been offered the job on the spot.

*I can't thank you enough,* she'd written. *It means a lot.*

Meg's heart felt full.

She took a walk through the woods. A peat-brown stream wove through the trees, and as she walked up the narrow path, brushing past fresh new ferns and crushing wild garlic underfoot she realised she could hear the roar and splash in the distance of a waterfall. The path twisted, and there it was in front of her. She sat down on the little wooden bench in a clearing, and Eliza hopped up by her side.

Meg buried her hands in the little dog's ruff of fur, gazing at the water and thinking. She'd bought the van on a whim, after reading an article about women in midlife finding themselves. Everywhere she looked people were rhapsodising about how much they loved the freedom of life on the road, and the adventure of waking somewhere new every day. The truth – which was slowly dawning on her – was that much as she enjoyed the adventure of travel, she preferred it when she arrived in a place and didn't have to set up camp.

She'd left Heatherby because she was running away from the past, and a life where she'd felt it was safest to stay invisible. Maybe Rilla was right about Applemore having some sort of magic about it. She'd arrived, and thanks to the library, she'd found a place where she seemed to fit for the first time ever. That little library was so much more than a book exchange... it was somewhere kindnesses were shared, and secrets kept.

She stood up to head back to the van, remembering as she did the teenagers who'd been exchanging notes. She hadn't seen either the boy or the girl in a while – when she got home, she'd have to go down and have a peek, in case another secret envelope had appeared.

It was only when she'd made herself some lunch, and was sitting on the step of the van reading her book that she realised what she'd said without thinking. Home.

That was an interesting thought.

# CHAPTER THIRTY-SIX

Gabe flipped the pages of the Metro newspaper that someone had left on the café table by the window. He'd arrived early, which had been pointless, because the only reliable thing about Rebecca was her lateness.

The coffee shop – which had been redecorated in his absence – was packed and noisy, but he'd managed to grab a decent table. Most importantly, it was dog friendly. He'd brought Stan along as a talisman, and he was tucked under the table looking with fascination out of the window as a constant stream of people walked by.

'Can I get you another?' The tall boy who'd brought him his coffee appeared, clearing his already-empty cup and raising a questioning eyebrow. Window tables were prime real estate on a Saturday and he knew he'd be pushing his luck to hang around for long without a drink in front of him.

'I'm just waiting for someone. Shouldn't be long,' he said, crossing his fingers under the table. Not strictly true, but it would buy him some time.

A moment later Stanley pulled at his lead, scrabbling under

the chair and getting caught as he pulled unexpectedly, his tail wagging furiously.

'Hello, darling.'

Gabe looked up in surprise. Rebecca bent to say hello to Stanley.

'At least he's pleased to see me,' she said drily.

Gabe stood up, his manners over-ruling everything. 'Rebecca.'

'Can I?' She tipped her head toward the chair opposite his.

'Of course. Sit down.'

She tucked herself in against the window, hanging her bag on the back of the chair and brushing her hair – lighter than he'd seen it – back behind an ear.

'You're looking well.' Rebecca put her hands flat on the table for a moment, then steepled her fingers and rested her chin. 'The outdoor life seems to suit you.'

'Thanks.' He cleared his throat and picked up the menu, which worked like magic to summon the boy in a black apron back to the table.

'I'll have a mint tea, please.'

Neither of them spoke as they waited for the order to arrive. They sat in an uncomfortable silence, Gabe looking out of the window, Rebecca stroking Stanley's long, silky ears.

It was strange to think how often he'd walked those streets. Barnes prided itself on being a cosy enclave of independent shops and tasteful boutiques, with drinks by the river and wholesome weekend walks on the common. Now it seemed claustrophobic and packed with people and traffic.

'Here you are,' said the boy, a few short moments later.

'Thanks so much,' said Rebecca, smiling up at him.

Gabe picked up his coffee cup and looked at her across the table.

'So,' he said.

'Thanks for coming. I appreciate it.'

He looked at her and waited.

'I said it's about the house. I want you to know that I'm putting it on the market.'

He sat back slightly. 'You are?'

'I want to move on. You must be able to understand that.'

Gabe gave a grim smile. 'Yeah, I'll give you that.'

'I know you spoke to Jacob. But it's not – it wasn't his place to try and explain. I wanted to see you face to face to apologise for – well, for everything.'

He felt his chest lifting as a deep sigh of resignation made its way out of his body. How many times had he heard her apologise over the years? They'd tried so many different times, and every time in the end it would be just one more glass or a night out with the girls, or dinner after a meeting... there was always a reason to open a bottle.

'I've made a lot of mistakes. Some of them I can't ever fix, but I'm trying my best to make a start at repairing the things I can.'

He put his mug down and looked at Rebecca properly then, realising that it wasn't just the shade of her hair that had changed. She looked different – her face was less drawn, and the loose linen shirt she was wearing over jeans was a far step from her usual slim-fitting black outfits.

'Go on,' he said, reaching down to stroke Stanley, who'd reappeared and was resting his chin on Gabe's thigh with a hopeful expression.

'I stopped drinking. I've been in recovery for a few months now, and away at a residential place where – oh, you don't need to know the details. But now I'm ready to start making changes. Selling the house is part of that.'

He shook his head. 'If you're serious, this probably isn't the right time to make drastic decisions.'

'I know what you're thinking. And I know if I tell you things are different, you'll say you've heard that a million times over.' She gave a small smile, twirling her spoon in her glass. 'But you walked away from the house, and half of it is yours by right.'

'And what about you? What are you going to do?'

She lifted a shoulder in a half-shrug. 'I'd like to join Jacob in New Zealand, if it's possible. When the house sells, I'll have enough money that it shouldn't be a problem. We both will.'

'I'm alright for money.' He gave a wry smile. His years working in industry had paid off, with share options and a pension which would mean retirement – something he didn't want to think about for a long time – would be comfortable.

Rebecca shook her head with a smile. 'Oh, I know.'

He laughed, despite himself. 'Believe it or not, I'm living in a tiny, rented cottage with an octogenarian as a neighbour, and I'm perfectly content.'

'I'm glad.' She met his gaze, and her brows dropped in an expression he couldn't quite interpret.

He cocked his head slightly in a silent query.

'I want you to be happy,' Rebecca said quietly.

'Oh,' Gabe said, realising in that moment where he wanted to be, and what he wanted to do. 'I am.'

She stayed a while longer, and together they talked through the practicalities of selling the house he'd bought into when they'd got together, splitting the equity, dealing with lawyers, and all the rest of it.

'Take care,' Gabe said as they left the café.

'I will.' Rebecca nodded briefly and touched him on the arm. 'You too. Thanks for being so kind. Not everyone would be.'

'Everyone deserves a second chance.'

Rebecca looked at him sideways. 'Or a ninety second.'

He watched as she disappeared into the Saturday afternoon crowds on the pavements. It was as if someone had loosened the final knot tying him to his old life back here in London. All he wanted now was to get back to Applemore, where the hope of a new life was waiting.

He'd broken the journey down with a few hours' uncomfortable sleep in a Travelodge, and much as he wanted to turn straight around and head back to the Highlands, he had the wisdom to recognise that he was getting a bit long in the tooth for a twelve-hour drive. On a whim, he picked up the phone and called one of his old university friends.

'Tommy. Yeah, I know, it's been too long. I don't suppose you're around this evening, are you?'

'I'M SO GLAD YOU CALLED,' said Tommy's wife Mel the next morning. 'Can't believe you thought we'd be doing something exciting on a Saturday evening, mind you.'

They were standing on the doorstep of Tommy's house in Warwickshire. Stanley was dashing around the lawn with their two red setters, delighted to have a chance to burn off some steam after his trip back to the city.

Gabe shrugged, laughing. 'You might have been off for the weekend now the kids are at uni and out of your hair.'

He pulled the car keys out of his pocket and Stanley, sensing his fun was about to end, hurtled off towards the far end of the garden and hid in some bushes.

'We can't afford it, mate,' Tommy chuckled, clapping him on the shoulder. 'You dodged a bullet there.'

Mel slapped her husband on the arm. 'Darling, for goodness' sake.'

'What?' Tommy looked injured. Mel shot him a look which clearly said *shut your mouth.*

Gabe, who'd sent a bank transfer Jacob's way only a week ago, kept his mouth shut. It might not have made sense to everyone that he still supported his ex-stepson, but he knew it was the least he could do for the boy he'd grown to love over the years.

Along the way he'd lost touch with most of his friends – the constant round of excuses and apologies that were part of life with Rebecca became too much for even the longest friendships in the end. But Tommy and Mel had always been there – the ones he'd turned to when he'd walked away for the last time, giving him a room for as long as he wanted. It felt fitting that they were here for him now when everything was finally falling into place.

'Right, I'd better hit the road.'

Tommy, who'd overheard Mel giving him the third-degree last night while they were standing in the kitchen, waggled his eyebrows.

'I want an update on what happens with this nice girl,' said Mel, wrapping an arm around his waist and squeezing. 'Life is for taking chances, remember.'

'I don't know what she's on about,' said Tommy, fondly. 'This is the woman who's ordered the same thing from the takeaway every Friday night for as long as I can remember.'

'Romance is not the same thing as curry, darling,' said Mel, shaking her head and laughing.

It was a long drive back – long enough for Gabe to decide what to do. He arrived in Applemore as the sky was still streaked with light and headed straight for the lighthouse.

# CHAPTER THIRTY-SEVEN

There was a knock at the window of the van, and Meg – midway through trying to reverse out of the little parking bay where she'd been lodged for the last two nights – opened her window to see the campsite owner looking at her.

'Leaving so early?'

She was wearing a pair of rainbow-patterned Crocs with purple dungarees and – completing the slightly eccentric air – had a fluffy grey chicken in her arms, who looked at Meg with a disapproving expression.

'Oh, yes, um, I –' she tried to think of a polite way to say that she'd been woken for the second morning in a row by a cockerel yelling outside her van at four thirty in the morning.

'Ah, I get it, don't worry. I'm a morning person myself.' The woman beamed and released the chicken, which flapped to the ground and scuttled off.

'Yes, best part of the day,' agreed Meg, who felt as if she'd been subjected to sleep deprivation torture and was very much looking forward to climbing into bed back at the cottage for a restorative mid-morning snooze.

'Hope we'll see you again,' said the woman, giving the van a slap of farewell as Meg started to reverse again.

Highly unlikely, thought Meg.

She trundled along the roads towards Applemore, stopping for a coffee at various little parking spots along the way when she started yawning once or twice every minute. In the end she pulled over and closed her eyes for half an hour, waking feeling slightly more human and heading down the glen towards the village with a sense of overwhelming relief.

She arrived back at the lighthouse, surprised to discover that the gate was closed and there was no sign of Kenny's van. He'd finished the fencing job, and the little gate and ramp that led up to the doorway looked wonderful. She pulled up the van, climbing out and letting Eliza out for a leg stretch. It was grey and cloudy, and white horses danced on the waves on the distant sea.

She wandered down towards the library, taking deep breaths of sea air and letting it fill her lungs. This was what made her feel free, not driving in the van. It wasn't the van's fault that she wasn't that sort of person. It was just one of those things. She'd tried it, and at least now she could accept that it wasn't for her. That was progress, of a sort. The old Meg probably would have just gritted her teeth and thought it was all she deserved.

Eliza beetled about, catching up on all the delicious scents that a weekend of visitors had left behind. Meg picked up a couple of pieces of litter which had been blown up from the beach and headed towards the library cupboard to see what sort of state it was in.

She opened the chest first, and was amazed to discover it full of all sorts of things – a little bag of vegetable seed packets with a note inside urging people to help themselves, some chocolate brownies from Anna's café, a four pack of tinned

255

soup… it seemed to have taken on a life of its own in the short time she'd been gone. Meg closed it carefully, smiling to herself, and straightened up to look inside at the library shelves.

She gave a little gasp of happiness when she saw a brown envelope sticking out from between two novels on the top shelf. Ah, the teenagers had been at it again, sending love notes. It was so cute. Tipping her head sideways, she frowned as she caught sight of the neat writing inked on the front.

**Meg**

Her heart thumped unevenly as she pulled it out from the shelf, turning it over to see if there was anything written on the back. Nothing. She slipped a finger underneath the seal and tore it open. Inside was a pretty card with a hand-painted watercolour of two trees on the front.

**Sorry I couldn't make our date on Saturday, but I'd like to make it up to you with dinner. Let me know what you think? – G**

Meg closed the card and looked around. There was nobody there, but she half-expected someone to appear from behind the sand dunes on the beach path and tell her it was a joke. Her heart was crashing against her chest.

She opened it again – no, she wasn't imagining it. It was the sweetest gesture.

She headed back to the cottage and sat down on the sofa.

*Hello,* she typed, feeling suddenly shy. *I just got back.*

The message was read straight away. That was unusual – she'd already noticed that Gabe, working outside as he did, was often slow to reply.

*How was the van trip?*

She laughed, shaking her head in amazement.

*How do you know I was on a van trip?*

*You said it yourself. The Applemore News Network misses nothing.*

*Of course... I forgot that part.* She glanced at the card, which was lying on the little wooden table by her side. *And yes, I would love to go for dinner,* she added, a moment later.

# CHAPTER THIRTY-EIGHT

It was Tuesday morning, and Meg – fully prepared for the third-degree about her non-existent Saturday date – was driving up the road to the flower farm. The little trees which had been newly planted along the edge of the drive were swaying gently in the wind.

As Meg passed the café car park, she noticed that despite the early hour, it was packed with visitors who had arrived for a new showing at the gallery opening that day. It was funny how she'd come to know the patterns of life in the village so quickly, when she'd never felt at home in Heatherby in all the time she'd lived there.

The road tracked left, and she headed on, past the woods and into the big gravel driveway that opened up to reveal Applemore House.

Rilla was standing outside the door with a sea of dogs at her feet and her arms full of what looked like the long, silver branches from a rosemary bush. She beckoned Meg with a wave of her hand and Meg pulled the car up beside her, Eliza yapping with excitement at the sight of all the dogs outside.

'Shush,' Meg said, laughing. She got out of the car and was hit with a wave of a familiar, resinous scent.

'I hoped I'd see you,' Rilla said, putting the branches down on the front step and opening the huge, studded door. She shooed the dogs inside and turned back, smiling warmly. 'I was going to pop up and join you all for a coffee at the flower farm, but I've just had a message from Lachlan – he's in Inverness for a meeting – and they want me to join them on a Zoom call at half ten. I'd far rather be getting on with making this rosemary into gin than dealing with the business side, but needs must.'

Meg made a sympathetic face.

'Anyway.' Rilla brightened. 'I was dying to hear how the van trip went. Did you love it?'

'How did you kn–' Meg began, then laughed. 'Don't tell me, the Applemore News Network strikes again.'

'Got it in one.' Rilla grinned, her freckled nose wrinkling slightly. 'So…?'

Meg shook her head. 'It was nice, but –'

'But van life isn't for you?' Rilla raised her brows slightly.

Meg pressed a hand to her mouth for a moment in thought.

'Was it that obvious?'

'I just had a feeling.' Rilla bent and broke off a sprig of rosemary, stripping off the needle-like leaves and filling the air with perfume. 'If I had a gorgeous new van like that I would be off adventuring every moment I could, but you seem really happy right here.'

'I am,' agreed Meg. 'I didn't expect to be.'

'Ah, Applemore has that effect on people, I think. I've seen people head straight back to civilisation as soon as they realise they can't order takeout food or go clothes shopping, unless you happen to like outdoor clothing,' she said, waggling her walking boots with a laugh.

'I didn't even think about that side of it. It just feels like...' Meg paused for thought. *Home,* she wanted to say. But that was crazy, wasn't it?

Rilla gave her a knowing look. 'Like you were meant to be here?'

'Is that weird?'

'I don't think so. I think sometimes we spend ages in the wrong place – I travelled for years, because I never found somewhere I wanted to stop. Then I came back here, and found Lachlan again, and...'

She gestured to the imposing castle behind her.

'And now you live in a castle.' Meg laughed, looking up at the tall spires of the turrets which glinted in the sunlight.

'Oh, don't get the Fraser family started on that. It's a house, apparently, not a castle. There's a difference.' She giggled. 'But I have to admit that to a girl who grew up in a perfectly normal house, it looks very much like a castle to me.'

'And me.' Meg glanced over at the car to check on Eliza, who'd clearly had enough of barking at nothing and had curled up out of sight.

'So what are you going to do with the van?' Rilla looked at her with a thoughtful expression.

An odd noise startled Meg, and she turned to see a peacock appear from behind a tree, wandering towards them with his tail leaving a trail in the newly raked gravel.

'Oh, that's Humphrey. He always turns up at this time of the morning for a treat – he likes to eat Kitty's leftover toast.' Rilla fished in the back pocket of her jeans and pulled out some crusts, tossing them towards the huge bird.

'I'm going to sell it,' Meg said, admitting to herself what she'd been thinking all the way home on Sunday.

Rilla's eyes widened slightly. 'Ooh.'

It was Meg's turn to raise her brows in query.

'Don't do anything until I've spoken to Lachlan.' Rilla said, pressing her palms together in a hopeful gesture. 'I think we might just be able to kill two birds with one stone.'

'I won't,' laughed Meg.

'I better get on this Zoom call,' Rilla said, checking her watch. 'I'll speak to you later.'

'IT WAS LOVELY, THANK YOU,' said Meg, laughing, ten minutes later, when Miranda passed her a cup of coffee with an expectant look on her face.

'Your date?' Miranda was wide-eyed. She glanced across at Beth, who was potting on tiny strawberry plants by the window of the orangery that ran along one side of the walled garden.

'My van trip.' Meg waited a moment.

'I thought you were going on a date?' Miranda sipped her coffee. 'I was looking forward to living vicariously through you.'

'So the Applemore rumour mill doesn't always work at full power,' Beth remarked, tapping the little terracotta pot on the wooden table before slotting it onto a crowded tray full of identical baby plants.

'Not always.' Meg thought of Laurel, who'd sent a message to say she'd pop by later in the week to tell her how her new work-from-home job was going. 'We rescheduled,' she added a few moments later.

'Ah, I'm glad to hear it. So my vicarious love life is just on hold, not cancelled.'

'Your love life is quite exciting enough,' said Beth.

'Don't listen to her,' Miranda said, chuckling. 'Anyway, if you haven't been on a date, what have you been up to?'

Heading back to the cottage an hour later, Meg stopped in a layby to let the farmer pass by with his tractor and trailer. He gave her a cheerful wave as he drove by, the trailer rattling loudly as it bumped over the edge of the narrow road and crunched in a gravel-filled pothole.

Like the little geranium cutting, she was growing tiny roots. All the time she'd been married to Michael she'd kept herself out of reach of friendship and a feeling of community and now, quite by accident, she'd found it in Applemore. As she drove down through the open gate towards the lighthouse, she saw that there were two white vans parked outside.

Kenny the builder spotted her and gave a wave of greeting.

'How's it going?' he said, as she let Eliza out of the car and wandered over to the cottage.

'Good thanks. How's the visitor centre progressing?' She peered in through the door, where she could hear a lot of banging and some off-key singing along to Rick Astley on the radio that was blaring out at full volume. Meg smiled. Maybe – despite the van trip being a bit of a washout in some ways – it hadn't been a bad idea to get away.

'Aye, we're coming on great guns. Do you want a sneak peek?' Kenny beckoned her over, and she followed him inside.

'This is amazing.' Meg stood in the doorway, astonished at what she was seeing. The once-grimy walls were now bright white, and the place smelled of a mixture of wood shavings and fresh paint.

'This wall over here is where they're putting all the old equipment so people can have a look at it,' Kenny explained, pointing towards the window, which was now framed by chunky wooden shelving. 'And here's where the information boards will be,' he said, waving an arm at a framework which lined one wall. 'We're putting a rail up here so people can see some of the old workings, but not actually touch them – we don't want health and safety getting their knickers in a twist – and there's a ramp going in here at the doorway as well to make sure we're accessible.'

'And you've done all this already?'

Kenny beamed with pride. 'Pulled a late one last night, but aye, we're almost done. I don't normally work weekends, but it's a bit different when it's for something like this. It's always good to give a wee bit back to the village, and the lighthouse means a lot to me.'

'It does?' Meg looked at him curiously.

'Oh aye, my grandpa was one of the lighthouse keepers. He lived in Helen's cottage.'

Meg put a hand to her heart without thinking, her eyes suddenly filling with tears. 'That's so amazing.'

'Aye.' Kenny's voice thickened. 'So it's nice to have this place as a testament to his hard work. It's the least I can do. This place is special to me.'

'I had no idea.' Meg ran a hand along the rail he'd installed, noticing how smooth it felt. The workmanship was impeccable – her years of watching Michael creating beautiful designs had given her an eye for the tiny finishing details that showed a real commitment to doing the best job possible. He'd have appreciated the precision with which Kenny had done those joints.

She said her goodbyes and headed back to the cottage, pausing for a moment to look at the lighthouse, gazing upwards as it stood tall and bright against the blue of the sky. It was strange – Michael had popped up in her head a few times over the last week or so – as if time, that age-old healer, had given her the perspective she needed. All those months she'd spent working through the paperwork and never-ending

263

administration that came hand-in-hand with death, all while trying to make the pieces of the stories fit.

She turned to watch as Kenny and his workmate carried in a long piece of timber, carefully manoeuvring it through the doorway. Overhead, a gull seemed to hang in the cloudless sky. In the distance she could hear the waves crashing against the rocks. After all those years where she'd been isolated and trapped with only her garden for consolation, here she was, with the freedom of the huge sky above her head and the roar of the sea in her ears.

She realised with a start that the feeling she'd been trying to pin down when she thought about Michael now wasn't grief – which had been complicated by the tangled threads of everything else that their marriage hadn't been. No, it was pity. In trying to live a double life, he'd somehow ended up with half of one. Not just in terms of time, but in what he'd lost.

That was his tragedy – but it didn't have to be hers. She had the second half of her life ahead, and whatever it might bring, she was going to grab it with both hands.

# CHAPTER THIRTY-NINE

Saturday night came, and the weather turned.

Gabe was standing on the step of the cottage, his broad frame filling the doorway. It was raining, with the wind blowing off the sea in splattering flurries. He was dressed for winter in a thick blue sweater which matched his eyes, his long legs clad in jeans and sturdy dark brown leather boots.

Meg found herself laughing at the ridiculousness of the situation.

'Only in Applemore,' she said, after a moment, reaching for an umbrella.

'I don't think that'll last long in this wind.' Gabe stepped out of the doorway in a gentlemanly manner, allowing her to pass through.

No sooner had she opened it than it had blown inside out. A ragged gust of wind almost tugged out of her hands, and she stepped sideways, bashing her arm against the wall with a gasp of surprise.

'Steady,' said Gabe, catching her elbow for a moment. She looked up, taking in the strong jaw and the rain-darkened hair falling over his forehead. He pushed a hand through it, sweeping it back as he raised his brows slightly.

'Is it bad luck if your umbrella turns inside out?' Meg battled it for a moment longer, then gave up, tossing it back into the hall with a shake of her head. She stood in the doorway, looking out at the rain.

'Fortunately I don't believe in bad omens.' His eyes twinkled as he gave his slow, lopsided smile. 'But I do think that those nice boots might get wrecked in this weather.'

He tipped a head toward her feet, which were clad in her favourite black suede heels. The path was already shining with puddles of water. By the time she got to his truck they'd be completely soaked.

'I think you might be right.' That was annoying. She headed back into the hall, slipping her feet into wellingtons instead. She'd thought her favourite boots would be a nod towards some sort of glamour, paired with a soft black v-neck sweater and a pair of black jeans. Trying to find something that was dressy enough for a meal out but didn't scream *Townie* in a seaside village where nobody ever seemed to get dressed up was a bit of a challenge.

They ran to Gabe's truck, where the engine was still running. He held the door open for her and she climbed inside. It smelled faintly of his aftershave, mixed with an outdoorsy, pine tree scent which must just be an occupational hazard of working in forestry.

'This is definitely one of the downsides of Highland life,' he said as they headed into the village. 'It's all very well making plans for a stroll to the village along the beach path, but the Scottish summer doesn't always co-operate.'

Meg brushed some raindrops off the front of her sweater. She looked down, realising that she was still in her wellingtons, which made her smile. All that time agonising over what to wear for a lovely early summer meal sitting outside at the Applemore Hotel watching the fishing boats heading out from the harbour, and now she looked like she was all set for a wander around the vegetable garden.

The tables outside – normally packed in the evenings – were sodden and deserted, with water splashing down on them from a leaky gutter above. Gabe's phone buzzed as he pulled up on the side of the road nearby.

He picked it up and looked at it, frowning.

'What was that I said about omens?' He shook his head with a smile. 'Give me two moments while I check something.'

He climbed out of the driver's seat and headed into the hotel. Meg flipped down the visor and checked her make-up quickly. Thank goodness for waterproof mascara – at least she didn't have any smudges under her lashes. Her hair had turned fuzzy, as it always did in the rain, but there wasn't much – apart from a vague smoothing with both hands – she could do about that. Thank goodness she hadn't gone over-board on the blusher, because she somehow looked quite pink-faced. Probably the result of all the blood that was swooshing around her body thanks to her heart, which was thumping as if she was a sixteen-year-old on a first date. She caught a glimpse of movement in the side mirror and closed the visor.

Gabe surprised her by getting back into the car, turning to look at her with a mildly amused expression.

'The text I had was the restaurant cancelling our booking for a table.'

'Oh.' Meg felt her stomach sink.

'Something to do with a leak in the kitchen, so they've had to shut everything down.'

'Oh well,' she said, trying to sound cheerful. 'Never mind –'

'I do mind,' Gabe said. 'I've been looking forward to this all week.'

Meg bit her lower lip.

'I've had an idea.' He fastened his seatbelt. 'It's not award-winning cuisine at the Applemore, but it'll do in the interim.'

He pulled the truck forward and started driving down the deserted street; the wipers working in double time against the downpour.

He pulled into the car park at the far end of the street that overlooked the sea, and looked at her questioningly.

'Not allergic to anything, are you? Specifically seafood?'

Meg shook her head, looking out at the Airstream caravan where two young girls stood in blue and white striped aprons, looking out at the rain from under their canopy.

'Quite the opposite,' she said, realising his plan. 'I love it.'

'Excellent.'

Five minutes later he returned with two parcels wrapped in paper, the familiar scent of vinegary chips filling the air.

'It's not the most exotic dinner you've ever had, I suspect, but hopefully we can get to that another time.'

Meg smiled to herself as she held the warm parcel on her knees. Dinner out at the hotel was all very well, but there was something curiously intimate about sharing fish and chips on a rainy summer evening.

Gabe drove the truck up out of the village, through the dark shade of the tall pine woods and past rocky moorland studded with gorse bushes. They reached the top of the moor, parking at the start of a forestry track which looked down over the harbour. In the distance, the lighthouse and the buildings looked like a toy village.

Gabe turned to look at her, unfastening his seatbelt. He looked down at her feet. 'Still in wellies, I see.'

'Oh,' she laughed. 'I was going to change when you went into the hotel, but I forgot.'

He looked out through the rain. 'If that weather does what I think it will, you might need them – if you're up for a walk, that is?'

Meg nodded, pushing her hair back over her shoulder. 'I think you might have more faith in the weather than I do. It's still pouring.'

As if to order, the rain crashed down against the windscreen, and Gabe laughed.

'I've got a bit of a handle on it after working outside. You learn to gauge when a scrap of blue –' he leaned over towards her side of the window, his shoulder brushing hers as he pointed, '– like that one, might just be the herald of some sunshine.'

'I like your optimism.' Meg lifted the parcel from her knees. 'Shall we…'

Gabe took it from her and unwrapped it, tossing the bag and the paper onto the back seat. 'I must remember to move that before tomorrow morning,' he said, laughing. 'Stan would eat the lot. He's like a dustbin in canine form.'

'Eliza isn't much better.'

'Fish and chips,' he said, handing her a box, 'are not the most romantic thing on the planet.'

Meg popped open the lid. Inside was a beautifully presented piece of fish, which had miraculously survived the journey and was still crisp in its batter, and golden chips which smelled absolutely delicious.

'It's not quite asparagus and smoked salmon,' she said, teasing him.

'Oh hang on, I've got some in the back.' He made to get out of the car, making her laugh.

'It's like Valentine's Day meals, though,' said Meg, biting

into a chip. 'I always think they look like the most awkwardly uncomfortable thing. Performative romance on the one specific day of the year, versus being nice to each other the rest of the time.'

'You say that like you've got an axe to grind.' Gabe grinned. 'Although we've both established that we've got a past.'

'It would be a bit weird if we were our age and we didn't.'

'Yeah.' Gabe broke off a piece of the golden batter. 'All that time spent planting trees gave me a lot of time to process stuff.'

'I was thinking the same about driving.'

Gabe looked at her, his eyes narrowing in thought, but a smile playing at his lips. 'And did you come to any profound conclusions?'

'Funnily enough, I did.'

He raised a brow.

'It's not exactly profound.' Her chest rose and fell as she tried to find the words. 'It's more a feeling. I think it's probably got something to do with turning fifty, and a realisation that we only get once chance at this life.'

'Ah, yeah.' Gabe grinned. 'It's a bit of an eye opener, that birthday.'

'It really is.' Meg looked out of the window, realising that the rain had eased off and over in the distance the purple clouds seemed to be clearing. 'I guess what I worked out was that if you find out what makes you happy, you should probably do more of it.'

Gabe held her gaze for the briefest moment, his blue eyes looking directly into hers. Then he looked away, cleared his throat and picked up a chip, examining it on all sides with a smile.

'These are pretty good,' he said, taking a bite. 'But I promise you I will take you somewhere much nicer next time.'

She looked at him sideways.

'That's assuming there is a next time,' he added, his mouth tipping up into a half-smile that she felt in her knees.

'I think there might be.' Meg popped a chip into her mouth.

'I don't like to chance my luck.' Gabe switched the wipers down to the lowest setting. 'However, if I did believe in omens, I'd say that the weather improving was a good sign.'

They ate in silence for a few moments, watching the distant sea through the rhythmic swishing of the wipers.

'So did you get whatever it was sorted down south?' Meg looked at Gabe.

He nodded. 'I'm sorry I had to drop you in it. It's a long story…' He thought for a moment. 'Long and short, I guess. I told you about my ex. We had a house together, which was hanging around my neck like an unfortunate reminder of the past I didn't quite know how to deal with.'

He told her the saga as they finished eating, and then Meg placed the cardboard box on the dashboard in front of her.

'I think in a funny way we've both come to the same point.'

Gabe cocked his head and looked at her. 'Is this the moment when you suggest I take all my money and buy a campervan?'

She made a face. 'Quite the opposite.'

'I get the feeling you haven't been bitten by the vanlife bug.'

Meg shook her head. 'Definitely not. But sometimes you have to try something to realise it's not for you.'

'That's a good way of looking at it.' His voice was thoughtful.

'Oh look at that!' Meg turned, catching sight of a rainbow which had appeared in the first rays of sunlight, rising from the rocks and the heather, and reaching across the sky. She leaned forward, gazing out of the windscreen to follow its path.

'I was going to suggest we went for a drive,' Gabe said, laughing. 'But now I'm wondering if we should search for the pot of gold over there beyond your lighthouse.'

'I don't need any gold,' said Meg, without thinking. She felt Gabe's eyes on her and turned for a moment to see him looking at her with an unreadable expression.

He rubbed the already dark stubble of his jaw.

'In which case,' he said, his voice gruff, 'it's lucky you wore those waterproof boots after all.'

# CHAPTER FORTY

Gabe turned the truck away from Applemore, the wheels splashing through rivulets which crossed the narrow road as they headed steeply downhill before turning up and into the first long stretch through the neat rows of pine trees that had been planted years before by forestry workers like him.

They chatted as he drove, Meg telling him how happy she was to discover that Laurel was enjoying her job and laughing about her description of Una in the office.

'It sounds like she's got Una's number,' he grinned. 'She's good at heart, but she's a bit like a terrier. She guards that office as if her life depends on it.'

'I think Laurel's so glad to have found a job she'll do whatever Una says.'

'That sounds like a match made in heaven.' Gabe pulled off the main road and up the private track which marked the entry to Lochbrannich Estate. He looked across at Meg, who was gazing out of the window at a white camper which was driving parallel to them on the road towards Inverness.

'So you've decided you're not the sort of person who lives in a van?'

'I'm not.' She made a rueful face. 'Do you think that means I'm a bit boring?'

He snorted with laughter. 'Is that the official measurement?'

'It feels like it these days. Everyone seems to think it's the most amazing adventure. Turns out I like my adventures to be more... catered.'

'Nothing wrong with that.' He looked at her again. Her mouth was parted slightly, her short upper lip turned upwards in that way that made him want to pull over the truck and find an excuse to kiss her. Not that he needed an excuse, but –

'I think Rilla up at Applemore House is going to buy the van.'

His heart quickened, and he shot her a sideways glance.

'Does this mean you're going to be stranded in Applemore for the foreseeable future?'

Meg's mouth tipped upwards in a little smile and she put a fingertip to her mouth, as he'd noticed she did whenever she was thinking before she spoke.

'It turns out my friend Helen's staying in Santiago for a while longer.'

He shook his head slightly and couldn't suppress the smile that spread across his face.

'Well, that's good news.'

Meg took a breath as if she was about to speak, but said nothing. She paused for a moment, and he watched as she looked out of the window as they drove through the green canopy of the trees.

'So this mysterious walk we're going on,' she said a moment later. 'Where exactly are we going?'

'Well,' he said, smiling to himself in anticipation as he

drove towards the summit of the hill, 'I'll show you rather than tell you. It'll be worth it, though.'

'And we're not trespassing?' Meg pointed to one of the discreet signs hanging on a gate that blocked entry to a forest path.

He shook his head. 'No, not at all, I promise.'

'This is so beautiful.' She wound down the window for a moment and he caught the coconut scent of the gorse bushes. 'And it smells amazing. It's like being on a tropical beach.'

'Only slightly colder,' he said, making her smile. He caught a movement to the left ahead of them and pulled up the truck to show her. 'Look at that.'

'What am I looking at?'

'Just there. A hare. Can you see him?' He tapped the window gently to direct her focus and a moment later she gasped in surprise.

'He's huge!'

'They're enormous, aren't they? I'd never seen one in real life until I came up here.'

'It must be amazing working outside and seeing so much wildlife.'

He watched her watching as the hare stood frozen for a long moment, staring directly at the truck, as if trying to gauge whether they were a threat. Eventually he seemed to make a judgement call, and with a leap over a tussock of grass, he hurtled off into the safe cover of a hawthorn bush.

He drove on, lost in thought.

It didn't matter about the skipped dinner, or the fact that they'd eaten fish and chips on their knees in the truck in the rain. The truth was he wanted to spend time with her, and he didn't care what they were doing. Una had made a million jokes about trying to set him up with single friends of hers, and the lads had teased him about finding a nice girl in the hotel bar on a Friday night, and he'd laughed them off every time, saying that he'd been there and done that and he was more than happy single.

He glanced at Meg as they reached the top of the hill, wanting to see her reaction as the view of the glen opened up.

'Oh,' she said, mouth dropping in surprise. He felt himself break into a huge smile as he watched her.

Loch Brannich sparkled in the strange bright light that followed a storm. The trees – now in leaf – danced in the breeze, and the fields were jewel bright and dotted with distant cattle and sheep. The place had changed since his last visit, as if it was a kaleidoscope picture.

'Look at that.' Meg pointed ahead. A bird of prey hovered for a moment and then plunged into the undergrowth.

'It's pretty amazing, isn't it?' He pointed ahead. 'Still snow on the mountains, look.'

She shook her head in amazement. 'I can't believe how beautiful it is.'

'It really makes you think, doesn't it? Why would you live in the city when you could have all this on your doorstep?'

'It helps if you're landed gentry with a castle,' she said, laughing.

'Funny you should mention that…' Gabe said with a wry smile.

# CHAPTER FORTY-ONE

Meg looked across at Gabe as he slid the truck back into gear and they started a slow descent towards the loch. At this time of year the light went on forever in the evenings. It could have been mid-afternoon, not seven thirty at night. At least the midges might have stopped biting – she crossed her fingers, hopefully. It was the one downside she'd discovered so far about life on the west coast of the Highlands. The lighthouse cottage garden was blissfully free of them, thanks to the near-constant sea breeze. But she'd encountered them on many an evening stroll up towards Applemore, coming home to discover her skin was covered in tiny bites.

'What do you do about midges when you're up on the moors planting trees?'

Gabe made a face and laughed. 'I swear a lot.'

'Does it help?'

'Not at all. But it makes me feel better. The funny thing is I arrived in late autumn, by which time they'd all buzzed off to wherever they go in winter. I'd read about them but I had no experience and then one day as if by magic, there they were. Everywhere.'

'Everywhere?' She looked at him sideways and burst out laughing at his expression.

'Not quite everywhere, thankfully.'

They drove through a stone gate and turned a corner and once again Meg gasped.

'Is this where we're supposed to be?'

She had visions of a furious Highland Laird armed with huge dogs and a rifle appearing to defend his territory.

A moment later, as Gabe raised a hand in greeting, she had to suppress a giggle.

A very tall, thin man in his late seventies with a patrician face appeared from the side of a filthy and battered Land Rover, followed by a grizzled and equally greying terrier. He had white hair swept back over a receding hairline, and a surprisingly sweet and welcoming smile.

Gabe pulled the truck to a halt and climbed out, striding across and shaking the man's hand with an equally warm smile. He said something, and then beckoned to Meg.

Feeling slightly shy, she got out of the car and looked down at her feet, realising she was still wearing a pair of pink polka dot wellington boots. There was nothing for it – she'd just have to style it out.

'So I thought we'd take that walk up to the bothy,' Gabe was saying. 'Ah, here we are. This is Meg,' he said, taking her hand for a moment – she felt her eyes widen in surprise – and drawing her towards them in a welcoming gesture.

'This is the duke of Lochbrannich,' said Gabe, as if being introduced to a duke every day was a common occurrence.

'Hello,' she said, wondering if she was supposed to curtsey but shaking his extended hand instead.

The duke beamed at her. 'Felix,' he said. 'We don't stand on ceremony here. Well, I don't, in any case.'

A moment later a woman – also tall, but pale and slender, and moving quite slowly, appeared from behind the enormous door of the house. 'Jennifer, darling, look. It's Gabe, the nice chap I told you about from the forestry. Well this is splendid,' he said, looking at them both and rubbing his hands together in a thoughtful manner.

His wife came and said hello and there was another flurry of handshaking and some chat about the weather and the terrible rain they'd had.

Meg patted the little dog, who was sniffing delightedly at her feet.

'Right, darling,' said the duke's wife, 'We really must get off if we're to get to the shop in Applemore before it closes.'

'It doesn't close for ages,' protested the duke, checking his watch.

His wife caught Meg's eye and shook her head. 'Honestly, this man,' she said, laughing. 'He takes a while to catch on.'

'Catch on?' The duke said, frowning.

Meg looked sideways at Gabe to see him suppressing a smile.

'If you want these young people to enjoy their walk to the bothy, then you and I really ought to let them get on with it,' she said firmly.

'Oh.' He gave a slow nod, as if something had just dawned on him. 'Yes, right. Very good. I shall see you during the week, Gabe, and we'll have a chat about the rewilding programme. I have some new ideas.'

'Looking forward to it.'

'Darling,' the duke's wife warned, hooking her hand through his arm in a practised manner.

The duke raised his hands in surrender. 'I am putty in her

hands,' he said, allowing himself to be steered towards the Land Rover, the little terrier trotting along behind him.

'Shall we?' Gabe gestured toward the truck, standing back to allow her to go ahead. They'd closed the doors and were just about to set off when the duke pulled up so his window was parallel to Gabe's. He opened it and Meg looked across to see the duke leaning forward to smile at them approvingly.

'Strike while the iron is hot, old boy, as I said to you the other day.'

'For goodness' sake, Felix,' the duchess said, shaking her head in disbelief. 'You are an absolute horror.'

Gabe dropped his head into his hands and let out a groan, then looked across, grimacing.

Meg's heart, which had settled down slightly, was now skipping about all over the place as she looked at him with an uncontrollably large smile on her face.

'Should I ask?'

'Probably best not,' said Gabe, shaking his head and laughing.

They bumped along a track which led through the woods and up to the opening to a woodland path. The white starry flowers of wild garlic danced above a thick carpet of green foliage, and a track wove up into the dappled shade of the trees.

Meg looked down again at her pink and white spotted boots.

'They're not very glamorous, but I think they're probably a better bet than the suede ones.'

'I think you're right.' Gabe looked at her, his gaze sweeping upwards over her body from her ridiculous but practical boots to her face, which she was certain was flushing pink. Meg steepled her fingers because she didn't seem to know what to do with her hands.

They set off up the path, climbing up and up through dripping trees and then out onto a stretch of path where the land was jagged with rocks covered in lichen and dotted once again with the coconut scented gorse and scrubby patches of heather.

'There it is,' said Gabe, as they climbed over the final ridge of a hill.

A rugged stone building stood nestled in a dip by a rushing stream. With a window on either side of the door and a low slate roof, it looked like something from a fairy-tale.

'It's so pretty.' Meg rushed over to the stream. The water was peaty and clear. It cut a path through the moorland, bubbling over rocks which had been worn smooth over centuries.

'I think there's probably a waterfall, look.' Gabe led her over to the edge and they peered at the water which tumbled down a few metres, landing in a natural pool which had formed below.

'I think it's a bit cold for wild swimming, don't you?'

Gabe pressed his lips together in a mischievous smile. 'I'm game if you are.'

'I am very definitely not.' She shook her head vigorously. 'I think wild swimming in ice cold water might be up there with living in a van as things I'm not designed for.'

She patted her hips as an afterthought. 'Even if looks might be deceiving.'

She stepped backwards, losing her footing on a clump of heather, and crashed into the solid wall of his chest, turning round and trying to step back but slipping sideways. Gabe caught her in his arms.

'I'm so sorry,' she gasped, taking in the prickly sensation of the sweater he was wearing and the feeling of his body against hers and looking up into his amused dark blue eyes.

He looked back at her and his mouth twitched in amusement.

'I'm not exactly complaining.'

Meg bit her lip and let out an unsteady breath. Using him as a sort of handsome but practical balancing post, she stepped backwards carefully and looked at him with a slightly embarrassed expression.

'So this bothy,' she said, in a slightly too-high tone of voice, walking towards it in her wellington boots, hoping he was following her. 'Tell me about it?'

She heard his footsteps behind and kept on walking until she reached the stone building, running a hand along the low granite sill as if she was suddenly fascinated by Scottish vernacular architecture.

'This is nice, isn't it?'

Gabe smiled slowly at her, looking at her fondly as if she was slightly insane. He was standing just in front of her, hand shading his eyes from the sun as he spoke.

'So – the rewilding project,' he said.

Meg nodded. 'Go on.' She settled back against the wall of the bothy, which had remained dry under the shelter of the roof, and crossed her arms. The air was loud with the evening song of birds, and dramatic plum-coloured clouds lurked at the edges of the sky, as if waiting for another chance to empty their contents.

'The plan is to plant broadleaf trees – in swathes – some in little forest groves, some individually.' He motioned for her to follow him around the bothy, so they were looking out across a vast stretch of moorland. 'Careful,' he said, laughing, as he pointed out a dark patch of water. 'I can't tell you how often we get stuck in those little hidden peat bogs when we're working... I've been soaked up to my knees so many times I've lost count.'

'Is that when you wish you were still jet setting to and from New York flying business class?'

Gabe shook his head slowly and vehemently. 'Not for a single moment.'

She was standing close by his side, aware of the warmth of his body, as he carried on explaining.

'As time goes on, hopefully more species will arrive as the habitat diversifies, and the whole ecosystem will flourish.'

'That sounds like magic.' Meg looked up at the sky, where a single bird soared overhead.

'Eventually the skies should be full of birds of prey and buzzing with dragonflies, and then as we plant the riverwoods we should see an increase in salmon coming back to the rivers, and –' he stopped mid-sentence.

'Go on,' said Meg, touching his arm without thinking.

'Sorry, I didn't mean to go on about it,' said Gabe with a rueful shake of his head.

'Don't apologise. I like it,' Meg said softly.

His eyes met hers for a moment and then he looked away, his tone almost casual as he watched the bird swooping through the air.

'I came here to get away... to find a new life by myself. I never expected to find something I really cared about.'

Meg followed his gaze, looking out at the huge sky and the sweep of moorland that stretched out for miles before them.

'I can see why you love it. It's beautiful.'

Gabe turned, catching her by the shoulders gently, turning her body to face his.

She looked up at him for a moment and gazed into his eyes, realising almost as he spoke the words that she knew what he was going to say.

'I'm talking,' said Gabe, dropping the gentlest of kisses onto her forehead, 'about you.'

And Meg reached up almost without thinking, her arms sliding up across his broad, muscled back. She felt his hands cupping her face softly in his hands, a thumb tracing across her mouth for a moment, and then he bent to kiss her, and everything surrounding her was forgotten.

Eventually Gabe broke away, looking down at her with such a gentle expression on his face that Meg felt her knees might be in danger of giving way again, so she held onto his arm for fear of landing in a puddle of peaty water.

'So,' he said, with a teasing smile, 'as I was saying. Rewilding.'

Meg gave a solemn nod. 'Go on.'

'He's a lovely old boy, the duke. He's determined to make a difference before he – as he would put it – pops off. I don't think his daughter is exactly on board, but he's hoping she'll come round.'

It was difficult to concentrate fully with his thumb gently stroking the back of her hand. Meg watched his mouth twitch with amusement.

'He seems sweet,' Meg said. 'If a bit eccentric.'

'He is both of the above. But he made an excellent point when I was talking to him the other day.'

'Go on.'

'He told me he'd met his wife forty years ago, and how happy they were together. And I think we've both figured out we've waited long enough.'

Meg shifted and took hold of his other hand as he stood before her, his voice low as he continued.

'If you're offered a chance at happiness, you'd be mad not to take it.'

Meg looked at Gabe, biting her lip as her heart thumped against her ribs.

'So I'm going to kiss you again now, if that's alright.'

Meg nodded. 'I think it's probably a good idea.'

# EPILOGUE

## TWO MONTHS LATER

'I can't believe you forgot to mention one vital detail.'

Meg stood on the grass by the entrance to the visitor centre. Helen grinned at her, swinging the hand of a tall, tanned man who looked down at her with affection. He was wearing a thick sweater, despite baking hot weather, which was almost unheard of for summer in Applemore. The shiny new hire car they'd picked up at Inverness Airport was parked in the space outside the cottage, alongside Helen's beaten-up old Fiesta, which had been Meg's only mode of transport since Rilla and Lachlan had bought the campervan. Now they were somewhere on a beach in Portugal, according to Miranda, and their daughter Kitty was having the time of her little life.

Meg looked across at the crowds of people who were milling about outside the lighthouse visitor centre, waiting for the official opening. They'd had to wait for approval from the tourist board (Kenny had muttered about his work being of a high enough standard that it was a load of old nonsense, if you asked him), but now it was official.

'Not that they haven't had it open unofficially,' explained Meg, laughing. 'But you didn't hear me saying that.'

'Said like a born and bred Applemore resident,' said Helen, tucking her arm around Meg's waist. 'Sorry for springing Luis on you,' she said as they wandered across towards the crowds. 'I thought I'd surprise you.'

Meg looked over at Luis, who'd dropped a kiss on the top of Helen's head and strolled off to take a look at the lighthouse.

'Well, you've done that. There I was thinking you were having a lovely time being a grandma and enjoying some painting in Santiago.'

'I was,' said Helen, waggling her eyebrows and making Meg giggle. 'I was also having a lovely time *not* being grandma, but being Helen again. I'd forgotten how nice it was.'

'So what's the plan?' Meg, who'd deliberately not let herself worry about the future, looked at her friend for a moment. She looked at the newly cut grass that rolled down towards the sea, and the huge sky overhead which could change in minutes, and across to the little white cottage she'd grown to love while she'd been house-sitting for her oldest friend. Helen turned to follow her gaze, letting go of her waist and standing close by her side, as if she was reading her thoughts.

'I'm going to stay for a while. I'm not sure how long. At least a year?' Helen lifted both hands in a vague gesture.

'I can't believe you've just gone and found yourself a whole new life in –'

Meg stopped mid-sentence and Helen stared pointedly across towards the visitor centre. Her heart gave the same skip of excitement that it did whenever she saw Gabe, and he turned – as if sensing her presence – and waved in their direction.

'– Found myself a new life,' said Helen, with a teasing expression, 'In a completely unexpected place?'

'Meg,' called Greta from the doorway of the visitor centre, 'can you come and double check this with me?'

'Duty calls,' said Helen, laughing.

Meg set off to find a harried looking Greta, who was frowning at the interactive screens that lined one wall of the visitor centre. Two out of the three were working, but the third was blank.

'We're ready to go, but this blooming thing is refusing to come to life. I don't know what I've done to it.'

Kathleen appeared, calm and unruffled as ever, dressed in a grey and white striped blouse and a pair of elegant wide-legged grey linen trousers.

'What's going on here?'

'It's this interactive thing. I swear it'll be the death of me.' Greta closed her eyes and tried to take a calming breath.

'Have you tried switching it off and on again?' asked Kathleen, peering behind the screen. She flicked a switch and the screen obediently flashed into life.

Greta's shoulders dropped.

'Okay,' she said with a short laugh. 'Let's get out of here and get this thing officially open before I go completely crazy.'

Outside, Helen had caught up with Luis and they were standing by the new fencing, surrounded by a group of Applemore locals. Miranda waved from their midst. Beth, who was carrying a huge bouquet wrapped in the flower farm's signature brown paper, rushed over.

'I thought I was going to be late. These are for the guest of honour.'

'Ladies and gentlemen,' Greta began, after clapping her hands. 'We are here today with a very special guest, who has come all the way from Applemore's twin village, La Mardelle, in the middle of the Loire Valley.'

A petite, dark-haired woman in a chic blue shirt dress and cream espadrilles gave a little wave.

'Merci de votre visite,' said Greta, in an accent which could only be described as *Mrs Doubtfire visits Paris.*

Meg noticed Laurel in the crowd, standing beside Jamie, one of the fencing lads. He hoisted a delighted Kai on his shoulders, and Laurel looked up at him with a smile. Jamie leaned over and kissed her, making her giggle. She looked up a second later and caught Meg's eye, giving a wave. Meg, who was babysitting later in the week so they could go out for the evening together, smiled and waved back.

Greta's speech went on, thanking everyone for coming and telling them how delighted they were to have an opportunity for everyone in the village to gather and celebrate such a wonderful event.

'There's one consolation,' said Gabe, his voice low as he whispered in her ear.

Meg turned, delighted, as he pulled her close and kissed her briefly for a moment.

'Go on,' she said, looking up at his eyes, which sparkled with amusement.

'With all this going on, we've dropped right down the Applemore gossip list.'

Meg looked around. Everyone was listening intently to Greta's speech.

'Which means,' said Gabe, taking her hand and leading her away, around the back of the cottage and through the long sea-grass at the back of the cottage garden wall, 'that nobody will notice we're gone.'

'You are impossible,' said Meg, laughing. 'We're supposed to be there doing our bit.'

He led her down towards the library, where a newly printed sign explained that the brand-new expanded community cupboard could now be found up at the Applemore Village Hall.

'You did that,' Gabe said, squeezing her hand. 'If we're talking about doing your bit. And you've looked after the library, and been the keeper of its secrets.'

Meg pressed her lips together, feeling a wave of unexpected emotion.

Gabe tucked a strand of hair behind her ear and let the back of his fingers trail down her neck for a moment. He'd been doing some last-minute repairs on the fencing and smelled of pine wood and fresh air.

She took an unsteady breath.

'And you did all the interactive stuff, not to mention building the website.' Gabe held her gaze. 'So I think we can be excused for sloping off for a moment alone.'

Meg looked up at the lighthouse and back at Gabe for a moment.

'It's weird, isn't it?'

Gabe cocked his head to one side and looked at her for a second with a curious expression. 'What is?'

'The lighthouse. All those years of guiding people safely home.'

She watched as his face lit up with that gorgeous, lopsided smile she loved.

'And here we are.' He drew her close.

She reached up, wrapping her arms around his neck.

'And here we are,' she echoed - but her words were stolen by a kiss.

# ACKNOWLEDGMENTS

It feels quite strange to think that I've been writing acknowledgements for eleven years now and every time they get shorter, not because I'm not grateful but because I know that the people who deserve the biggest thanks won't ever read them... so to my darling James, and my beloved children Verity, Archie, Jude and Rory even though none of you will see this, I love you all enormously.

To my lovely friends - you all know who you are - I love you.

To my cover designer Diane Meacham, thank you so much for the most gorgeous look for all of the Applemore stories, and especially this one.

To my agent Amanda Preston and all the team at ILA who have found readers for Applemore all around the world - I am so grateful and thankful - it is such a lovely surprise to wake up to messages from readers from a different country every morning!

Enormous thanks to every one of you who reads these stories... there are so many books out there and it's an honour that you've chosen to read one of mine!

Made in the USA
Middletown, DE
29 September 2024

61675955R00179